SHOWDOWN IN FEATHERSTONE VALLEY

☙

LONDON JAMES

ONE

CRAIG

If there was one thing the Klondike taught Craig, it was how not to quit. "If you quit, you die," his partner Flynn told him once. Truth be told, it was probably more than that. It was perhaps once an hour. No matter the number of times, though, it didn't matter. If you quit up there, you died. Period.

If you quit visiting your claim, someone would kill you for it. Of course, even if you continued to visit your claim, someone would still try to kill you for it.

If you quit keeping your fire going, you'd freeze to death.

If you quit mining your claim, you'd starve to death.

Heck, even if you quit moving some days, the relentless frontier would claim your life.

Which is why Craig never quit. He never stopped mining his claim, never stopped making money, always kept his fire going, and always kept moving.

It was exhausting, but he wouldn't have lived it any other way.

If there was another thing the Klondike taught him, it was that resilience is the key to life. Well, resilience and God.

"So, when is this contest supposed to start?"

Craig looked up as Wyatt stood over him and his desk. The

young man chewed on his lip and twisted his hat in his hands. A nervous energy seemed to flow through his shoulders as he rocked his weight back and forth on his feet.

"I have a meeting with Mayor Duncan and Mr. Miller later this afternoon to discuss the details." Craig looked back at the map of Featherstone Valley spread across his desk, glancing between Old Bear Mountain, where his men were already mining, and Rattlesnake Mountain—the mountain he was currently fighting for in a purchase deal with the town.

Ever since moving to Featherstone Valley nearly five years ago, he had had his eye on the mountain, but given the price of the land then, he couldn't afford it. Instead, he purchased Old Bear—the lesser of the two prices. Old Bear had done a lot for his company. It had given him several prominent veins of color, building not only his wealth but also allowing him and his company to become one of the biggest employers in the small town. It had been a satisfactory purchase then, suiting his needs and allowing him to build. But this was a new time, a new year, and it was time to expand.

Rattlesnake Mountain was just the site to do it.

Or so he thought.

It wasn't until Mayor Duncan rejected his first offer that he realized this might not be as easy as he thought.

And it only got more complicated from then on.

"Do you think Mr. Miller is as bad as you say he is?" Wyatt asked.

"I wouldn't have said it if I thought otherwise."

"I suppose that's true. He's made a lot of money in Deer Creek, hasn't he?"

"Yes, he has."

"Must be nice to be so rich."

Craig shot his gaze toward the young man, trying to ignore the hint of admiration and curiosity swimming inside Wyatt's words. "I wouldn't be too keen on believing the money is worth having. Not when you consider the source of how it was made."

Wyatt's smile faded, and he ducked his chin toward his chest. Embarrassment seemed to wash through him, making his cheeks blush. "Yes, sir."

A glint of guilt prickled in Craig's chest. He didn't mean to belittle his young head foreman. "I'm sorry for my tone. I just… that man is not someone you should admire."

"I don't admire him."

"Good. It's smart of you not to."

The young man inhaled, and his shoulders hunched as he exhaled. He stared at the floor, his eyes darting back and forth as though thoughts swirled inside his mind, but he wasn't sure if he should utter them.

"Is there something wrong, Wyatt?" Craig asked.

"Well, sir, I… what's going to happen if…" Wyatt clamped his mouth shut. His eyes continued to dart around the room, looking at everything but Craig.

"If Mr. Miller wins the bet?" Craig finally finished. Although he knew those words were on the young man's lips, he wished he had been wrong.

Wyatt opened his mouth to answer but closed it and nodded as though he wouldn't let himself say the answer out loud.

As Craig stared at his head foreman, he couldn't help but feel the same way. He wasn't sure he could allow himself to say the things he needed to, either. He had thought about the less-than-favorable outcome a few times since the deal and bet were made, and he'd hated every second of it. He only wanted to think of a win. He didn't want to think of a loss.

Knowing what he did about the town and the mountains, if he did lose, there would be nothing for him to do but either leave for greener pastures or continue to mine Old Bear Mountain until it was dry and then move on to a different town, leaving the workers to find new work with Mr. Miller.

He didn't like either of those options.

He just had to win.

He just had to.

"We're just going to have to make sure that doesn't happen, won't we?" he finally asked Wyatt.

Wyatt smiled and nodded. "Yes, sir."

Craig dropped his gaze back to the map, tracing the route between the two mountains. While Old Bear was closer to the Humbug River that weaved its way around most of Featherstone Valley, Rattlesnake was closer to town—a fact he knew the miners would be happy to learn. Closer to town meant that they wouldn't have to leave their homes for a week at a time, fending for themselves in tents or a rundown cabin, eating beans and cornbread for more meals than they cared to admit to each week. Closer to town meant they could go home each night, spending time with their wives and children and enjoying homecooked meals and warm beds at night.

He couldn't deny that the realization even made him happier. While he didn't have a wife or children to go home to, the thought of better meals and his warm home each night was nothing short of a dream he wanted to cling to. Of course, he could camp and rough it in the wilderness. He'd done it for years in the Klondike. But doing it and wanting to do it were two different things, and if he had the choice of a tent or his home, he'd pick his home—every time.

"Are we going to keep any men working at Old Bear? Or do you want me to tell all of them they will be moving to Rattlesnake when the contest starts?"

Craig furrowed his brow. While Wyatt impressed him most of the time, there were other times he just wanted to smack the boy upside the head for merely opening his mouth.

"They all will go to Rattlesnake. I need every man working that job so I can win this contest. Once we secure the mountain, we can hire more men and divide the teams."

"Oh. Yeah. That's probably a good idea, huh?" Wyatt's shoulders hunched as though he realized how foolish his question had been. "I shouldn't have asked such a question."

Craig raised an eyebrow, half-smiling at the head foreman. "Don't worry about it. You're still learning."

Of course, he wanted to believe his words as much as he wanted Wyatt to believe them. Truth be told, a tiny part of him worried the job was too much for the young man. However, he also always wanted to see the hardworking side of people. The side where they live by their determination to make something of themselves in this world. For all the youthful faults Wyatt had, he was determined to make a name he could be proud of.

It was this quality that made Craig give him a chance.

"So, I guess I'll let the men know to prepare to move the equipment?"

"We will move some, but not all."

"How will they mine the mountain, then?"

"We're going to buy a few new things." Craig moved some papers on his desk, exposing the latest copy of The Featherstone Gazette. He hadn't had a chance to read it yet, but he'd wanted to ever since he saw the glaring headline from Prudence Chatterton's gossip article. Whoever had been writing it for the last several weeks had certainly garnered a readership, and the article had gone from the back page to the front because everyone wanted to know the latest from the person who seemed to have his or her nose stuck in everyone's business.

He eyed the headline again but left the paper on his desk, instead reaching for another piece of paper he'd received in the mail from a friend a few weeks ago.

"I need you to go to the mercantile and send a wire to the New Holland Machine Company in Holland, Pennsylvania."

"All right. What is it for?"

"For this." He laid the paper in front of Wyatt and pointed to the drawn image of the stone crusher advertised on the flyer.

He'd seen the machine once, a long time ago, when a salesman came into town, hoping to talk him into purchasing one. He had wanted to at the time, but he didn't think the need was as significant as it was now. Not to mention, he hadn't wanted to spend the money, even if he'd had it. There was a small part of him that regretted saying no.

Oh, to live and learn.

Wyatt furrowed his brow and grabbed the paper, reading it aloud. "For making roads, paving, concrete walks, troughs, etc. Make big money crushing stone for neighbors. This is a strong, durable crusher. Write for low prices." He paused and looked at Craig. "You think we need a stone crusher to mine Rattlesnake Mountain?"

"I do. I probably should have ordered one a long time ago for mining Old Bear, but I haven't had the need as much as I do now. Rattlesnake is farther from the river…" Craig let his voice trail off. "It's a machine I want and believe we need."

"I can head over to the mercantile right now."

"Good. Here." Craig handed him a list he'd been working on for a few days. "I need to order these other supplies as well."

"Yes, sir." Wyatt fetched both pieces of paper, glancing at them before he turned toward the door. He reached for his hat and coat, slipping on both before leaving the office and shutting the door behind him. A cool gust of air filled the space, making Craig turn toward the window and look outside.

Men and women walked past, and he caught their movement between the sheer curtains as they made their way down the street to unknown destinations while the sun shone down on their shoulders. A few sunny days this week—a rarity in Montana in February—had melted some of the snow, causing the streets to become muddy. Dirt footprints littered every building in town, and as Craig looked at the ones Wyatt left on the office floor, his thoughts turned back to the deal and the two outcomes.

His life had always been left up to chance. Well, it had since the day he left everything he knew in California and headed up to the Klondike. He'd been nothing short of an ignorant fool when he got off the boat in Skagway, trudging across to the beach after the tide had gone out to the small town full of both dreamers and those out to do harm or scam people out of every last penny in their pockets. He hadn't known what to expect, and while he figured it would be nothing but grit and hard work—which it was—the risks had left his head spinning most days.

He wondered daily if he'd made the best choice.

Surely, a life lived with comforts far outweighed a life where the constant struggle for survival leaves an indelible mark on one's soul. Between the biting cold, the aching muscles, and the relentless hunger, the haunting companions had carved deep lines into his weathered face, callusing his once-soft hands. At times, he thought he looked a decade older than twenty-six.

He heaved a deep sigh, pulling his gaze from the window and looking over his desk at all the papers—contracts with miners, housing requests, and the lists he made each day with all the tasks that needed his attention. What would it all mean if he lost this deal?

He didn't want to think about it.

Out of the corner of his eye, the words from Prudence Chatterton's gossip article caught his attention, and he reached for the newspaper, sliding it across his desk. He picked it up, shaking it as he opened it.

The printed words seized his attention...

RUMORS SWIRL OVER RATTLESNAKE MOUNTAIN: A DUEL OF TITANS

HELLO ONCE AGAIN, DEAR CITIZENS OF FEATHERSTONE VALLEY! IT'S YOUR TIRELESS CHRONICLER OF LOCAL LORE, PRUDENCE CHATTERBOX, HERE TO UNVEIL YET ANOTHER RIVETING CHAPTER FROM OUR BUSTLING TOWN. THIS WEEK, THE WINDS OF RUMOR HAVE BROUGHT

WHISPERS OF A BURGEONING CONTEST THAT'S GOT EVERYONE'S EARS PERKED UP.

THE STAGE IS SET WITH RATTLESNAKE MOUNTAIN, THAT MAJESTIC LANDMARK THAT LOOMS OVER OUR PEACEFUL VALLEY. THE PLAYERS? NONE OTHER THAN MR. CRAIG HARRISON OF THE ESTEEMED HARRISON GOLD MINING COMPANY AND MR. SIDNEY MILLER FROM THE NOTORIOUS DEER CREEK. YES, YOU HEARD THAT RIGHT! THESE TWO TITANS OF INDUSTRY ARE RUMORED TO BE LOCKING HORNS OVER THE OWNERSHIP OF RATTLESNAKE MOUNTAIN.

NOW, FOR THOSE WHO MAY NOT RECALL, MR. HARRISON IS WELL-KNOWN TO US, A MAN WHOSE ENDEAVORS IN MINING HAVE OFTEN SPARKED BOTH AWE AND CONTROVERSY. ON THE OTHER HAND, MR. MILLER, WITH HIS VENTURES THAT SOME MIGHT CALL... LESS THAN SAVORY, REMAINS A FIGURE SHROUDED IN WHISPERS AND SIDELONG GLANCES. HIS ESTABLISHMENTS IN DEER CREEK HAVE LONG BEEN THE SUBJECT OF HEATED PARLOR DEBATES AND A FEW RAISED EYEBROWS.

ONE MUST PONDER WHY OUR OWN MAYOR DUNCAN, EVER THE JUDICIOUS LEADER, WOULD ENTERTAIN DEALINGS WITH A MAN OF MR. MILLER'S REPUTE. THE PLOT, DEAR READERS, THICKENS AS THE COMMUNITY STANDS AT A CROSSROADS. DO WE, THE PROUD DENIZENS OF FEATHERSTONE VALLEY, REALLY WANT A CHARACTER LIKE MR. MILLER LAYING CLAIM TO OUR CHERISHED LANDSCAPES? WHAT INDEED IS AT STAKE IN THIS HIGH-STAKES GAME OF MOUNTAIN AND MIGHT?

REST ASSURED, FOR YOUR DEVOTED PRUDENCE CHATTERTON IS ALREADY WEAVING THROUGH THE WEB OF RUMORS AND HALF-TRUTHS. I VOW TO UNEARTH THE REAL INTENTIONS BEHIND THIS RUMORED CONTEST AND TO BRING TO LIGHT WHAT OUR BELOVED MAYOR MIGHT BE SCHEMING.

THE IMPLICATIONS OF SUCH A DEAL COULD RIPPLE THROUGH OUR TOWN'S VERY FOUNDATIONS. WE MUST ASK OURSELVES WHAT THE FUTURE HOLDS IF RATTLESNAKE MOUNTAIN FALLS INTO MR. MILLER'S HANDS. THE THOUGHT ALONE IS ENOUGH TO STIR A SENSE OF URGENCY IN THE HEART OF ANY LOYAL TOWNSPERSON.

FEAR NOT, FOR I SHALL KEEP A VIGILANT WATCH, READY TO REPORT back with all the facts and findings. Stay tuned, dear readers, and keep your eyes sharp and your minds clear. Featherstone Valley deserves the truth, and I, Prudence Chatterton, will stop at nothing to deliver it.

Until our next encounter, keep your spirits high and your gossip low.

Featherstone Valley counts on us all!

TWO

SIDNEY

The last person who had tried to best the likes of Sidney Miller hadn't lived to tell the tale. No one would even dare try anything over his eyes—and if they were stupid enough to attempt something, let's just say that was the last foolish thing to cross their minds.

What part of 'hadn't ever lived to tell the tale' did they not understand?

Knowing this fact, one could bet that for the last few weeks, since it was decided Sidney and Mr. Harrison would compete for the property in Featherstone Valley, Sidney hadn't been in the best of moods.

In fact, he'd been downright malicious.

Not that he cared.

Not even in the slightest.

Honestly, being in such a horrible mood almost made him in a better one.

If that made any sense.

Sidney shoved open the mayor's office door, not caring that it bumped into the wall behind it. The door rattled, knocking over a candlestick sitting on a shelf. The wax stick rolled from the shelf and hit the ground, bouncing a couple of times before rolling an inch and stopping.

Mayor Duncan was sitting at his desk, and he flinched as the door hit the wall. He spun in his chair, staring at Sidney with wide, blinking eyes.

"Mr. Miller, I wasn't expecting you..." He cleared his throat.

"Save it, Mr. Duncan." Sidney fought the instinct to roll his eyes as he crossed the room and sat in the chair on the other side of the desk. He leaned against the back, exhaling a deep breath.

"You could have at least announced your arrival by knocking or let me know in some way you were coming."

"You lost that privilege when you borrowed money from me and again when you agreed to this ridiculous bet with Mr. Harrison over the mountain property."

Mayor Duncan sucked in a breath. "I already told you I had no choice."

"A man always has a choice. You just chose the easier route."

"Don't underestimate this town, Mr. Miller, and don't underestimate the families who live here."

Sidney rolled his eyes again. "It's them who should not be underestimating me. Do you think all the families of Deer Creek were happy with all the gifts I brought to their town? They weren't, and if you believe they were, you are a fool. In the end, though, they have realized how much my businesses have done for the town, and every family here will do the same."

The mayor shifted uncomfortably in his plush leather chair, unable to meet Sidney's piercing gaze. "It's not that simple here in Featherstone Valley, Mr. Miller. The people of this town have... expectations. I can't just go selling off land to the highest bidder without giving them a say."

Sidney let out a harsh bark of laughter. "And you can't just disregard the deal we had when I loaned you the money you needed to save this town, either. Have you forgotten about our little arrangement already?" He cocked his head to the side, digging his gaze deep into the depths of the mayor's fear.

Mayor Duncan slumped in his chair and furrowed his brow as though trying to drum up any courage he could find. "No. I haven't. But we agreed that I would pay back the loan in cash. Nothing was written that I had to give you first choice on town land."

A smirk spread across Sidney's lips. "Ah. So, you do have a backbone. I suppose what you just said is true. Perhaps I should change the wording of the contract, then." He chuckled, glancing around the room as he propped one leg onto the other's knee. "I must say, I'm slightly impressed with you finding such a loophole."

"Why do you want the mountain so badly, Mr. Miller? Gold mining isn't exactly on your list of professions."

"That's for me to know, not you."

"Still, people will ask. What am I supposed to tell them?"

"Tell them whatever you want. I don't care. Since when do you give a hoot about the people of this town?"

"I've always cared about the town and the people. Why else would I borrow money for them?"

"Borrowed money to pay back what you stole?" Sidney blinked. "Seems to me that a man who cared about a town and its people probably wouldn't have used town funds to make poor business investments."

"I didn't know they were poor investments!" The mayor clenched his hands into fists and slammed them down on his desk. He sucked in a breath, holding it until his face turned a slight shade of red. As he finally exhaled, he glanced toward the office door. His eyes widened as though the thought suddenly occurred to him that someone could have overheard him. He lowered his voice to a whisper. "I thought I would make money on the deals, and I could just pay it back."

"But they weren't town investments. You had every intention of pocketing the earnings."

"So? I've heard about business owners doing that sort of thing all the time."

"Yes, with their own business income. Not town funds." Sidney chuckled again. He'd encountered idiots in business hundreds of times and even foolish politicians who couldn't tell a man which direction was north or south. Still, he expected people to trust them enough to uphold the state's laws and manage the town's funds.

But Bartholomew Duncan was in a class all to himself.

Mayor Duncan's eyes darted toward the door again. "Money aside, you have to understand my position here. If word got out that I sold that prime real estate to you for your... establishments, there would be heck to pay come re-election time."

"That sounds like a *you* problem," Sidney said, straightening up and crossing his arms over his chest. "I'm not here to discuss re-elections and such. I'm a businessman, Duncan. I don't give a darn about public opinion. All I care about is securing that land and expanding my business. And you'll help me do it, contest or no contest."

The mayor sighed heavily, removing his spectacles and pinching the bridge of his nose. "What exactly did you have in mind? Harrison is no pushover, you know. He's got the support of half the town behind him."

A slow, wicked grin spread across Sidney's face. "Harrison is nothing more than a bug waiting to be squashed. He may have the town's favor now, but I have something better."

"Like what?"

"Money and influence. And I intend to use both to secure my victory."

Duncan leaned forward, slipping his spectacles back on as his interest piqued despite himself. "Go on..."

"Aside from having a few tricks up my sleeve, I also intend to call upon a few... favors."

"What kind of favors?"

"Let's just say that with some well-placed bribes, a little blackmail, maybe even a scandalous rumor or two about our upstanding Mr. Harrison, by the time I'm done, the good people of Featherstone Valley will be begging me to take that land off their hands."

The mayor's eyes widened again, and he blinked a couple of times. "That's a dangerous game you're playing. If anyone found out..."

"They won't," Sidney cut him off sharply. "Because aside from what I'm doing, you will be in the background making sure this contest is rigged in my favor. I want everything tilted toward my interests."

Mayor Duncan swallowed hard. "And how am I supposed to do that? The agreement says whoever finds the most gold wins the mountain."

"Ah, but we have yet to finalize the details. Instead of casting the rule that the winner finds the most gold, you make the rules about quality, not quantity."

"And what will that do?"

"It will give you the power of judgment." Sidney paused, waiting to see if the mayor understood. However, judging by how he raised one eyebrow, looking confused, Sidney continued. "I want the judging criteria, the scoring, everything to go in my favor. Do that, and we won't have a problem. Do I make myself clear?"

Mayor Duncan closed his eyes and nodded as he opened them. "I see. Of course, you make yourself clear. I'll see to the details personally."

"Good." Sidney stood and moved around the chair, facing the mayor as he reached into his pocket and yanked a handkerchief out, wiping the back of his neck. "I need a few weeks to *gather* all the necessary supplies and workers. Once I have everything secured, we can meet to finalize the details and sign all the contracts and paperwork. Agreed?"

"Agreed."

"Then I suggest you get it all done."

Before the mayor could utter another word, Sidney spun and left the office, slamming the door just as hard as he'd opened it. A low rumble vibrated through his chest, and he stomped down the street with the mercantile in his sight.

These fools have no idea who they are dealing with.

Sidney had worked his entire life, building everything from the ground up. He started with a single saloon won in a crooked card game he'd figured out how to rig by watching the men play for a few weeks. Studying the cards had always been easy, and from that single game and that single saloon, he now owned a string of taverns and brothels across three states. Featherstone Valley was just a pin in his wheel, but it was a necessary pin. One that could expand everything he already had.

If one controls the workers, one controls the town.

And he intended to gain that control.

If one employs the men, one controls the men.

And he intended to gain that control, too.

What did he care about gold?

Well... of course, he loved it. Gold was, after all, money. He'd be stupid not to love it. But loving it didn't mean he wanted to make a living digging it from the ground. It took too much time, effort, and work for that nonsense. But if owning a company and employing the men who could do that work would gain him power over the town, allowing him to bring in businesses or, even better, gain the upper hand by buying them out of their homes and land...

Well, that would just be... what was the saying again?

Icing on the cake.

Much like this bet.

While he couldn't deny he'd been angry about the bet. Who wouldn't? Oh sure, there was a part of him that relished the idea of a challenge. After all, where was the satisfaction in an easy win? Not to mention, walking in and having everything handed over would have been a little boring. Enjoying the darker side of the deal, allowing his ruthless hunger to demand nothing less than total domination, though...

Now, that wasn't boring.

Neither was the thought of teaching Mr. Harrison that Sidney wasn't a man to be trifled with. Mr. Harrison would learn—the hard way, too—that when Sidney crushed him into dust and took everything he held dear.

The so-called "nice guy" act might work on the simpletons of Featherstone Valley, but Sidney saw right through it. Men like Craig Harrison, with their righteous morals and blinded ideals, were too weak to seize absolute power. They didn't have the guts to do what needed to be done, to bloody their hands and step on a few backs on the climb to the top. But Sidney did. He'd prove it, too.

Nothing was off-limits, and there was no tactic too low. Ultimately, Sidney would be the last man standing, the law of Featherstone Valley in all but name. And as for the town itself... well, they would learn to embrace their new future under his reign. The "good old days" of Sunday sermons and church potlucks were over. It was time for progress of a different sort— the kind that lined Sidney's pockets and kept the miners and cowhands pouring into his establishments night after night.

He knew what to do.

And just who to send word to.

Mr. Harrison could preach and plot all he wanted. In the end, it would all be for nothing. Because Sidney Miller always got what he wanted, and what he wanted now was Featherstone Valley, bent and broken to his iron will.

He trotted up the stairs and entered the mercantile,

acknowledging the few women standing at the counter, their baskets laden with supplies for that night's dinner. They froze, looking at him with wide eyes.

"Good morning, ladies," he said, tipping his hat. Even a conniver can be a gentleman, right?

They both looked at him and while one's mouth fell open, the other squared her chest. "Good afternoon." Her words sounded forced from her lips, as though she uttered them not because she wanted to but because she had to.

Her face flushed slightly pink, and she glanced over her shoulder, nodding to the other woman. The other nodded back, and the two walked off toward the other side of the store. Sidney's gaze followed them momentarily before turning toward the store owner behind the counter.

"What can I help you with today, sir?" the store owner asked.

"I need to send a telegram."

"All right. Let me grab a pencil." The store owner bent down, fumbling around the shelves under the counter, straightening up after finding what he was looking for. He fetched a piece of paper and readied himself. "What do you wish for me to say, Mister?"

"Inform Mr. Adams that Mr. Sidney Miller of Deer Creek is offering him the position of Head Foreman of the Miller Mining Company in Featherstone Valley. Quality wages will be paid, plus room and board until suitable housing is found, and I will reimburse all travel expenses. I expect him in Featherstone Valley in three weeks."

The store owner etched each word on the paper and glanced at Sidney. "Anything else, sir?"

"No, that's it."

"And who shall I send this to?"

"Mr. Bert Hinkle, Great Basin Mining Company in Tonopah, Nevada."

"Nevada, you say? That's... that's a long way away." The store owner chuckled as though he wanted to make a slight joke to lighten the conversation. Sidney didn't know which, nor did he care.

"Yes, it is."

The store owner eyed Sidney as though he expected Sidney to elaborate on the nature of the telegram. *Did he expect me to tell him what the business matter of the telegram was about?* Sidney stared at the man, furrowing his brow until finally, the store owner took the silent hint.

"Well, I suppose I should get this sent off for you. Do you need help with anything else?"

"No, that's all."

"All right... well..." The man hesitated momentarily, then scurried off toward the back room. As he vanished behind a long, thick curtain, Sidney returned his hat to his head and strode out of the store, ignoring a few men who stared at him as they passed by. He returned to his carriage, motioning to the driver it was time to leave as he sat. He looked around the town. It wasn't much to look at, but it would be nothing but dollar signs after he was done with it.

Even if a few rocks in the road slowed him down, it didn't matter. He had an empire to build, and heaven help anyone who stood in his way.

THREE

AVA

Ava's silver spurs rattled as she made her way down the street. With the straps hitched around the heels of her boots, the silver and gold rowels spun, their spiked tips sharp enough to cut the hide of any animal.

Or the skin of any man.

For nearly four years, since 1899, she'd strolled down the same dirt roads of Tonopah, Nevada, watching as the once dusty little town of a few tiny buildings made from scraps of wood had spread through the sagebrush, growing to dozens and dozens of brick dwellings three and four stories tall—all built with the hunger for the precious metals hidden deep within the earth.

News had spread like wildfire about the rich strikes along the Comstock and down south through the Tonopah basin, bringing hordes of men who trekked westward seeking employment with either the Tonopah Mining Company or the Goldfield Consolidated Mining Company. Their sixteen teams of mules left trails in the Nevada sand, stretching so far and wide that one could see them for miles until a dust storm covered the evidence. With their sights set on wealth and power, they all wanted a share of the money.

Just as she did.

The only part of this life she hadn't planned on was being forced to work in the mind-numbing dark below the ground for the likes of someone else. She wanted her own claim, somewhere on the outskirts of town where she could carve her own path through the Sierras, far away from prying curiosity and self-indulgent men whose ignorance tied them to the warrants of a suit-clad boss whom they didn't know and never would.

She never wanted to be destined for that life, only lived with the scraps she earned, just like all the other muckmen who now followed behind her to the assessor's office to turn in the last bit of gold they had for money. It would be the last of their pay since the mining company had fired them all that morning.

She didn't want to think about what she would do now.

Beads of sweat dripped down the back of her neck, moistening the collar of her button-up shirt. Although February was still cold in Tonopah—the desert of Nevada—the stress of the morning had left its mark, leaving her feeling like it was a hot summer day. Summer was always the worst in Tonopah and the one thing she hated. With skin-cracking dryness, the cloudless skies, and the discomforting scent of sagebrush, those hot days could leave one's head spinning as though they'd drunk too much whiskey even though they hadn't had a drop.

Or at least that was Ava's guess.

Being that she'd never had a glass of whiskey in her life, she didn't know for sure how it felt. She'd seen enough drunk men in her life, though, to understand how one acted when they'd partaken a little too much in drinking.

"Ava! Ava!" Mrs. Pruett darted from the Buckhorn General Store, forcing a groan from Ava's chest. The woman's canary voice bellowed with a pitch as shrill as the bell hanging from the door, and she waved one hand while crossing the street. "I'm glad I caught you. I wanted to let you know Howard ordered those extra supplies you needed. They should arrive sometime next week."

"Thank you. I'll let Griffin know."

"Oh, should we expect him to fetch them when they arrive?" She batted her eyes and cocked her head to the side, continuing before Ava even had a chance to think about answering the question. "I guess that's foolish to ask. Of course, we should expect him. I mean, I couldn't help but notice something, perhaps, going on between you... well, I don't wish to pry into the business of another—"

"I'm sorry, Madeline." Ava gave the woman's arm a firm, warning squeeze. "But as much as I'd love to stay and chat, I'm in quite a hurry."

Before the nosy store owner's wife responded, Ava headed down the street, shaking her head. Of course, it was known around town that Mrs. Pruett was the nosiest of all the women. She lived to spread gossip, and her tongue mirrored a wildfire burning dry brush as the flames devoured all in their path. She never seemed to miss any moment when she could question Ava's relationship with her mining partner, Griffin. Surely, her hinted question, masked as a statement, would turn into several more.

None of which Ava desired to answer.

Whatever love affair she thought she saw between Ava and Griffin, and however strong she believed it was, she was wrong.

He was nothing more than a brother figure.

And Ava was nothing more than a sister figure to him.

Ava continued down the street beyond the Hotel Esmeralda. Beaten by the sun and pelted by the sand blown around from the occasional windstorm, the colors of its plated glass windows didn't seem to gleam in the early morning light as they once did. Built with three stories, the owners had spent far too much money on the place, decorating each room with luxurious furniture and beautiful linens that, unfortunately, the revolving door of dirty mine workers had tarnished. A few horses stood tied to the hitching posts out front, and they slept as they swished their tails at the relentless flies swarming around them. The coarse strands slapped their hides with a smacking sound. Although they slept, their ears still perked, twisting with each sound they heard.

Ava's hand wrapped around the doorknob to the Great Basin Mining Company's office, and as she opened the door, familiar laughter rasped through the air, filling her with dread. It was the joy of one she wished she didn't know.

"Well, well, well. Look who it is." Billy Jack slid from around the corner, and with his back against the building, he inched closer to her. A smirk spread across his face, and he straightened his shoulders to puff up his bony chest. He failed. "I haven't seen your smiling face around here in a while."

"I wasn't aware my travels were any of your business," she said.

With a slight chuckle, he rolled a toothpick from one side of his mouth to the other. His breath smelled of rotting teeth, a scent as foul as the stench of his stained clothes and the chunks of his unwashed hair framing his face. The dull, mud-colored strands were so long that they touched his shoulders. He licked his sunburned lips and nodded toward the two men behind him, their attention trained on her. One of them pretended to blow her a kiss while the other rubbed his dirty chin with one hand.

"Oh, come on, don't play like that. Where have you been hiding out, Ava?"

"You act as though I'm going to divulge such information to you."

Long ago, there was a time when this man's existence didn't repulse her. Growing up together in the orphanage in Virginia City, Billy Jack had been, dare she say, a friend and even a courted lover when they were young. He had been someone she'd known all too well who was now so twisted by evil that he was nothing more than a stranger and a foe.

With the sickness of his greed and lust for power, the once shy young man who shared his meals with her, held the door for her, tipped his hat, pulled out a chair, and treated her with respect had vanished, leaving only a vengeful horse thief and a criminal. A man who only lived to point his gun in someone's face to steal from them or, worse, murder them for his own gain.

He wasn't the kind soul she once knew. He wasn't the gentleman she once cared for or who cared for her. Now, he only loved money and authority, leaving little concern if the people he gunned down were women, children, or if they were men with families.

"I only ask because I'm concerned for your welfare."

"You shouldn't tell lies, Billy Jack."

"I wouldn't dare do such a thing as to be untrue to a woman such as yourself." He laid his hand on his chest and attempted a slight bow. He looked less than anything she would consider regal.

"You should also work on your performance before the day comes when you sit in front of a judge and claim innocence for something you've done."

"And what about all the crimes you committed all those years ago? Or are those somehow forgivable?"

"I did nothing I haven't repented for. I may have stolen a wallet or two in my youth when we needed a meal, but I've never committed the transgressions you have. Now, if you'll step—"

He clasped a lock of her hair between his fingers, letting the soft strands slide over his dirty skin. Memories of their time together swam in his irises, blurring in the brown shade. She knew the thoughts running through his mind, the visions of riding through the trails, laughing and chatting about how they would never take life too seriously. Plans only the young make when they believe they are more intelligent than everyone else and that they have their whole lives ahead of them. They ran away from the orphanage the second they could—two sixteen-year-olds with a passion for freedom. They lived by obtuse notions of life and the philosophies of the imprudent, only to realize the world wasn't as giving as the sisters of the Church to a pair of young fools. Without work, they soon had to resort to petty theft just to survive.

A time in my life I would forever regret.

"We had fun, though. Didn't we?" he whispered. "You and me and our crazy plans for the future."

"Which plans? The ones you worshiped or the ones you betrayed?"

His smile vanished.

"I'm here to meet with Mr. Hinkle and Mr. Owen, so if you'll step aside..." Her words hissed through her gritted teeth, and she shoved her shoulder into his chest, knocking him off balance enough for him to retreat a couple of steps. The disgusting odor of his clothes stuck to hers, churning in her stomach as she twisted the doorknob once more and stepped inside the office.

Through the haze in the air, the sunlight brightened the gloomy interior with its plain white walls and bare furniture. Mr. Hinkle and Mr. Owen sat at their desks, and while Mr. Owen only peered over his spectacles, Mr. Hinkle stood, buttoning his jacket as Ava crossed the room. He held his hand out for her to shake.

"Good afternoon, Miss Adams."

"Good afternoon, Mr. Hinkle." She glanced at the other partner. "Good afternoon, Mr. Owen." He nodded, glancing at her momentarily before returning his gaze to a few papers on his desk. His spectacles slid down his nose slightly, and he pushed the thin lenses and delicate frames back up without moving his head. She waited for him to say something, but when he didn't, she turned her attention back to Mr. Hinkle. "I received your note asking for a meeting this morning, so I'm here for that meeting."

"Yes. Thank you for coming." Mr. Hinkle motioned toward the chair on the other side of his desk. "Please have a seat."

His tone caused her stomach to twist, and her teeth clenched as she sat.

"I'm sure you're wondering why we called you into the office this morning."

She nodded, glancing between the two men again. Only one gave her any attention back. "That is a correct assumption."

"Miss Adams, we brought you in this morning to inform you of a telegram we received about a job offer for you."

She froze. Her heart thumped. "What did you say?"

"We got a telegram requesting your employment with another mining company."

"Requesting my employment? I don't understand. Who is the telegram from?"

"It's from Mr. Sidney Miller at the Miller Mining Company." Mr. Hinkle fetched a paper from his desk and handed it to her.

She took it from him, reading each word twice to ensure she understood it.

INFORM MR. ADAMS OF JOB OFFER
MILLER MINING COMPANY IN FEATHERSTONE VALLEY
QUALITY WAGES AND ROOM AND BOARD PAID
TRAVEL EXPENSES REIMBURSED
ARRIVE IN TOWN WITHIN THREE WEEKS

"I don't understand this." She handed Mr. Hinkle the slip of paper back.

"Well, it means you have a job waiting for you in Featherstone Valley with a good wage, room and board paid, and Mr.

Miller is offering to reimburse your travel expenses. The only requirement is that you arrive for the job within three weeks."

"Arrive? Where is Featherstone Valley? I've never heard of it."

Mr. Hinkle looked at his partner, who shrugged and shook his head as though he refused to answer. Mr. Hinkle answered instead. "I believe it's... it's in Montana."

"Montana?" She looked at the telegram again. "I'm not going to Montana... this telegram isn't even addressed to me. It's addressed to Mr. Adams."

"We are aware of that, but we have every reason to believe it's an oversight."

She raised one eyebrow. "An oversight? That's a big oversight, Mr. Hinkle."

"I understand your concern. But we still firmly believe it's addressed to you."

"And why would it be addressed to me? Do you know this... Mr. Sidney Miller?"

"We do."

"How?"

"He was an investor in our company many years ago, and he's stayed in touch. We might have mentioned to him a time or two about the type of miner you are."

"The type of miner I am? And what type is that?"

"You know you were one of our best."

"One of your best? If I am one of your best, why are you firing me?"

"We aren't firing you, Miss Adams. We are simply letting you go so you may accept this job offer."

"Is that how you hear what you are saying?"

"With all due respect, Miss Adams, despite what you may think, we are doing you a favor."

Ava cocked her head to the side and cleared her throat. "You know, Mr. Hinkle, I have often found it funny that when someone says *with all due respect*, they follow it with derision. It's almost as if they mean disrespect; however, they attempt to justify the disdain instead of owning it."

Wyatt didn't answer but instead brushed a few fingers over his lips; his shoulders bounced with silent laughter.

Mr. Hinkle raised one eyebrow and glanced at his partner. "My apologies, Miss Adams. I meant no disrespect."

"I'm sure you didn't." She glanced between them again, and both men glanced down at the floor, and Mr. Owen cleared his throat. He was always the weaker of the partners. He was never the one to speak and was the first to shy away if confronted. "So, what *did* you mean, Mr. Hinkle?"

"You have been loyal to the Great Basin Mining Company and have far exceeded what we have asked of you. Please let us help you. This job will mean more money and more opportunity." He paused. "We have decided to give you three weeks' pay that should more than cover any of your travel expenses."

"And what if I don't want to take the job?"

Mr. Hinkle's eyes widened, and he blinked. "But you must."

"Why?"

The two men dropped their gazes to the floor again. "We wish to do right by you, Miss Adams. We believe this is right."

Although a slight part of her desired to continue refusing, she couldn't help but feel that she'd be a fool to do so. She closed her eyes and inhaled a deep breath through her nose, exhaling as she looked at the men again. "All right. I will take the job."

Mr. Hinkle wrenched open his desk drawer and yanked a few thick leather-bound ledger books from the depths. He flipped the pages, licking his thumb every few sheets to help separate the parchment. After finding the correct page, he jotted down a few words in chicken scratch handwriting, then reached into a drawer again. He pulled out an envelope, fumbling with it as he overturned it and slipped several bills from it. One by one, he counted each one, then set them in front of her. "Here you are. There's three weeks' worth of wages." He slid the ticket book across the desk and pointed toward a few lines. "Sign here, here, and here."

She grasped the pen and dipped it in the inkwell, swooping the letters of her signature across the lines before Mr. Hinkle tugged the ledger book back toward him and signed his name.

No matter how many times she'd penned Ava Adams, seeing it in print always seemed to leave a hole in her chest, yet swell it with pride. It was a name not given to her at birth nor left with her when her mother abandoned her with Sister Mary at the orphanage. Instead, she'd given it to herself when she arrived in Esmeralda County.

"Thank you for all you've done for the Great Basin Mining Company, Miss Adams. Mr. Owen and I wish you nothing but the best."

After gathering the money, she stood, shoving the pay into her pocket as she glanced at the men one last time. "Of course you do."

She turned to leave, and Mr. Hinkle stood, calling after her. "Miss Adams?"

"Yes," she faced him.

"Take this. I know it's not much information, but it's something." He handed her the telegram, and as the paper touched her fingers, she looked down at it, reading the words.

She had so many questions, and while she could ask them, she wouldn't get any answers—at least not from the two men in the office wearing expensive suits.

"Good luck to you," he said.

"Thank you."

FOUR

AVA

Tumbleweeds rolled across the dirt road as Ava made her way back through town. Their branches broke from the bouncing movement, and the twigs scattered in the breeze, which also blew through her waist-length raven hair. A chill ran through her coat, inching up the back of her neck, causing goosebumps to fleck her arms.

She longed for a bath and to feel the hot water on her skin, not only warming her up but also cleaning her of all the dirt filling deep into her pores. While the money she'd just collected could secure her a nice hotel room for the night, the thought of it would remain just that—a thought that she could only dream about. She had to save every dollar she could for the supplies needed to get to Montana.

Montana?

Was she ready to leave all she'd known for the last several years? Did she wish to leave the only bosses she'd known, the only miners she'd known, and the only home she'd known?

What about Griffin?

He was the brother she'd never had. A far better and more

trustworthy friend than Billy Jack had ever been. How was she supposed to tell him goodbye?

She didn't want to think about that.

She headed back toward where she'd come, passing all the familiar places in town, like the general store where she had purchased her first pair of sturdy boots for work, the blacksmith's shop where she would take her tools to be repaired, and the livery stable, where the scent of hay and horses mingled with the dust in the air. She'd lived in this town for many years, and while she hated it a time or two—or several—it now suddenly felt like a place she didn't know if she could live without, even if she knew she had to.

As the morning hours gave way to the afternoon, more townsfolk stirred from their homes. Of course, most meandering the streets with her were men, either alone or with other men. Wives were a rarity in the Tonopah Basin, and the lack of femininity in the town only stoked the flame she didn't belong. The only woman miner in their world, they often mocked her as though they believed she, too, should either work in the brothel at the edge of town or parade around the saloon clad in a scandalous dress for all the men to see. To them, she was only worth the price of their enjoyment and nothing more.

Oh, how I loved proving them wrong.

As she neared the edge of town, she crossed the road, and the scent of hot ham sandwiches wafted from Mr. Johnson's café. The business's weatherworn sign came into view. Its green and white paint had faded over the years; however, the words—*The Northern Mr. Wyatt Earp*—were still readable—a joke by the owner, Wyatt Johnson, and his wife, Josie.

Ava continued toward the lone structure, surrounded by dozens and dozens of empty hitching posts—except for the one her buckskin horse was tied to. Usually barren during the day, as soon as the sun dipped in the sky and the men quit their work underground, the hitching posts housed more horses than a herd of wild mustangs roaming the range. The only place in town to hide away in the arms of the best food in town, everyone enjoyed the place—some more than others, a little far too often for their own good, she thought, filling their bellies until they cried out in pain. However, of course, such wasn't any of her business unless *the someone* was her—which, unfortunately, had happened several times.

What could she say other than she was a sucker for those sandwiches?

Rays of sunshine beamed through the windows, lighting the smoky air inside the café as Mr. Grant and Mr. Watson, two men she knew from the mines, sat around one of the many tables, the only patrons this lazy afternoon. Cigar smoke billowed above their heads, and with cards in their hands, they greeted her while the third man in their poker game, old man Pritchard, ignored her. Not that such bothered her much. The foolish loudmouth of a man had traveled here from Canada with some cronies, thinking he could make his fortune swindling miners by selling overpriced horses.

Mr. Johnson, the owner, stood at the counter on one end of the room, wiping out a glass with a dirty dishtowel as she meandered through the mess of empty tables and chairs. A half smile inched up the side of his face while tiredness fixed in the arches of his eyebrows and slumped shoulders.

"Good afternoon, Miss Adams. Did you come in for a hot sandwich?" he asked.

"Good afternoon, and yes, I did." Her rump slid on top of one of the stools, and she rested her elbows on the counter.

He threw the dishrag over his shoulder. "One hot ham sandwich coming up."

After pouring her a glass of water and setting it down, he retreated into the kitchen, appearing several minutes later with a plate in his hand. He set it down in front of her, and she closed her eyes, sniffing the ham-scented steam rising from the meat and bread.

"So... anything new going on at the Great Basin Mining Company?" he asked.

She shrugged. "I don't know. They fired me this morning."

"They fired you?" Mr. Johnson blinked. His mouth gaped open. "But... you're the best miner they got working in those mines. They are fools if they think they will find anyone to replace you. What did they say exactly?"

"They told me they'd received a telegram from some man they know wanting me for a job, and they said they are doing me a favor."

"I don't understand."

"I don't either. But that was what they said."

"So, what are you going to do?"

She shrugged again, ignoring the flicker of anger bubbling in her chest. "I don't know. I suppose I will take the job since there isn't another mining company in Tonopah."

"What about starting one of your own?"

"I don't own any land, and I don't have the money to buy any." She snorted a slight laugh, shaking her head. While another in her shoes would probably be concerned, she was just annoyed. She'd spent several years below the ground, digging through the depths of the earth for Mr. Hinkle and Mr. Owen, and what had they shown her for that loyalty?

The door.

That's what they'd shown her, and they had tried to disguise it by saying they were doing her a favor.

She rolled her eyes and shook her head. The disbelief proved too much for her patience, and she inhaled, picked up the sandwich, and took a bite. Although she wanted to dwell in the deliciousness without caring about anything else around her, she couldn't. Not this time. A growl swept through her exhaled breath.

"I know you won't want to hear this, but perhaps this is a blessing."

"A blessing? How?"

"Perhaps the path you've been on isn't the one you're supposed to be on."

Her shoulders deflated, and she rested her elbows on the counter. "Please don't start in on the paths in life. You know I don't believe in that stuff."

"That stuff? Do you mean God and the Bible? Didn't the sisters teach it all to you at the orphanage?"

"They did." She inhaled, holding it as she fought the memories. "They taught me other things about the Bible that weren't in there, too, and if that is believing in God..." She let her voice trail off, not wanting to finish her sentence.

"Ava, the things they did, that's... that's not..."

"It doesn't matter." She waved her hand at him. "Can we just talk about something else?"

Mr. Johnson stared at her. She could tell he didn't want to change the subject, but thankfully, when he opened his mouth again, he did. "So, where is this job?" he asked.

"Montana."

"Montana?" The bar owner jerked his head. "Wow. I have to say I never thought I'd live to see a day you'd leave Tonopah."

"You and me, both." She rolled her eyes again. "I never thought there'd come a day I'd leave this town."

"I said those same words to Josie just the other night."

"Oh." Ava blinked several times as she straightened her shoulders. Owning the only café in town left the Johnsons wealthy, and they lived in one of the biggest houses in the area —a rarity out in the middle of nowhere. "Are you thinking about leaving Tonopah, too?"

"I'm not. But she has been trying to talk me into moving to Virginia City. She doesn't care for Tonopah as much as I do. She feels too alone. I understand her reasons; however, I'm not convinced yet." He chuckled, shaking his head.

"I told him he'd be stupid to leave and close this place down," Mr. Pritchard grunted hoarsely as he shuffled the stack of playing cards.

His voice inched across Ava's already flared anger, not only from the sound he made but just from knowing he'd overheard their whole conversation.

Mr. Johnson glanced at her. "Ava. Don't."

"Too late." She spun on her stool, facing the poker game. Amusement tickled through her mind. "Unless he desires to close up so he can get away from *certain* people of this town. I can't say I blame him. I wouldn't want *your* company all day long either."

Mr. Pritchard's eyes narrowed, and he scowled while Bradford and Tucker smirked and snorted a chuckle through their noses.

"Should have known such scorn would come from the likes of a woman—especially you, Miss Adams," the old grump scoffed. He spat tobacco in a tarnished copper pot on the ground near the table. His utter loathing burned through his wrinkled, sulky frown.

He spat again. "I don't like ya. In fact, I think this world would be a better place without ya."

She fanned her face, then laid the back of her hand against her forehead, lightening her voice in a lady-like dainty tune. "Oh my, I just don't know what I'll ever do without your favor."

"You're nothing but an infuriating, loudmouthed wench."

"Why, Mr. Pritchard." She laid her hand on her chest. "Wherever does this hostility toward me come from? People will begin to think you don't like me if you keep acting like that." She looked at Mr. Johnson, dramatically widening her gaze as if to pretend the old man's words hurt and shocked her. They didn't. "I'm not loudmouthed. Am I?"

Mr. Johnson laughed, unable to answer her question, as he poured himself a glass of water and took a few gulps before waving his hand toward the men. "He's just sore at you for ruining his business. He was making quite the killing by robbing people blind for years until you came into town. Now he's having to barter for every dollar he can get his grubby hands on."

"I didn't cheat nobody." The old man pointed his fat finger at Mr. Johnson. It trembled not only because of his age but also because of the anger building through his body. "I sold those horses for what they were worth and not a penny more."

"And how *has* business been for you, Mr. Pritchard?" A whispered chuckle breathed through Ava's words. This conversation had made her feel better than anything had all day—even better than when she got her pay from the Assessor's office.

The old man threw down his cards and shoved his chair from the table, growling as he stomped toward the door. His boots thumped against the hardwood floors, and he slammed the door so hard that the force rattled through the wall, shaking several bottles decorating one of the many shelves.

"Thanks a lot, Ava," Bradford said, tossing his own cards down on the table. "He's gonna be madder than a fox in a henhouse for a week, and I'll never get the money he owes me."

She flashed Mr. Johnson a smile, and he nodded as though he had read her mind. He vanished back into the kitchen, returning with two plates, one in each hand. He gave them to her, and without saying a word, she glided toward the table, setting the hot sandwiches between the men and giving them a wink.

"This should suffice for any hardship I have caused you, gentlemen," she said.

"Ava, will you marry me?" Mr. Tucker's hand reached for a plate.

"Get in line, Mr. Watson," Mr. Johnson called from the

counter. "Because there ain't no man in town who doesn't have that question on his mind. Unless, of course, he has a wife, and even then, I'm not sure he'd pass on the chance."

"You know I'm not the marrying kind, Tucker." She gave Mr. Watson another wink, hoping to mask her lie. "But if I ever change my mind, you'll be the first to know. I promise."

She returned to the counter, sliding on the stool once again.

"You sure have a way of making friends, don't ya?" Mr. Johnson asked.

"Friends and enemies."

As the two laughed, the café door swung open suddenly. Everyone in the café flinched, and Ava sucked in a breath as Griffin stumbled in, breathing heavily as though he had just sprinted there from the mines on the outskirts of town. His brown hair was disheveled, and his face was flushed. He scanned the room wildly until his eyes landed on Ava, perched at the counter.

"Ava!" He hurried over to her. "Please tell me it isn't true."

Ava growled, avoiding his gaze. Of course, word would spread like wildfire in the mines, but she expected that blaze to take at least a day or two to ignite.

"Tell you what isn't true?"

"That you aren't leaving."

"How did you find out?"

His eyes widened, and he blinked. "It's true?"

"Afternoon, Griffin," she said, ignoring his tone. "You look like you could use a glass of water. Mr. Johnson, would you please—"

"I don't give a darn about water right now." Griffin cut her off. He waved his hand as he rushed toward her and gripped her shoulders, forcing her to look at him. Worry creased his brow. "Is it true, Ava? Did they fire you?"

Ava sighed heavily. "Griffin, I... it's complicated."

"Complicated? What is complicated about it? Either they

canned you, or they didn't!" His voice rose in frustration and confusion.

"Keep your voice down," Ava hissed. "You're still in Mr. Johnson's place of business, and it's rude."

"Rude?" Griffin glanced around the café, looking at Mr. Tucker and Mr. Grant before meeting her gaze again. "Are you being serious right now?"

"Just keep your voice down. There's no need to shout."

"Fine. I will lower my voice if you tell me what is happening."

"It's nothing, really. Mr. Hinkle and Mr. Owen received a telegram from a man they know who wants me to come to work for him. They believe the job offer is rather good and thought they were doing me a favor."

Griffin released her and stumbled back a step, running a hand through his hair. "I don't understand... You're the best miner they've got. The whole operation would fall apart without you running things. Who is this man who offered the job?"

She shrugged. "I'm not sure. His name is Mr. Sidney Miller."

"I don't know anyone by that name around here."

"Mr. Miller isn't from here." Ava reached into her pocket and pulled out the crumpled telegram, handing it to him wearily. "See for yourself."

Griffin unfolded the paper, his eyes scanning the words. When he finished, he looked up at her in disbelief. "Montana? They expect you to pack up and head clear across the country just like that? Because this... this Mr. Miller, a man they know, requested you for a job?"

"That about sums it up," Ava replied dryly.

"Well... are you going to go?"

She inhaled. Unsure of how she would answer the question, she said nothing. She simply nodded.

His brow furrowed, and he shook his head. "But you can't

leave." Before she could say another word, he began to pace. Agitation grew through his stiffened shoulders, and he clenched his fists. "They can't do this. They can't make you leave."

"You're right, they can't. But I need a job, Griffin. Besides, it might not be bad in Montana." She wasn't sure if she said what she did to convince him or herself more, but in the end, it didn't matter. The sentiment was the same. She'd have to convince both of them just the same.

Griffin stopped pacing abruptly and spun to face her; his eyes were focused with a determination she'd seen in him countless times—especially when he was about to say or do something she couldn't talk him out of. "Then I'm coming with you."

Although she should have seen those words coming, she didn't. She hadn't thought about the what-ifs that would accompany her telling him she was leaving, and she'd been foolish not to.

"What? No, Griffin, don't be a fool. You have a good job here and a place in town. I can't ask you to throw that away."

"You aren't asking. I'm telling," he said firmly. "If you're heading to Montana, I'm going too—end of story."

"Be reasonable." Ava rolled her eyes. "What would you even do up there? You don't have an offer like I do."

"I'll figure something out," Griffin shrugged. "I'm a hard worker, and I have skills. I reckon somebody will have a use for me."

Ava pinched the bridge of her nose, feeling an argument brewing. "Griffin, I appreciate you wanting to come with me; I truly do. But I can't let you live your whole life because of where I'm going and what I'm doing. It wouldn't be right."

His brow furrowed again. "It's not about living a life on your account. Who's to say I won't find happiness up in Montana? Who's to say my future bride isn't living up there right now, waiting for me? You could be the one keeping true loves from finding each other."

Ava snorted a laugh. "You and your true love nonsense."

"It's not nonsense." He paused, taking a deep breath. "But all that aside. If you aren't here, I don't have anything in this godforsaken town. We're partners. We're family. And we've been so since I started in the mines, and you showed me the ropes. Where you go, I go. That's the end of it."

"It won't be an easy journey," she warned. "Montana is a long way off, and we have no idea what awaits us when we get there."

"I'm not afraid of a little hard traveling." He winked.

Ava sighed, a reluctant smile tugging at her lips. "You're a fool, Griffin Baker. Do you know that?"

"Maybe so. But you're stuck with me, so what does that make you?"

"That makes me a fool, too." She laughed and then pointed her finger in his face. "Don't say I didn't try to talk you out of it when you're saddle sore and miserable a hundred miles in."

"Wouldn't dream of it." Griffin held out his hand to shake. "Partners?"

Ava clasped his hand firmly in her own. His callused palm was warm and familiar. "Partners," she agreed.

FIVE

CRAIG

Resilience is a testament to one's innate ability to adapt, overcome, and thrive in the face of adversity. It is the force that propels us forward when the world seems to crumble around us, the light that guides us through the darkest moments, and the hope that sustains us when all else seems lost.

Craig didn't know how often he'd heard his grandfather utter that phrase—perhaps a hundred, perhaps two hundred, perhaps even more. He couldn't remember. All he remembered was that his grandfather said that phrase so often that his father had it etched on a wood marker and placed near the old man's grave—a reminder to everyone who walked past or visited.

Craig hadn't known in his youth how much he'd come to rely on his grandfather's words as he grew into a man—often finding solace in them after a hard day's work plowing the field long after the sun had nearly dehydrated him, or the long days and nights mining the Klondike when the temperatures could freeze a man's finger off.

So many times, he had sat by his fire, glancing up at the sky and praying so much that he wondered if any prayers were left to even say. Surely, one could never run out of words to say to God. But the thought still crossed his mind nonetheless.

"Good morning, everyone." Pastor Boone's sudden voice jerked Craig's attention, and he shook his head, focusing on the scent of the familiar aged wood as he sat in one of the last pews. The soft glow of sunlight filtered through the stained-glass windows, and the intricate patterns of colors flecked the hardwood floor, casting a kaleidoscope of hues across the worn boards.

"Good morning, Pastor Boone." The small room echoed with a collective greeting as men, women, and children responded to the pastor's words with their own greeting.

Pastor Boone smiled and nodded, looking at the faces of those who looked back at him. "I must admit that it took me a few more days than usual to find the right sermon I wanted to give today. Who would imagine it would be hard for a pastor to figure out what to say?" He chuckled, and several townsfolk joined him, chuckling, too. "I don't think I have to tell you where I found my inspiration. It seems to have happened quite often as of late, and I can't say that I haven't wondered if I should focus my attention elsewhere or not."

Craig leaned against the back of the pew, drawing in a deep breath as he glanced at the ceiling. He wasn't sure he had it in him today to sit and listen to the pastor's ramblings about influence and inspiration. Not when his mind was so heavy with the burdens of the past few days.

Confusion had spread through the miners, causing questions and tensions that had otherwise never bothered them before. Men had been quicker to argue, and the notion of being slow to anger had become nearly a myth among them. Couple that with the impending arrival of the crusher, and everything felt like it now weighed heavily on Craig's shoulders, threatening to break him like a twig.

"Folks of Featherstone Valley," the pastor continued. "Today, I want to speak to you about resilience in the face of adversity, and the scripture we will study today comes from *2 Corinthians 4:8-9,* 'We are hard-pressed on every side, but not crushed; perplexed, but not in despair; persecuted, but not abandoned; struck down, but not destroyed.'"

As soon as Pastor Boone spoke, his words perked Craig's ears. Each one hung in the air like a lifeline for those—mainly him—struggling to keep their heads above water. How had the man known he needed to hear this today?

Inspiration.

Ah. Prudence Chatterton's Parlor Patter.

That had to be it.

Craig leaned forward, his heart yearning for the comfort and guidance the pastor's message promised.

"Life is full of trials and tribulations," Pastor Boone continued, his eyes sweeping over the congregation until they found Craig. A slight smile spread across his lips. "We face insurmountable challenges and obstacles that threaten to crush our spirits. But as followers of Christ, we have a hope that cannot and should not be shaken."

Unsure if it was the belief swimming in his heart or just the idea of someone else saying the words to him, Craig felt the weight of the pastor's message. It was like a glimmer of light piercing through the darkness that had settled over his soul, a reminder that even in the bleakest of times, there was still reason to hold on to faith.

"Just like the apostle Paul, we may feel hard-pressed, perplexed, persecuted, and struck down. But we are not alone in our struggles. God is with us every step, giving us strength when we are weak, comfort when we are distressed, and hope when all seems lost."

Seems lost.

Although the words were like a knife to the gut, they had a

power, as though they no longer held him captive to their meaning. He couldn't describe it; he could only feel it.

As Pastor Boone's voice rose with conviction, Craig's eyes wandered across the congregation. He saw the faces of his neighbors, his friends, and his fellow townspeople. Each one seemed to carry their own burdens, their own fears and doubts. And yet, they gathered together in the church, seeking solace and strength in their shared faith.

Although he had known it wasn't just him that was affected by Rattlesnake Mountain, he hadn't thought much about how the sale to a man like Sidney Miller would affect the town. Sure, he had thought of it and had voiced his opinions, but the thoughts had been few and far between in the last several days. Consumed by his own needs, plans for the crusher, and figuring out the arrangement of moving miners and equipment, the thought hadn't crossed his mind.

As he continued to look around the room, wondering about the men, women, and children and how a saloon and brothel would impact their lives, his gaze settled on Mayor Duncan, sitting a few pews ahead. His shoulders were slumped as though his decisions and Pastor Boone's words weighed on him, too. As if to feel Craig's gaze, the mayor glanced over his shoulder, and for a moment, their eyes met, then the mayor looked away.

"In times like these," Pastor Boone continued, his voice cutting through Craig's thoughts, "when our community faces uncertainty and division, we must cling to our faith. We must remember that our true strength lies not in our own abilities, but in the power of God working through us." The congregation murmured their agreement, a chorus of whispered prayers and quiet amens. "Let us not lose heart, dear friends. Let us fix our eyes on Jesus, the author and perfecter of our faith. In Him, we find the resilience to face any challenge, the courage to stand firm amid the storm."

Amid the storm, indeed.

Craig closed his eyes as the pastor's words continued to wash over him. The road ahead was uncertain, the challenges daunting, but he had to have faith even if right now, at this moment, it felt fleeting.

"As we go forth from this place," Pastor Boone concluded, his voice softening to a gentle whisper, "let us remember that our circumstances do not define us. Our faith, our love, and our unwavering trust in God define us. May we be a light in the darkness, a beacon of hope to those who are struggling." With those final words, Pastor Boone closed his Bible, his head bowed in reverence. "Let us pray."

As the congregation joined in silent prayer, Craig bowed his head, too. He prayed for guidance, for strength, and for wisdom through the trials he faced.

He also prayed the mayor would come to his own senses, which was probably not the thing to ask God for, but he did it anyway, adding a little whisper of apologies if such a prayer was uncouth.

"Thank you all for coming and sharing your Sunday morning with me." Pastor Boone motioned toward the doors in the back of the church. "You are all dismissed."

Although everyone around him rose to their feet and gathered their belongings, Craig remained seated. He clasped his hands, holding them in his lap as he stared at the floor, trying not to make eye contact with anyone. He could feel their eyes boring into him, and heat warmed the back of his neck.

Surely, people had questions about the mountain deal. He did, too, for Pete's sake. But there were none he could answer.

That was the mayor's business.

Not his.

Let them ask him. Let them make him squirm. Let him deal with the tension in the air. Let him watch as the men gather, their voices low and urgent as they discuss the implications of a man like Mr. Miller. Let him deal with the angry mobs with fists clenched and eyes blazing with indignation. Let him deal with the others who were not so vocal about their concerns, walking around with worry lined on their foreheads as they wondered what the future might hold.

That was the mayor's business.

Not his.

He closed his eyes, holding them shut until the church was silent.

"Mr. Harrison?" a voice asked.

Craig opened his eyes as Pastor Boone sat next to him.

"Good morning, Pastor Boone," Craig said.

The pastor nodded and leaned back against the pew. "So, how did you find my sermon today? Was it helpful?"

Craig exhaled, the weight on his heart lifting slightly at the kindness in the pastor's eyes. "Yes, it was. It was just what I needed to hear, Pastor," he said.

"I'm glad. I didn't know what I wanted to say today, but then I saw the newspaper."

Craig snorted a laugh and nodded. "Prudence Chatterton certainly has a way of capturing the heart of the matter, doesn't she?"

"She or he?" The pastor flashed a smile and continued. "But yes, whoever it is writing those articles sure has a way of finding a story... and explaining one."

"You got that right." Craig paused. "Wait. Did you just say she or he? Do you think the person writing the article could be a man?"

"I suppose. Sarah and I have talked about it a few times, trying to identify who the writer could be."

"Do you know who it is?"

"Nah. We've both suggested a few names, but neither of us is truly interested in discovering the truth. Perhaps in the past, I was, like when I first arrived. But although the articles draw people's attention to the gossip around town, they also expose the heart of the matter, forcing those involved to broach topics out into the open that would otherwise be swept under the rug."

"I can see that. I must admit I was happy when she or he wrote about Mayor Duncan entertaining a deal with Mr. Miller."

"Do you think he would have not told anyone?"

"I know he wouldn't have."

"And why is that?"

"You'll have to ask him." Craig exhaled a deep breath. Although such an action would usually calm his anxiety, it didn't this time.

"I hope my son, Patrick, didn't cause you problems by suggesting the bet for the mountain."

"No, he didn't." Craig shook his head. "Truth be told, I think it might have helped by giving me a chance to buy the property since Mayor Duncan kept rejecting my offers. I'm afraid there would have come a time when Mr. Miller would have outbid me."

"Is what you said about Mr. Miller and the businesses he brought to Deer Creek true?"

"Every word."

"One would think that the mayor would consider the town when making such a decision—especially if the townsfolk are against such businesses or a man like that."

"Yeah, one would."

Craig caught the pastor's one raised eyebrow out of the corner of his eye. A look of intrigue seemed to settle on the man's face.

"This Mr. Miller... I assume all his businesses make him a good income."

"I believe so."

"And I assume this income could allow him to... oh, I don't know... perhaps loan people money should they find themselves in need."

Craig's teeth clenched. "I believe that is so, too." He glanced at the pastor, cocking his head to the side. "I wasn't aware that a man of the cloth would be so observant."

"Oh, we see more than one would think. However, I must admit that I wasn't always a pastor. I'm not sure you know this about me, Mr. Harrison, but before I turned my life over to God's calling for me, I was a Texas Ranger."

Craig sucked in a breath, and his head whipped toward Pastor Boone. "Really?"

"Yeah. It was a hard job but rewarding, especially when those who committed the crimes were brought to justice."

"I can imagine it was."

The pastor made a *humph* sound as he glanced down at the floor. He leaned forward, resting his hands on his knees before reaching over and patting Craig on the shoulder. "If there's anything you need to help you with buying this mountain, don't hesitate to ask." He paused, rising to his feet. "It's not just a pastor who protects the sheep."

"I understand, and I appreciate that." Craig paused, furrowing his brow. I know there are many Bible verses about asking God for what you want. But I must admit, after so many rejections from Mayor Duncan, I've wondered if God's rejecting me, too."

"Ah, yes. *Matthew 7:7-11*, Ask and it will be given to you; seek and you will find; knock and the door will be opened to you. For everyone who asks receives; the one who seeks finds; and to the one who knocks, the door will be opened. Or even in *Matthew 21:22*, If you believe, you will receive whatever you ask for in prayer."

"I've asked. And asked, and asked, and asked." Craig chuckled, letting his voice trail off.

"I know how that feels. Trust me." The pastor folded his arms and leaned against the back of the pew. "From my experience, people put far too much thought on the *asking* and not enough on the receiving. They believe that what they are asking for is what's best for them, and they never think that it might not be or it might be but not at that time."

"Are you saying that Rattlesnake might not be best for me?"

"That's not for me to judge or decide. We don't live by my timing. We live by His, and sometimes unanswered prayers lead to greater things."

"So, you think perhaps He's up there telling me to wait?"

The pastor shrugged. "Perhaps. Or perhaps Rattlesnake Mountain is meant to be yours. But not this very instant. The only thing to do is ask and have faith that no matter what happens, He knows what is best, and His timing will make every question and every doubt worth it in the end."

Craig inhaled a deep breath, and this time, doing so brought calm back into his mind. "Being patient is hard."

Pastor Boone laughed. "I know it is. I can't lie and say that I don't worry about what will happen if Mr. Miller has free rein in this town. But it's not my job to worry about the what-ifs that can happen. It's my job to help the people seek and come to Christ. When we do this, there is nothing we can't face."

The pastor laid his hand on Craig's shoulder, pausing before he stood. "Let me know if you need anything."

"I will."

With a final nod, Pastor Boone moved up the church aisle and vanished behind his office door. The click from the knob echoed in the empty church, and Craig sat for a minute, dwelling in stillness and peace. He closed his eyes, willing the courage he lacked, and as he stood, he opened them, giving one last glance to the rows of pews and the cross hanging on the wall above the podium.

As he left the church and stepped out into the bright sunlight, he spotted Wyatt standing with his parents, Mr. and Mrs. Cooper. He made his way over to the family, nodding a greeting as they noticed him.

"Good morning, Mr. and Mrs. Cooper." He shook Mr. Cooper's hand.

"Good morning, Mr. Harrison." Although Mr. Cooper spoke, his wife only nodded. "We hope you've had a good morning so far."

"I have. Thank you." Craig glanced between the three, then ran his hands through his hair.

"We were just talking about the sermon today. It was quite the message, wasn't it?" Wyatt asked, pointing toward his father.

"It was." Craig paused, remembering the pastor's words. "It gave me a lot to think about."

Mrs. Cooper sighed, and her brow furrowed. She brushed her fingertips against her collarbone and blew a slight breath. "I just can't believe the mayor and the position he's taken. The thought of Mr. Miller opening any businesses in town..." She let her voice trail off as she hooked her arm in her husband's. She let out a sigh.

Mr. Cooper patted his wife's arm. "I've heard talk around town," he said. "You should know men aren't happy about it, not one bit. That newspaper article from Prudence Chatterton got this town riled up."

"The wives aren't happy either," Mrs. Cooper added. She clutched her husband tighter as a chill seemed to spread through her. "The last thing they want is women who work at the brothel walking around town, flaunting themselves in front of our husbands and sons."

"I can imagine they aren't happy about it." Craig ran his hand through his hair again. "I'm not either."

"What will happen if Mr. Miller wins the bet?" Mr. Cooper asked.

Craig hesitated, the weight of the question settling heavily on his shoulders. He shrugged as the words he didn't want to say rested on the tip of his tongue. Not knowing the answer to any question never sat well with him. His pride got too much in the way. "I don't know," he finally said.

As his shoulders hunched, deflated with his own thoughts, he glanced around the town and saw Mr. Lockhart approaching, a telegram clutched in his hand.

"Mr. Harrison," the mercantile owner said. "I have a telegram for you. It just came in over the wire." He held out the slip of paper, releasing it as Craig took it from him and scanned the message.

He glanced up at Wyatt. "It's from the New Holland Machine Company. They want me in Butte by tomorrow morning for the crusher's arrival on the afternoon train."

He folded the telegram, his mind racing as he shoved the paper into his back pocket. To make it to the city in time, he would have to leave Featherstone Valley within the hour and ride most of the night.

"Wyatt," he said, turning to his head foreman, "I need to leave for Butte, and I need you to keep the men on schedule while I'm gone. We can't afford any delays."

Wyatt nodded. "You can count on me, sir," he said. "I'll keep things running smoothly."

Craig clapped him on the shoulder. "I know you will. I'll be back as soon as I can."

SIX

CRAIG

Of all the soreness in the world—even the whole-body kind that comes from mining gold mines—Craig doubted that there was anything worse than being saddle sore. He couldn't say what differed about the pain, but it seemed to hold onto one in places no one should have pain.

After riding to the train station, Craig dismounted his horse, his legs stiff from the long night's ride. He'd had only a few hours of sleep, and he rubbed his eyes, trying to shake off the fatigue that clung to him like a second skin.

The bustling town of Butte was already awake, with businesses opening for the day and city folk going about their morning routines. Men, women, and children meandered through the streets on their way to unknown destinations and activities. They mostly ignored one another, keeping their gazes focused on other things around them.

Craig tied the horse to the hitching post outside the train station, making his way around the building and onto the platform. The train had yet to arrive, and only a few train attendants worked around the station, checking paperwork for the upcoming arrival and preparing the platform for the onslaught of people and luggage heading their way.

Craig headed over to the ticket counter. His boots thumped against the wooden platform, and he smiled as the agent greeted him. "Good morning, sir."

"Good morning. I'm expecting a rather large piece of equipment to arrive on this morning's train, and I need to arrange for it to be transported to a little town about thirty miles from Butte. Do you know with whom I should speak to about this?"

The man nodded and smiled again, adjusting his glasses. "Let me check my paperwork. Companies always send telegrams when large shipments are en route." Before Craig said a word, the man grabbed a clipboard and flipped through the attached papers. "Are you Mr. Craig Harrison?" he asked.

"Yes, that's me."

"All right. I see you are expecting a crusher from the New Holland Machine Company."

"Yes, that's it."

"Well, there are a few wagons for hire at the livery. If you head over there and speak with Mr. Collins, you can arrange for a wagon and team of horses to transport the machine to wherever you need. It should be ready by the time the train arrives."

"Where is the livery?"

"Just up the road that way. It's not far."

Although he didn't, Craig wanted to groan at the man's answer. Not that far when he wasn't sore wasn't a big deal. Not that far when every step hurt worse than the one before because he'd been riding all night... well, that was another story. "Thank you. I will head there now."

Psalm 46:1, God is our refuge and strength, an ever-present help in trouble.

After securing the wagon, horses, and driver, Craig made his way back to the platform. The sense of the train's soon arrival seemed to spur the few attendants working around the station. Instead of the casual pace they used before, they suddenly moved quicker, shouting orders at one another to check the to-do lists before taking a break.

Craig sat on a bench outside the station. The verse that had been in his mind since he left Featherstone Valley whispered again through his thoughts. So much of the last few days had been unknown, and he expected no less from the days to come. He wasn't sure of the outcome of any of it, and while he would never admit it, the fear was greater than anything he'd ever felt.

He inhaled, and the cool breeze around him brought the smell of coal and smoke that seemed to cloud the town. A few vendors set up stalls near the platform, getting ready to sell their different products to those arriving on the train. The various products ranged from baked goods, like bread and pastries, to tools men could use, like shovels and rakes. One man even tied several horses with saddles to a tree and set up a sign that read 'Horses for Sale.' The animals ignored everything around them as they hung their heads, slept, and swished their tails at flies bothering them.

A train whistle blew in the distance, and everyone on the platform rushed even more. City folk started to arrive, too, weaving around one another as they seemed to wait for their loved ones or whoever they were meeting on the train. Vendors shouted toward the crowds forming, announcing their wares and trying to gain any attention they could. One approached a mother and son and knelt before the child, holding a slice of bread. The man smiled as the child lit up, eyes wide in wonder over the delicious-looking offering. The mother did not return the warmth, and after jerking her son's arm, she moved away from the vendor without even a glance over her shoulder.

It wasn't long before the engine's chugging grew louder and

louder, turning into a deafening noise as the train inched down the tracks and stopped. The brakes squealed with a high pitch that pierced his ears and made a few people cover theirs. Steam billowed from the stacks, and the train hissed as the conductor jumped down and checked the wheels.

The doors opened, and people disembarked the train cars in a sea of smiles, waves, and utter confusion that made Craig's head spin. He stood, trying to keep his gaze on a few of the attendants. An older couple stepped in front of him, and with their hands locked, they searched through the faces that passed.

"Can you see her?" the woman asked her husband.

He shook his head. "I don't, but I wouldn't worry. She's not going to leave the station. We will find her as people start to leave."

Although the woman didn't look like she much liked her husband's idea of a solution to their problem, she didn't say another word, and the pair continued through the crowd. The only notion they'd been there was the idea they'd given Craig.

Just wait until the chaos dies down. The machine isn't going to leave without him.

More and more people disembarked the train. Men in suits with briefcases exited most of the front cars while miners with sooty faces and weary expressions stepped down from the cars further from the station. Their bodies were marked by the grueling work they endured.

Craig knew that work well.

Among the multitude of miners, a woman stepped off the train. Aside from her long raven hair and beauty, her clothes stopped Craig in his tracks. She didn't wear the long, flowing skirt like every other woman around her.

Instead, she wore pants.

And men's pants at that.

Craig's head jerked, and he trained his eyes on her.

She moved through the crowd, weaving around men and

women as if walking in slow motion. She glanced from man to man and woman to woman, meeting several people's gazes and smiling at a few of them. An air of confidence hinted through each step, each smile, and she carried herself as though, despite the unconventional attire, nothing but a woman's blood ran through her veins.

Craig's gaze followed her, and as she skirted around a couple hugging in a tight embrace, oblivious to everyone around them, her eyes met his. She paused, staring at him. He sucked in a breath. Overtaken by something that stirred within him, the curiosity nearly knocked him off his feet.

A man brushed up against her, tapping her on the shoulder. As she looked at him, he motioned for her to follow. She did. Their movement with one another caused Craig's stomach to clench. He furrowed his brow, dropping his gaze. He shook his head.

What's the matter with me?

He fought with himself to look for her again, and when he found her, he couldn't help but smile. Her magnetic presence drew his attention despite himself. His thoughts wandered, and he imagined what it would be like to know someone like her, to share moments of laughter and conversation.

The man with her nudged her arm, and after she smiled at him, the two vanished into the crowd.

Craig continued to search for her before he leaned back against the bench, exhaled, and shook his head. He had little room or time for daydreams and distractions, especially now.

Not to mention, the woman was obviously with another man.

The morning sun climbed higher, casting long shadows across the platform as the passengers soon dwindled in numbers. Once only a handful of people remained, he stood, stretched his stiff muscles, found one of the train attendants, and introduced himself.

"Good afternoon," he said, shaking the young man's hand. "My name is Craig Harrison. I have a package on this train."

"Ah. Yes. From the New Holland Machine Company?" The man scanned a clipboard much like the ticket agent had. "Have you made transport arrangements?"

"I did." Craig pointed toward the side of the platform where the horse, wagon, and driver had parked before the train arrived.

"All right. We will get it loaded for you."

∽

"Your wagon's all set, sir," the young train attendant's words jerked Craig's attention. He had stumbled away from the wagon a few steps to catch his breath after helping load the machine. His lungs burned, and he gasped for breath. He turned to the several other men who had helped him load the machine in the wagon. Only one other struggled as much as he did while the others stood, breathing normally. A thin layer of sweat glistened on their foreheads, the only indication that they'd just spent the last thirty minutes lifting a machine that weighed more than the wagon it now sat in.

"Are you all right, sir?" the young man asked.

Craig nodded, gasping for a few more breaths before he straightened up. His chest ached, his back ached, and his legs ached.

"Thank you for your help, gentlemen." He stuttered over his words—still gasping between breaths. As they each nodded and walked away, Craig turned to the driver. "Do you remember the schedule?"

"Yes, sir. I'll be waiting at the livery at sunrise, and we'll head out."

"Sounds good." He waved his hand at the man and turned to leave. "I'll see you in the morning." Another thought dawned on him, and he stopped and spun to face the wagon. Pain hitched in his gait, and he hissed a few breaths. "Before I go, can you tell me a good restaurant to go to tonight?"

"Well, there are lots of places around here..." The young man let his voice trail off and clicked his tongue before closing one eye and pointing toward Craig. "If I have to pick the best one, I would say it is Linguini's Italiano Bistro."

"Italian, huh?" Craig rubbed his chin as he contemplated a nice heaping plate of spaghetti or fettuccini alfredo. He hadn't had either of those in a long time—two dishes that weren't often on Miss Holden's menu. "I could go for some Italian," he said.

"Are you staying at the inn near the livery?"

"Yes."

"Linguini's is north down the street and around the left corner. You can't miss the place."

"Oh, yeah? Does it have a big sign?"

"No, but you can smell it from a mile away. I swear, it's like garlic; the scent oozes from the porous lumber and brick."

"Sounds like it will be a good meal."

"Yeah, you can't go wrong with anything at that place."

"Thank you for the suggestion. I'll see you in the morning."

The young man whistled a sharp noise and tapped the horses on the butt. They struggled slightly with the wagon's weight, but after a few steps, the wheels rolled smoothly down the road away from the train station. Craig waited until it vanished before he set off for the inn. He wanted to freshen up a bit before heading to dinner. The idea of a big plate of pasta made his stomach growl, and although his body still wanted to rebel against his soreness, he had a bounce to his step and a smile on his face.

SEVEN

AVA

After nearly three weeks of riding the trails and taking the train, Butte, Montana—the last big city stop before continuing to the small town of Featherstone Valley—had been a welcome sight.

Holding what little belongings they'd packed into a couple of traveling bags, Ava and Griffin made their way through the crowded train station platform. Men, women, and children meandered in all directions, and the conversations of tearful hellos and welcome homes echoed around them. The chaos seemed to tickle the excitement building in her chest. She hadn't realized how much this new adventure would stir up emotions she didn't know she had. But it did.

It stirred up more than she ever knew possible.

The pair continued down the road, traversing the cobblestone walk as it veered through the city's streets. Building after building lined the streets, and their second-story levels blocked out a little of the early afternoon sun. Wagons rolled past them, and the chorus of horseshoes with their clip-clop sound bounced around them.

The hustle and bustle of the city was nothing like the dirt-infested town in the Tonopah Basin. Money, wealth, and luxury oozed from the bakeries, dress shops, delicatessens, hotels, and restaurants on every corner.

Men, women, and children strolled down the sidewalks. Dressed in suits and elegant dresses, their attire far surpassed Ava's and Griffin's—a problem they should resolve with a quick trip to a few shops before they made their way to the hotel.

"Do you think we should shop for some clothes before we find a couple of rooms to stay in for the night?" she asked, raising one eyebrow. She'd never been one to suggest shopping for anything other than mining supplies, but by the time the tenth woman looked her up one side and down the other, scoffing at her pants, she couldn't take it.

Griffin furrowed his brow and shrugged. "I suppose we can. If you would like." He smirked. "I never thought you'd be one to care what other people think about you."

"I don't. But there is still a lady underneath my clothes."

"Really?" His head jerked toward her, and he chuckled. "Because you could have fooled me."

"Oh, be quiet." She slapped his arm and rolled her eyes. "I'm allowed to like or want to wear a dress now and then."

He laughed even harder as he glanced over one shoulder and the other before pointing ahead toward a sign hanging above a door. "Of course you are. I just didn't know that about you."

"Where is it written that you must know everything about me?"

"I guess it's not. Well, there looks to be a dress shop on the corner. Do you want to meet at the hotel in like an hour?"

"Where are you going?"

"I'll head to the livery and see if I can buy a couple of horses for us. Unless *the woman underneath your clothes* would like a wagon."

She slapped at him again, but he shifted out of her range this time. "Horses are fine. I don't need a wagon," she said.

"Horses it is. What do you want to do for supper tonight?"

"I don't know. Perhaps we can figure it out later."

Griffin nodded, then motioned across the street. "I'll see you in an hour."

∼

Building after building, the city grew and spread from the train station. A metropolis of stone, brick, and glass, the only vegetation bloomed from the planted trees along the sidewalk and the flowers in the various windowsills of the apartments and the occasional house down another set of streets.

As Griffin said, Ava found the dress shop on the corner. A red and white striped awning covering the sign flapped in the gentle breeze, shading the front door from the bright sunlight. As Ava opened the door and entered the store, a bell chimed with a soft ding.

Scents of roses and cinnamon whispered through the air, masking the dusty odor from outside. The pungent sweetness soothed and calmed, like a little delicious bakery filled with loaves of bread and pastries.

"Good afternoon," a woman's voice called from behind. Her thick French accent thumped on the letter d. "I will be right with you."

Ava continued through the shop, gazing upon the racks of dresses in all shades of color and styles made of lace, cotton, and satin hanging from hangers. Elegance and sophistication breathed from each stitch, unlike the stained pants and blouse now wrapped around her body, which had seen the depths of the earth, deep in the mineshafts for far too long.

"Hello, Miss," a voice said behind her.

Ava spun to find a tall, thin woman approaching. Her long legs seemed to glide across the floor. "Good afternoon."

"Good afternoon," Ava said.

"Welcome to my shop; my name is Miss Josephine De La Fosse. How may I help you?"

"I wanted to look around." She glanced down at her blouse and pants, clearing her throat. "I just arrived in the city and was looking for something nice to wear for a change."

The French woman bit her lip, and with a tilt of her head, she traced Ava from her worn boots to the stained collar of her button-up shirt. "Oui, I can understand that. I mean no offense, of course."

"I figured. And no offense is taken, I assure you."

She smiled. "Is there any particular color or style you wish me to pull out for you?"

"Unfortunately, I'm not too familiar with what a woman should wear. I'd appreciate it if you could pick a few things for me."

"But of course I will." Her smile broadened. "What sort of dress shop owner would I be if I didn't know what my customers desire? Please have a seat. I shall return in a moment with a few choices for you."

"Thank you."

She dashed off toward the back of the store again, leaving Ava standing beside a table full of gloves from elbow length to wrist length. The white and cream satin material glistened from the sconces on the walls. Next to the table, a couple of hat racks sat in rows. Their forked hooks were filled with brimmed hats layered in lace, bows tied around their crowns, or tiny cocktail hats decorated with elegant pearls or bright-colored, exotic bird feathers.

"How long are you planning to stay in zee city?" Miss De La Fosse appeared from around the corner, tugging a rack of dresses behind her. Each skirt rocked from side to side with movement.

"Just for the night. We leave in the morning."

"Oh." She cocked her head to the side and blinked several times.

"I know what you're thinking." Ava laughed. "It's just been so long since I've passed through a city such as Butte and I... I would like at least one dress."

She smiled and winked, waving her hand. "Say no more. I shall look through some more racks while you search these. Don't worry. We shall find you the perfect one."

While she made her way toward the back of the store, Ava moved toward the dress rack, brushing the hanging dresses from one side to the other as she looked over each one. A couple piqued her interest, and she moved them off to the side before continuing with the rest.

It wasn't long before she returned with even more dresses, and the two of them moved through the selections, fussing over whether a particular style or color would look good on Ava. The two giggled over a few selections and colors, and Josephine shook her head, repeating that she wasn't sure what she was thinking when she picked a bad one.

"I'm usually not this horrible with my selections," she said as they moved another dress into the 'no' pile.

"I don't think any of them are horrible. They are all beautiful." Ava hesitated, smiling. "Some seem to fit better than others. That's all."

As the two women continued through the dress rack, the bell above the door jingled again, and a pair of older women stepped inside. The brims of their large hats stuck out so wide they barely fit through the frame.

"Are you sure this was the place Miriam told us about, Esther?" One of them said. Her voice oozed with a hint of repugnance, and with a flick of her wrist, she whipped out her spectacle stick and lifted it to her face. The disgust from her scowl tightened through her willowy body as she looked down her long, thin nose.

"I believe so, Margaret," Esther answered. A foot shorter than her cohort, she was as round as Margaret was tall. Just as equal in her aversion, Ava caught a hint of confusion in her round face. "I thought Miriam had taste, but now... I don't know what she could be thinking."

"Yes, she isn't showing it by sending us here, is she?"

The once sparkling light in Josephine seemed to dim as all the happiness in her world vanished in a sea of blackness. Hopelessness seemed to cloak her as she listened to the women speak so carelessly about her store.

Ava recognized the woman's feelings instantly, having lived with the daily prejudice from the men of the mining company. She was nothing more than an unwanted woman in their world, and even if she was their boss, they always—with snide comments and physical teasing—reminded her she didn't belong every chance they got. She knew just how it felt to be mistreated by someone who thought less of you for no other reason than their misplaced ignorant opinions.

"Miss De La Fosse," she said, not taking her eyes off the two women. "I would like these two dresses. Could you please wrap them up for me?"

"Two? I thought you only wanted one?"

"Well, they are both just so pretty. I can't decide which one I want more. I want to take them both."

"Of course. I will get them wrapped for you immediately."

While the store owner scurried off carrying Ava's chosen garments high over her head, Ava approached the two older women, swaying her hips slowly as she stared them down.

"It's fortunate you ladies visited the shop this evening," she said, her voice deridingly sharp as she cocked one eyebrow. "Miss De La Fosse has quite the collection in her boutique. I'm sure if you perused around a bit, you will find something to suit your taste."

Once again, Margaret laid her spectacles against her face as she peered down at Ava. Judgment whispered through her stiffened body from the tips of her toes to her grayed hair tucked in a tight bun at the base of her neck.

"I highly doubt that," the woman said.

She traced Ava from head to toe with her eyes, wrinkling her nose at Ava's attire. A slight *humph* escaped through the disgusted-looking scowl on her lips. She lifted her gaze toward the ceiling, arching over to the window as she twitched her shoulder.

Ah, yes. Yet another burden I knew all too well: someone believing me to be penniless and inferior because of my clothes.

A chuckle left Ava's lips. "I'm afraid I have to beg your pardon for my appearance, ladies. As you can see, well, the life of a miner can be... not as sophisticated as the streets of Butte."

Miss De La Fosse appeared from the back of the store carrying a giant box with tissue paper hanging out of the sides.

Griffin will have quite the joke with that.

"Will you need matching hats or gloves?" she asked Ava, her voice sad.

"Not today. But thank you, Miss De La Fosse. You and your store are so lovely." Ava turned her attention back to the women. "Well, if you ladies will please excuse me, I must see to my purchases. You ought to have a look around. Miss De La Fosse has beautiful clothes to suit everyone's tastes—even the snobbish."

While Esther sucked in a breath with a mouse-like squeak and covered her mouth, a fire burned red-hot through Margaret's face. The angered woman shot Ava a look of loathing before grabbing her friend by the arm. With her back arched, she stuck out her chest, and the two women stormed out of the shop, one dragging the other.

"My apologies, Miss De La Fosse," Ava said, approaching the counter. "I'm afraid I may have cost you a couple of sales."

She set the dress box on the counter and waved her hand

toward them. "Do not even concern yourself. I am sure they did not intend to buy anything, anyway. I cannot stand women like that, and yet, when they come in, I clam up. I become flustered, and I do not know what to say. I wish I could be more like you."

"I'm not sure that is a wish you want to make. Sometimes, I wonder if my mouth will get me into trouble one of these days. You probably shouldn't wish for such a thing."

"Still, it would be nice to defend myself, at least, no?" The store owner finished wrapping the dresses, and after Ava handed her the money, she slid the box across the counter. "Thank you for coming in this afternoon."

"You're welcome. I appreciate your help."

"Enjoy zee dresses."

"I will."

∽

After leaving the dress shop, Ava made her way down the street toward the hotel in the center of town. Horse carriages and a few motorcars rolled past her in a never-ending stream of busyness that seemed to go on for miles and miles. The different wheels spun down the street, some quick, some slow, as they traveled in one direction or the other, and at times, a horn would blare, or a coachman would shout curse words, inciting arguments between the drivers as they traveled down a road neither wished to share, even if they had to.

Along with the traffic, dozens of people on foot overwhelmed the sidewalks. Men with newspapers tucked under their arms tipped their hats to women either pushing baby carriages, chatting with friends, or carrying shopping bags. Children played with one another, shouting as they darted to and fro, while some trailed behind dogs clipped to leashes; the animals were as excited as the pint-sized owners, jumping up and down or trying to sniff everyone and everything they passed by.

She rounded the corner, spying Griffin standing near the front of the hotel. He scanned the street from one side to the other, exhaling a breath as he saw her. He pointed toward the dress box, but she held up her hand before he could say a word.

"Don't say anything," she said with a crisp tone.

He covered his mouth with his hand and shook his head. The words 'I won't' mumbled through his fingers.

"There was a reason why I bought more than one dress, and it wasn't because I couldn't decide. I did it to help out the store owner."

"If you say so."

"I say so because it's the truth."

"And I believe you." A broad grin spread across his face.

She rolled her eyes, adjusting the box in her arms. "Did you get us a couple of horses?"

He nodded. "The horses and saddles are waiting for us at the livery."

"What about the hotel rooms?"

"I haven't even been inside. I was waiting for you." He motioned toward the door, and without waiting for him, she moved toward it. Before she could open it, he grabbed the knob, twisting it. The door opened, and they stepped inside.

Warm colors of gold, green, and maroon played off the cream-colored carpet while decorative vases filled with flowers sat on every table situated between chairs or next to one of the several luxurious couches. Their lush cushions reminded her of pillows. Amongst the blooms, candles of different sizes and shapes burned; their reddish-orange flames danced with the slightest movement. The soft glow blended with the beautiful chandeliers dangling from the ceiling; their pear-shaped diamond crystals shimmered with any light they could find, reflecting in rainbows along the walls and the mirrors hanging in the darkened corners. The reflections played with the mind, making Ava feel as though the room was bigger than she once believed.

"Wow. This is some hotel," Griffin said. "Do you think we have enough money for this place?"

"The only way to find out is to ask how much the rooms are. The expenses will be reimbursed."

"Yeah. Yours. Nothing was said about mine."

"Well, let's find out how much it is."

They approached the front desk, and a man in a suit and pillbox hat greeted them. A crooked smile spread across his long oval face, and his fire-red hair circled his head like a horseshoe, leaving most of his scalp naked and glistening under the chandeliers' lights. He reached for a leather-bound notebook and flipped it open to one of the pages.

"Good afternoon. How can I help you?" he asked.

"Good afternoon. We would like two rooms, please."

The man opened his mouth, but before he could answer, Griffin spoke up. "How much are the rooms?"

"One dollar and twenty-five cents a night."

Griffin's mouth gaped. "A buck twenty-five! Do your rooms have gold-covered furniture? I'm not paying a buck twenty-five for one night's stay. I'll sleep in the loft with the hay at the livery before paying that much." He nudged Ava. "There's got to be a cheaper place to stay than this. Let's see what else we can find."

While part of her agreed with him, there was another part of her that wanted to stay. How often would she get the chance to stay in a fancy hotel on someone else's dime? This was perhaps the only time the opportunity would present itself.

She looked at Griffin, cocking her head to the side.

"You want to stay the night, don't you?" he asked.

She nodded. "I will pay for your room."

"You don't have to." He turned to the desk clerk. "We'll take two rooms if you have that many."

"We do. The rooms include many amenities, and room service includes breakfast, lunch, and supper."

"Room service? You have room service?" Griffin's eyes lit up like a child's at Christmas.

"Yes, sir."

"Well, I know what I'm doing for supper." He chuckled, nudging Ava again. "I'm sorry if you wanted to go to a restaurant, but I'm going to treat myself to some room service."

She laughed and shook her head. "And I hope you thoroughly enjoy it."

The desk clerk penciled their names into the ledger. His handwriting was rather neat for a man with swooping, cursive letters. After he was finished, he fetched two tiny keys from a board behind his desk.

"I shall see you both to your rooms."

EIGHT

AVA

After a hot bath, Ava slid the satin dress over her hips. The silky material hugged her curves, and after she slid her arms in the sleeves and buttoned each pearl button at the cuffs, she tugged the material around her shoulders until the bodice tightened around her chest. The elegant shade of lilac satin brightened against her skin, and she traced her fingers over the white lace pattern on the top of the dress.

She checked her reflection in the mirror, adjusting her ponytail on one side of her head so her waist-length raven curls cascaded over one of her shoulders. The locks bounced with her movement, brushing against her face. A few loose strands whispered along her cheek, drawing attention to the rouge she'd painted on her cheeks. The only make-up she'd brought and the only make-up she had.

"It's not much," she whispered, turning from one side to the other, still studying her reflection. "But it will have to do."

She fetched her wallet, and after closing the room door, she made her way down to the hotel lobby. The streets became packed with people as the afternoon hours led to early evening. Men and women paraded around in their own black tuxedos and stylish gowns as she meandered through the foyer and out through the doors to the awaiting sidewalk. Another night of festivities seemed to swim through the expressions on their faces. With the city and all its pleasures at their fingertips, the nightlife would entertain them.

Cool air hit her face, along with sticky and damp humidity.

"Good evening, Miss," a voice said behind her.

She turned to find a young man in another hotel uniform and pillbox hat. "May I hail you a carriage?"

"Um... yes, please."

Before she could say another word, he whistled loudly between his two fingers and waved one hand in the air. A coachman shouted in return as he steered toward the hotel, slowing the horse from a trot to a walk before coming to a halt in front of her. The young man grabbed the door, opening it.

"Your chariot awaits, ma'am," he said.

She slid onto the leather seat of the buggy. Her heart pounded.

Was this how those who lived in the city spent their time?

"Where to, miss?" the coachman asked, his brow scrunched as he spoke over his shoulder.

"Um. I'm not sure. I want to go to a nice restaurant tonight."

"Nice, huh? How do you like Italian food?"

"Italian? Um. I like it just fine."

"All right. I'll take you to the best Italian food in Butte—Linguini's Italiano Bistro."

∼

While the carriage bounced down the street, the hanging lanterns lit only a few feet in front of them. Their yellow glow softened from the misty fog that seemed to settle around the city. Tiny droplets of haze sprinkled her face and neck through the window, and she wrapped her arms around herself, shying away from the chill.

Hopefully, the restaurant was not far from the hotel.

As the restaurant's sign appeared, the coachman maneuvered the buggy alongside the sidewalk and stopped.

"That will be fourteen cents."

She handed him a dollar bill, and his eyes widened.

"My apologies, ma'am, but I don't have enough change to give you."

"I don't need any change, thank you."

"But you're trying to give me a dollar bill."

"And your point is?"

"I can taxi all week and not be so fortunate as to see that much in tips."

"Well, consider this one lucky day." Her fingers wrapped around the door handle, twisting it before shoving it open.

"Oh, wait. Let me get it for you."

"Oh, I got it. There's no need for you to trouble yourself."

The coachman nodded as she slid from the seat. Her shoes touched down on the cobblestone sidewalk, slipping a little on the uneven, wet rock until she gained her balance.

"Would you like me to wait for you, miss? I'd be more than happy to do so. No matter how long you are."

"Um, that would be lovely. I've never been to this city and wouldn't know how to return to the hotel."

"Well, don't you worry. I'll be waiting for you right here when you're ready to return."

As she neared the restaurant's door, it opened, and a short, balding man nodded his greeting. "Good evening, ma'am." His thick Italian accent purred from his lips, and his bushy black mustache brushed from side to side as he spoke.

"Good evening."

He shut the door behind her, darting quickly for the maître d' desk as he dug a pencil from the lapel of his blazer.

"Welcome to Linguini's Italiano Bistro. My name is Marcello. Do you have a reservation?"

"I'm sorry, I don't. Did I need one?"

"No." He smiled, shaking his head. "Are you meeting someone here?"

"It's just me."

"The *perdere* is dining alone, then?" He cocked his head to the side. A faint sadness plagued him, eclipsing the previous curiosity from seconds ago.

"*Perdere?*"

"It's Italian for 'Miss'."

"Ah, yes, yes. The miss is dining alone."

He clicked his tongue, and his lips pursed together to accentuate the sound. "How could a pretty miss like yourself eat alone? Surely, any man would love to dine with such a lovely creature."

"Yes, but would the miss enjoy the company of just any man?" A smirk spread across her face as she winked.

"Ah yes, well, that is an excellent point."

He fetched the menu from the stack on the desk and led her through a maze of tall plants circling the dining room. Hidden from view, the numerous tables sat tucked away in a darkened corner where the only light came from the candle centerpieces and a couple of dim oil lamps burning along the walls. Flickering shadows played off the warm crimson wallpaper and stone-black hardwood floors as the soft light glistened against the bone-white china and silver cutlery lying elegantly on the crisp cream linens. Although other patrons filled several of the tables, most sat empty.

"Is this table to your liking?" he asked, pointing to one in the corner next to a window. "I thought perhaps you would like a view this evening, so…"

"Yes, it is. A view is always wonderful. Thank you."

He stepped aside to allow her by him so she could sit on the lush chair cushion. "Giuseppe will be your waiter tonight. He shall see to anything you need. Enjoy your meal, miss." He set the menu in front of her, shook her napkin free from its fold, and laid the thick white material on her lap. Then, with a slight bow, he strode away before she could say another word.

She flipped open the bill of fare, scanning the array of delicious selections. Her stomach growled as though the notion of food spurred its determination to gain her attention after she had ignored it all day.

Another plump, short man approached her table with an ear-to-ear grin. Unlike Marcello, who had a full head of jet-black locks, this man was bald as a rock. The only hair on his face was two bushy eyebrows, so full and long that they formed one line across his forehead.

"Good evening. How are you tonight?"

"Just fine. Thank you."

"Excellent." He lifted a silver pitcher and poured water into one of the glasses on the table. "My name is Giuseppe, and I will be your waiter tonight. May I start you off with a beverage and an appetizer?"

For a brief second, she scanned the menu, studying the various delicious-sounding options. As she glanced up to answer her waiter, her gaze drifted past him toward a man strolling into the dining room behind the maître d'.

Her breath escaped her lungs. The man looked at her, locking on her gaze as he crossed the room and sat at the table in front of hers. They faced each other, separated by the vacant seats at their tables across from them. She held her breath, studying him as he stared at her, unfailing even when he sat in his chair and took a menu from Marcello, the host.

"Miss?" her waiter asked again. "Miss? May I have your order?"

"Um..." She shook her head to regain her thoughts. "Can... can I have a moment, please?"

"Of course." With a slight bow, he backed away.

Her eyes fell upon the handsome man once more as he squared his broad shoulders and rested his forearms on the table. Despite the expensive suit perfectly tailored to his body, his subtle beard gave him a rugged quality most city men didn't share.

Their waiters approached each of the tables once, his for the first time and hers for the second; their mirrored actions blocked the man from her line of sight and her from his, and she couldn't help but lean to the side and peer around Giuseppe's rotund belly.

"Have you decided what you would like to order, Miss?" The waiter glanced over his shoulder as though trying to figure out what she was looking at, and he smiled when he figured it out. "Or do you need another moment to think about it?"

"Um, no, no, that's quite all right." She glanced down at the menu again, finding the first thing she saw. "I will have the lasagna, please."

"Very well, miss." He fetched the menu from her hands and strode off, tucking the booklet under his arm.

She lifted her water glass and took a sip, letting the coolness chill her lips as she snuck a peek at the stranger again. A smirk spread across his face as he caught her, and he mouthed several words to his waiter, who then hurried off, too.

She wondered what his voice sounded like. Was it deep and masculine, a tone you'd expect from a strong soul, a protector, and someone who commanded those around him instead of taking orders? Or was it high-pitched, almost boyish, like that of some of the men she'd known throughout the years in the mines?

In need of a distraction, she leaned into the back of her chair, training her attention on everything in the dining room except him. Although his eyes still burned into her, she denied him the pleasure, fixing her entertainment on studying the other patrons, whether they were parties of people celebrating in a group or cozy-looking couples sharing a night out with one another.

While the men wore either black or gray suits, the women wore differently designed dresses in a variety of spring-like pastel colors of pink, yellow, and a baby blue so light that it appeared white in the darkness of the dining room. The only similarities among the ladies were their hairstyles—curled up-dos that showed their long or short necks and the earrings dangling from their ears. The diamonds in them glistened in the soft candlelight.

Her fingers twisted through her curls lying over her shoulder.

A smile curved through her cheeks as laughter and insignificant chatter filled the air from several tables. Conversations of family and friends, of recent travels or holiday plans, and of raising children drowned out even the slightest hints of noise filtering from the street through the glass window next to her. She didn't know which she would have liked to listen to more.

She took another sip, and as she set the glass down, Marcello and Giuseppe rushed past her table.

"But what are we going to do?" her waiter asked. "We don't have another table available."

"We're going to have to think of something. It's Mr. and Mrs. Sheffield," Marcello responded. A slight growl hinted in his tone.

Giuseppe glanced around, looking back at his boss. His eyebrows were raised, and he shook his hands. Panic was etched in every inch of his stance. "But we have no tables to give them."

"Find one." Marcello stomped off, leaving the waiter standing with his mouth agape. He continued looking around the room, spinning in several circles.

Her gaze danced between him and the stranger sitting at the next table. He watched the scene, too, and as if they had the same thought, they glanced at the empty seats across from each of them. If they shared a table, the couple would have a table, and her waiter's problem would be solved.

Their eyes met again, and he shrugged as if to silently tell her he was thinking the same thing and wanted to know what she thought. She hesitated, wondering which would be more awkward—saying no after learning the waiter's problem and that the stranger had suggested they help or sharing a meal with a stranger.

Finally, she shrugged, too, and nodded.

It would be rude not to help the waiter.

∽

CRAIG

Craig's heart thumped as he lifted his hand to catch the waiter's attention.

"Excuse me," he said.

The waiter spun and faced him. A look of panic brewed in his bushy eyebrows. "Yes, sir?"

Craig cleared his throat, pointing at his chest and the young woman sitting at the next table. "The... the lady and I... we can share a table. Then the couple you are trying to seat can have my table."

The waiter's eyes lit up, and a smile spread across his face. "You... you mean it?"

"Of course." Craig swallowed hard. He hadn't ever done anything so bold before, sitting with a strange young woman, much less inviting himself to do so. Sure, she nodded, which he took as a yes to his silent question, but still.

"Thank you, sir. Oh, thank you." The waiter bowed and fetched Craig's water from the table. He set it on the young woman's table, also thanking her several times before he grabbed the back of the chair and held it out for Craig to sit. "You have no idea how much this means. You know what I will do for you... yes, I will make sure your meal is on us. Yes, that is what I will do."

"You don't have to do that," Craig said, shaking his head. "Or I suppose I should say you don't have to do that for me. I will pay for my supper."

"I will pay for mine as well," the woman said.

"No, no, no. I won't hear of it. Tonight, you dine for free, and I shall tell the kitchen to make an extra plate of garlic bread." Before Craig could say another word, the waiter darted away.

"Well, he was excited, wasn't he?" Craig turned his attention toward the woman. His heart thumped, and he inhaled. While surely he had only waited a few seconds to see if she would say anything, he wouldn't have been surprised if someone had told him it had been a year that had passed. Time seemed to stand still. He cleared his throat again and stuck out his hand. "I'm Craig Harrison, by the way."

She stared at his hand, studying it before she grabbed it.

Her hand was firm in his, and she met his gaze with an unyielding fierceness as though she was every bit a woman, yet there was a man's toughness to her that was unlike anything he'd ever known or seen in the fairer sex.

"Ava Adams." The delicateness of her voice calmed his heart, but only for a moment, as the curiosity swimming in her emerald eyes hit him like a stick of dynamite. Their bright green shade deepened against the fans of her black eyelashes and caramel skin.

"That's a beautiful name." His voice cracked, and he coughed. "Excuse me."

"Are you all right?"

He nodded, reaching for his water glass and taking a sip. "Yeah. I'm fine."

"Well, that's good."

They stared at one another. He could almost hear the seconds tick by on the pocket watch in his jacket pocket. Tick. Tick. Tick.

This was turning into one of the worst ideas he had ever had.

"I'm... I'm sorry if I shouldn't have suggested we share a table," he said.

She held up her hand. "No, no. It's fine. I had the same thought about us sharing a table, I think, around the same time as you when I overheard their conversation. There's no sense in us taking up two tables when someone is in need."

"That was my thought."

The host walked through the restaurant holding two menus tucked under his arm. An older couple followed behind him. They had an air about them, something that told Craig if the host or waiter hadn't found a table for them, it would have been the downfall that perhaps ended the place in the not-so-distant future. The man held the chair for his wife, and while he took his seat, she whipped out a pair of spectacles on a long stick. She laid it against her face, peering through the small frames down at the menu.

"What shall we have tonight, darling?" the man asked. "How about the fettuccine?"

"Oh, no. The fettuccine was dreadful. It tasted like a box covered in milk." Her raspy voice was about as harsh as the words she used.

Craig looked at Miss Adams, and the two both dropped their gazes to the table, covering their mouths to stifle their laughter.

NINE

AVA

Ava's heart hammered as she sat across from the stranger. She'd never had a second thought about dining with a man in the past. Of course, to be fair, meals and conversations with men in Tonopah were often more amusing to her than anything. The time spent in their company was mainly for a free meal and nothing more. The young men coming into the dusty town were far too focused on gold and securing their place; they left little to the imagination of not only their intentions—which were never good—and their desire for finding gold, not a wife.

Not that she was wife material.

She wanted to find gold, not a husband.

But this man... there was a difference about him. He wasn't one of those young men with nothing between their ears but gold dust. Or at least that's the feeling that hit her square in the chest.

He sat across from her and set his glass of water on the table, moving the chair closer to the table. "So, what did you order for dinner?"

She blinked at him. "I beg your pardon?"

"What did you order for dinner?"

"I ordered the lasagna. Why do you ask?"

"Well, in my experience, there are two types of women. One type is rather recluse. They don't wish for uncomfortable change or to venture into the unknown." His eyes narrowed as though he studied whether or not she fit inside such a box.

She didn't.

For some reason, she doubted he believed she did either.

"Then there is the other type of woman," he continued. "Those who seek out adventure. They have many layers to their character and personalities, which cause them to stand out among those around them. They are so different; they leave everyone in wonder."

"And you know which type I am just by what I ordered for dinner?" she asked.

"No. I just had to come up with something stupid to say to lessen the awkwardness of the situation."

She laughed. "Well, you did a good job."

"Noted." He leaned back in the chair, folding his hands in his lap as he glanced around the room.

The silence between them brought back the very same awkwardness he was trying to avoid with his question, and she rested her elbow on the table, laying her chin in the palm of her hand. Men had never been so quiet around her before. Usually, they were chatting non-stop, telling her about themselves—boasting, she liked to call it—or about what they had to offer her. They acted as though she were searching for a husband, and they were the pick of the litter, the perfect fit. None of them had ever sat silently, looking at everything around the room except her.

"Tell me something, Mr. Harrison," she finally said.

"You may call me Craig if you want."

She cocked her head to the side. "First name basis already?"

His eyes widened. "Well... that's why I added if you want."

"I was only teasing." She chuckled.

"Why do I feel you do that a lot?" he asked.

She raised one eyebrow. "Perhaps people just make it too easy for me to."

"Perhaps they do." He paused, fiddling with his water glass by moving it an inch to the side of where it was, and continued before she could say anything. "So, Miss Adams—"

"You may call me Ava... *if you want.*" She winked.

He smiled and nodded. "So, Ava, do you live in Butte?"

"No. I'm just passing through. I arrived on the morning train, and I leave tomorrow."

His brow furrowed, and he blinked. A thought seemed to cross his mind, and he pointed at her. "You... you were at the train station. I saw you there."

"You did?"

"Yeah. I was there on business, and... I saw you and another man walking through the crowd on the platform. You were wearing pants."

She chuckled. "Ah. Yes, we arrived today, and usually, I am in pants."

"Not particularly common for a woman to wear pants."

"Well, I suppose that means I'm not a particularly common type of woman."

"Who was the man? Is he your husband?" Craig seemed to stiffen as though he didn't desire to ask the question but had to for one reason or another.

"The man is Griffin Baker. He is a friend."

"And where is your friend tonight?"

"He is in his hotel room enjoying room service for the first time." She laughed.

"Room service, huh?" Craig chuckled, too. "I guess I can't say I blame him, although he is missing out on your company."

"He's had more than enough of my company since we left

Tonopah, I assure you. And, admittedly, I have had more than enough of his."

"So, you two..." Mr. Harrison cocked his head to the side and lifted his hand, wiggling his finger as though to insinuate Ava and Griffin were a couple.

"Oh, no. He is like a brother to me. Nothing more. And I am like a sister to him, and nothing more."

"Ah. I see." Craig's shoulders softened. "So, you're from Tonopah? Where is that?"

"Nevada."

"Nevada? You're quite a distance from home, aren't you? And you said you're just passing through? That seems like an adventurous journey."

"It has been. But I'm headed to a little town not too far from here, so it's almost over." She paused. "Do you live in Butte?"

"Nah. I'm just here on business."

"And what kind of business are you in?"

"I own a mining company in a little town near here."

She froze. The question of what little town sat on the tip of her tongue. Should she ask? Or should she leave it alone? Her own questions stumped her nearly as much as his words. Just what was this man playing at? Did he know who she was? Had he known all along? Was that why he asked to sit at her table? How could he have known, though, unless he had connections in Nevada?

She shifted in her seat and straightened her back against the chair. She had thought it nothing short of serendipity that they'd happened upon one another this whole time.

Should she now doubt it?

Unsure of how much she wanted to divulge, she bit her tongue to keep from saying anything else. She still didn't know exactly who Mr. Sidney Miller was, what kind of man he was, or if he had connections to Mr. Harrison, and she wasn't about to get herself wrapped up in a battle she knew nothing about.

"Mining, huh? Like for gold?" she asked, trying to ignore the pit rolling around in her stomach.

"Yeah. That's what I've found the most around these parts." Mr. Harrison took another sip of water. "I did a little mining for silver and copper in the Klondike, but I wasn't much good at it."

Her head jerked, and she blinked several times. "You've been through the Klondike?"

He nodded. "I mined up there for a good few years with a couple of friends named Flynn O'Neill and John Colton. I never made more than what it cost to live up there, though. Land sold fast, and what was left for the rest of the men who traveled up there was picked clean in a matter of months." He chuckled. "At least, the land I checked was, which is why I moved to Montana."

As she opened her mouth to ask how long he'd lived in the state, the waiter appeared behind her and set a plate in front of each of them. The earthy scents of the garlic, tomato sauce, and cheese from the lasagna tickled her nose and made her stomach growl. She checked his plate, noticing that he, too, had ordered the lasagna.

She raised one eyebrow, and he laughed, holding his hands up.

"I ordered it before I knew what you ordered," he said.

The waiter glanced between them. "Can I get you two anything else?" After they both shook their heads, he nodded. "Enjoy your meal."

Mr. Harrison shoveled a bite into his mouth as the plump waiter disappeared. His eyes closed as though the burst of flavors were too much to handle.

"Oh my. This is delicious." He pointed to her plate. "You should try it."

She looked down at the food. Although she was still hungry, the questions about how this man had happened upon her still churned in her stomach. She hadn't told anyone her travel plans, but for him to be at the train station on the same day she'd arrived? And now he was at the same restaurant out of all the places to eat in the city?

She'd let her guard down. And now she regretted it.

She grabbed her fork, cutting off a small bite.

All she could do was get through this meal and walk away.

"Do you not like it?" he asked, seemingly noticing her less-than-enthusiastic excitement over the meal.

"Huh? Oh. No, I like it. It's delicious." She chewed and swallowed the one bite, cutting off and enjoying a few more before she even looked up from her plate.

He cocked his head to the side, raising one eyebrow. He opened his mouth but shut it briefly before pointing to her hand holding the fork.

"What happened there?"

She looked down at the jagged scar across her wrist and down her hand. It was the last few inches of an old wound that continued up the length of her arm. The dress's sleeve covered the rest of the scar.

"Oh, it was nothing."

"It doesn't look like nothing."

She cut off another bite and waved her other hand. "It was just an accident with a saw."

"A saw?" He blinked at her, his mouth gaping open. "You... you... what were you sawing?"

"A tree. The saw got away from me and sliced my arm. At first, I thought I would lose my hand, but I lucked out."

"It looks like it was a pretty bad wound."

"It was, especially when I was out in the middle of nowhere and lacked the luxury of a hospital or doctor. But I survived, and Griffin saved the hand."

"May I ask why you were cutting down a tree?"

She shrugged. "It was in my way."

He blinked at her for another few minutes. "Well, I suppose

that is understandable then that you would cut it down." He chuckled slightly as he shook his head. If he wanted to say something else, he didn't. He simply smiled and took several more bites of his supper.

Ava ate what she could of her own meal, washing it down with a glass of water. Questions still lingered in her mind, swirling around one another as they both finished their meals.

Unable to take them any longer, she broke their silence. "You said your mining company is in a small town near here; which town is it?"

Please don't say Deer Creek.

"Featherstone Valley."

Although she wanted to close her eyes and exhale a relieved breath, she didn't. The reaction wouldn't have made sense.

"It's a great little town." He paused, furrowing his brow for a slight second. "You should visit it if you ever get the chance."

Before she could respond, Giuseppe appeared at their table, nodding to them. "Are either of you interested in dessert?"

Mr. Harrison looked at her, raising his eyebrows.

The thought sounded tempting as images of cakes, ice creams, or even fruity pastries flooded her mind. However, given the situation, passing on the offer sounded like the better choice.

She shook her head. "Not tonight. But thank you."

The two men exchanged glances as Mr. Harrison shook his head. "I don't know that I have any room myself. Just the checks, please."

Giuseppe held up his hand. "The meals are on the house."

"You didn't have to do that."

"No, no. It was our pleasure. Thank you for you... help." The waiter winked, glancing at the older couple at the other table with just his eyes and without moving his head. The two were oblivious to anything but the food sitting in front of them.

Mr. Harrison chuckled. "It's I who should thank you. You

spared me from a night alone, and instead, I got to dine and share a conversation with a lovely woman."

Giuseppe smiled and grabbed the plates. "If there is anything else I can get you, please let me know."

He made his way back to the kitchen, and as he vanished behind the swinging door, Mr. Harrison inhaled a deep breath and threw his napkin on the table.

"So, what are your plans for the night?" he asked.

Ava hesitated. She didn't want to reveal too much about her plans, especially not to a stranger, no matter how charming he seemed. She still didn't know if he knew who she was or that she was working for Sidney Miller. "I'm heading back to my hotel to get some rest. It's been a long day, and I'm sure Griffin is waiting for me."

"Traveling can be exhausting."

She scooted her chair from the table, cringing slightly as the legs slid along the hardwood floor, making a loud sound that caused the older couple to look up from their dinner. The woman scoffed as though annoyed by the interruption.

Ava ignored the old woman's glare, making her way to the door. Mr. Harrison followed behind her, and she stopped as the evening air outside was cool and refreshing after the warmth of the dining room.

After finding her carriage and driver still waiting, she turned to Mr. Harrison. "It was a pleasure meeting you. I wish you good luck with your mining company and hope you have safe travels home."

"Thank you. It was a pleasure meeting you, too, and I hope you have safe travels as well."

They stood there momentarily as though neither were ready to part ways. Finally, Ava stuck out her hand. "I guess this is goodbye, then."

Mr. Harrison returned her handshake. "Goodbye."

CRAIG

What was the saying again? Something about not letting something slip through your fingers?

Was it just those words?

Or was there more?

As Ava's carriage rolled down the street away from the restaurant and vanished in the darkness, Craig muttered the phrase at least twice—or at least he muttered the phrase he could remember. He had long since resolved not to have any regrets in life. He decided early on that everything that happened to him not only happened for a reason but also shaped him into the man he was.

And he rather liked the man he was.

Not in a boastful way or a way that one would consider him full of too much pride, but just enough that he could still consider himself humble.

Surely, life wasn't always grand. He'd lived through good times, but he'd also lived through hard times. Times when he wondered if he'd live to see the next day. The Klondike could do that to a man. It could weigh down so heavily on one's shoulders that it would make one almost wish to fall asleep and never wake up. A few men he knew even took matters into their own hands just to end their suffering. Something he knew he'd never do for himself, but he still understood why they did what they did.

Even living through those experiences, Craig never regretted a day spent in the snowy mountains. He held onto each day, each memory, letting it be his foundation. He couldn't fault any of it.

Nor could he regret any of it.

But tonight?

Tonight, he couldn't help but notice how his gut twisted at the thought of letting Ava vanish in the dark. The weight of those words he wanted to say but didn't pressed down on him. He had so many questions he could have asked her about her travels, Tonopah, and, most importantly, where she was headed. She mentioned a small town outside of Butte but never said which one and in which direction. Surely, there weren't many, but there were more than he could count if he considered north, south, east, and west. Not to mention just how far she still had to travel opened it up to more miles he wanted to think about. He should have asked her so much. Now, he would never have the chance to see her again.

Standing in the cool evening air, he replayed their conversation in his mind, trying not to think about all the missed chances. She was unlike any woman he had ever met. Her confidence, her wit, her mysterious nature—all of it intrigued him more than he cared to admit. He didn't know why he felt such a strong connection to a woman he had just met.

But the reality was—he had.

Craig sighed, shoving his hands into his pockets. A pang of regret inched through his chest, churning in his stomach as he made his way down the street to his hotel.

He'd never felt this before in his life.

Tonight, he wasn't sure he could continue to say that.

TEN

AVA

"So, you never told me how dinner was the other night." Griffin rode beside her as they headed down the trail. The town of Deer Creek had already begun to peek in the distance, with the tops of buildings poking through the trees and smoke billowing up from the chimneys.

Ava's head whipped to face him. "What do you mean? It was dinner. Dinner is dinner."

His brow furrowed. "No, I know that. I suppose I just meant... well, you looked rather nice when you left the hotel. Did you have a good time?"

"Yes, I did. It was just a nice dinner, though. Nothing more."

Her heart thumped. She hadn't told him anything about the night at Linguini's Italiano Bistro or meeting and sitting with Mr. Harrison. It wasn't that she didn't want to...

No. It was.

It was that she didn't want to.

The problem was she didn't know why she didn't. What did it matter if they left the encounter intent on never seeing one another again? Knowing that, then why would she care if Griffin knew? He knew about all the other men she had dinner with over the years. What about Mr. Harrison was stopping her?

"Was it a nice restaurant?" Griffin asked.

She nodded, *mm-hmm*.

"Where did you go?"

"It was a little Italian place."

"I haven't ever been much for Italian, myself. I've always thought it had too much pasta and sauce for my taste. Give me meat and potatoes, and I'm happy." Griffin chuckled. "Well, it's good that you had a nice evening."

She nodded again, *mm-hmm*, thankful he didn't ask her any more questions.

She hated lying to him but didn't want to tell him.

Not now.

Not yet.

Ava rode in front of Griffin as the two came into town and headed down the streets of Deer Creek. One and two-story buildings lined the town, and while it wasn't as big as Butte, it was larger than she had expected. It reminded her of Truckee on the border of Nevada and California with timber structures that appeared as though they'd seen better days and tall Ponderosa pine trees. Their thick pine scent tickled her nose. She'd always loved that smell.

Deer Creek didn't look much different from Truckee, and as she looked around, it reminded her of Tonopah. She could never figure out how, with so much money coming out of the Comstock, towns could look as they did.

Griffin used to say that gold didn't matter because it didn't flow through the streets—at least not in the right places.

Apparently, he hadn't been wrong.

Men, women, and children meandered along the street with dirt-stained faces and dusty clothes. A few stopped to stare at Ava and Griffin, but most ignored them.

They continued, passing the general store, a hotel, and a

bank, and as they rounded a corner, another building came into view, stopping Ava in her tracks.

Of all the buildings she'd ever been in or seen, only one brought a chill to her bones. Of course, this wasn't the same orphanage asylum she'd grown up in, but it didn't matter. They were all the same in her eyes. Her childhood was nothing more than a mix of memories she loved and memories she wished to forget. Like old wounds that have never fully healed, no matter how desperately she wanted them to, they still haunted her.

"Are you all right?" Griffin asked.

As she nodded, the front door opened, and several children ran outside, making their way to a rundown playground in a fenced yard. The sight of them chasing one another caught Ava's breath. Just like them, she had once run and played around the orphanage asylum she grew up in—her home for more years than she cared to admit.

A place of happiness and pain.

A place where she lived through excitement and where she lived through fear.

A place of love and loss.

A place for children who lost their parents or for the children like herself who were never wanted.

"Yeah. I'm all right."

"Are you thinking about her again?"

Ava shrugged her shoulders, not wanting to answer the question. The truth was, it had been years since she had thought of her mother or how she had left her at the orphanage in Virginia City as a young child. She spent so much of her life wondering why the woman had abandoned her to a couple of nuns—forgotten about and unloved.

A little boy playing in the yard screamed as they passed, and as Ava whipped around, she spotted him lying face down on the ground. No more than three or four years old, he picked himself up and continued running around with the other young children, unfazed by what had happened to him. Upon hearing him scream, a nun rushed out of the building, trotting down the stairs toward the boy. She grabbed his face, wiping his tears before giving him a slight hug. Seeing the nun reminded Ava of Sister Katherine at the asylum where she grew up. She'd been the kind one whose love spread through all the children, wrapping around them like warm blankets in winter. She often snuck treats into their rooms and protected those misbehaving to keep them from punishment.

"Sister Gretchen!" A shrill voice pierced Ava's ears. "Come here at once."

Another nun strode toward the first. Her robes swooshed through the dirt, and dust followed her in her wake, puffing in the air as if it, too, tried to escape her ferocity.

"I'm sorry, Sister Helen, but I just wanted to ensure Jacob was all right."

While the sweet nun cowered, the older woman folded her arms across her chest. Her eyes narrowed through her tiny spectacles.

"Please return to the care of the children inside. It is almost time for them to wash up for dinner."

"Yes, Sister Helen." The holy woman scurried off, giving the little boy a pained nod before leaving.

Just as the one nun reminded Ava of one she knew, the mean one reminded her of another nun at the asylum—one who was the opposite of everything Sister Katherine stood for. Just thinking about Sister Bethany made Ava's backside sting with a pain she remembered all too well—pain inflicted upon her more times than she cared to think about. Leather belts don't let people forget, and Ava had the scars to prove it.

The older, gruff nun watched as the other nun went inside. She glanced over the children still playing as she straightened the sleeves of her dress, tugging on each cuff a couple of times before she stuck her nose in the air. "Children! It's time to come inside for lunch." A few of them tried to protest, but taking one look at her, they hushed and ran inside. She followed behind them with a brusque gait Ava had seen in Sister Bethany after she scolded a child for one crime or another. Her bitterness was un-nun-like, and Ava could never understand how she felt called to such a mission by God. She seemed to hate it instead of love it.

Griffin cleared his throat, jerking her attention. He smiled as she glanced at him. "Where did you say we were supposed to meet Mr. Miller?" He knew his question would distract her just as she needed it.

She returned his smile. "The Crazy Eight Saloon."

"Well," Griffin pointed down the road ahead of them. "I think that's the sign up there."

∽

Growing up in a world where Ava never mattered, she stuck to the places she knew. Places where she felt kindness. Places where she felt welcomed. Places that would allow her to dwell in calm thoughts, a reprieve from the stressful madness of homelessness and poverty.

Saloons had never been any of those things to her.

In fact, they were just the opposite.

They were places of chaos, places of maddening thoughts and bitter resentment, and places where men would hide away in the arms of a drink. Walking into one would cause the hair on her neck to stand, and the Crazy Eight Saloon was no different.

Rays of sunshine beamed through the windows, lighting the smoky air inside the saloon. While they always looked different in the light of day, much like a restaurant without patrons, the many nights of inhibitions had left the walls and floor seemingly drunk, as though the hooch oozed from the porous lumber.

The bartender looked up, eyeing Ava and Griffin as they made their way across the saloon to the bar.

"What will it be for you today?" he asked.

"We're here to see Mr. Miller," Ava said. As soon as she said Mr. Miller's name, the few patrons sitting around at a couple of the tables silenced and stared at her. While Griffin looked around at them, Ava kept her gaze on the bartender. She wasn't a fool.

"What is this regarding?" The bartender grabbed a glass and wiped it with a towel before slinging it over his shoulder. He fetched a toothpick from his pocket, stuck it in his mouth, and rolled it to the side. Only a tiny part of one end stuck out.

"He sent a wire to my bosses, offering me a job with his mining company. He said to be here in three weeks. That was three weeks ago. I'm here per his request."

"Wait right here."

Before she could say anything, he moved around the bar and trotted up the staircase. His boots thumped on the hardwood floors, and she glanced up at the ceiling, listening to each step as he walked down a long hallway and knocked at a door. Dust floated around her from the boards.

A few moments later, he returned, followed by another man in a suit. Tall and thin, the older gentleman with salt and pepper hair looked at her and furrowed his brow.

"Are you Mr. Miller?" she asked.

"I am." He cocked his head to the side. "And just who might you be?"

"I'm Miss Ava Adams. You sent a wire to Mr. Hinkle and Mr. Owens about a job opportunity with your mining company." She stuck out her hand to shake his, but he didn't return the gesture.

Instead, he just looked at it, keeping his hand to himself. His eyes narrowed, and he scratched his chin. His shoulders stiffened, and his eyes moved from Griffin back to Ava. "With all due respect, ma'am, I don't believe my business is with a woman."

A flicker of annoyance bubbled in her chest. She always hated the stance men took around her. She glanced at Griffin. "Isn't it funny when someone says *with all due respect* and then follows it with derision? It's almost as if they mean disrespect; however, they attempt to justify the disdain instead of owning it."

"I wouldn't start, Ava," Griffin whispered, shaking his head as if to tell her not to say such things around a man like Mr. Miller.

"I would listen to your friend, or whoever he is, Miss Adams." Mr. Miller folded his arms across his chest. "If I want to disrespect someone, I don't hide it."

She shrugged. "If you say so."

Mr. Miller exhaled through his nose, continuing to study her. "I did wire Mr. Owens and Mr. Hinkle; however, I offered the job to Mr. Adams, not Miss." He glanced at Griffin, who took a few steps back and held up his hands, shaking his head.

"Don't look at me." Griffin motioned to Ava. "She's the only Adams I know of."

Ava stepped to the side, blocking Mr. Miller from Griffin. "This is Mr. Griffin Baker," she said for her brother-like friend. "He's my right-hand man and has been for several years."

"So, who is Mr. Adams? Your husband? Your father, perhaps?"

"I am unmarried and never have been, although I don't believe that is your business. As for my father, I never met him, and I have no idea where he is or even if he's alive anymore. I am the only Adams in the Tonopah Basin."

"But you're a woman." Mr. Miller narrowed his eyes again as the insult slipped from his tongue.

"Which means what, exactly?" Familiar with this mindset from men, hearing the words never seemed to shock her, and yet, no matter how many times someone uttered them to her face, they burned hot anger in her chest.

Ava stood toe to toe with Mr. Miller, and although he towered over her and had more men watching his back in the saloon than she had watching hers, she wasn't about to back down. If she did, surely he would pounce on it. He seemed like the type to search out any weakness in someone and then use it against them.

"I suppose it means nothing," Mr. Miller finally answered. "It's just not every day I come across a woman in this business or line of work."

"Ava is the best miner I've ever known," Griffin said. "She's known all over Nevada from Tonopah to Virginia City. I don't think there's a miner in the Comstock who doesn't know about her."

Mr. Miller glanced at Griffin, staring at him until Griffin dropped his gaze to the floor and shoved his hands in his pockets.

This man's intimidation tactics were getting on Ava's last nerve.

"Mr. Miller, I'm here because you sent for me. If you still wish for me to work for you, I will. If not, then I will return to Tonopah. The choice is up to you." While part of her hesitated to say what she did, knowing Mr. Miller was obviously not a man to mess with, another part of her didn't care. She needed to get to work, and whether that was in Deer Creek or Tonopah, it didn't matter.

Mr. Miller's eye twitched, and he inhaled a deep breath. "Come back tonight. The saloon will be packed with men, most of whom are looking for work. You can hire who you want. Even him." He glanced at Griffin and then back at her. "Just be ready to leave for Featherstone Valley in the morning."

She'd heard that name before, and hearing it again churned her stomach. "Featherstone Valley? I don't understand. I thought the job was in Deer Creek."

"Nope. It's in Featherstone Valley, Miss Adams." Mr. Miller turned to leave again.

"Wait. I thought another man owned the mining company there."

"There is another mining company in Featherstone Valley. But soon, there will only be one—mine."

"I don't understand."

"We are in a competition for a chunk of untapped land near the town. Whoever mines the most gold wins the land." He paused, and the glare of his dark eyes chilled her blood through her veins. She'd never feared a man before. Now she did. "Since you are the best in Nevada, or so you claim to be, I expect you to win me that mountain."

"Mining isn't like that, Mr. Miller. It's not something you can bet on with a whim."

"Then I suggest you find a way to make it that way, Miss Adams. Because you don't want to find out what will happen to you if you lose."

Before she could say anything else, Mr. Miller returned to the stairs. He didn't look over his shoulder, not even once. It wasn't until after he vanished that Griffin moved around Ava.

"What just happened?"

"I'm not even sure myself." She glanced around the saloon, ignoring all the men still watching them.

"I don't know what you have gotten yourself into, Ava, but we can't take this job. We need to return to Tonopah."

"I can't. If I leave here, I have no work."

"You don't know that. I'm sure tons of mining outfits would love to have you."

"I'm not going back, Griffin. It's too long of a trip."

"So, what are we going to do now?"

"Well, I suppose we should find a hotel, then come back here tonight. I guess I should be happy he's letting me pick my men. Although, I'd rather have experienced men going underground."

"Yeah. And that's if you can find enough who will work for a woman."

"I'm purposely not thinking about that part." She chuckled and headed for the door. Griffin trotted after her, walking as he caught up.

"May I ask you something?" he asked.

"What?"

"How did you know another man owned a mining company in Featherstone Valley?"

ELEVEN

AVA

"So, are you going to answer me this time or not?" Griffin leaned against the hallway railing as she closed her hotel room door. He cocked his head to the side.

"I don't know. What was the question again?"

"You know exactly which question I'm referring to. Don't you dare play dumb with me."

She closed her eyes, exhaling. While she liked Griffin's quick wit and sharpness, she sometimes wished he didn't know her so well. "For the last time, it doesn't matter how I know there is a man who owns a mining company in Featherstone Valley."

Of course, the truth of it was that it did matter.

It mattered that she was headed to the one town she never thought she'd visit in the morning. And it also mattered that, from the sound of it, Mr. Miller was intent on running Mr. Harrison out of business. *'There is another mining company in Featherstone Valley. But soon, there will only be one—mine.'*

She wasn't sure what that meant, but it was enough to know that Mr. Harrison might not be happy to see her when he found out why she was in town.

"If you don't want to tell me, that's fine. I know I'll find out soon enough, anyway." Griffin pushed off the railing and followed her as they descended the stairs.

They stepped out into the night air, weaving through the crowds of people strolling the streets. Even in the slight breeze, the stench of unwashed men permeated the air.

"Are you sure you want to do this?" Griffin asked. "And by this, I mean take this job?"

"Yeah. Why?"

"I just don't get a great feeling about Mr. Miller. He seems..."

"Motivated by greed and crushing everyone in his path?" Ava finished Griffin's sentence, and although she chuckled as she said the words, he didn't even break a smile. "Oh, come on, it was a joke."

"I don't think it is. I'm not quite sure how powerful the man is, but are you sure you want to get yourself tied up to a man like that?"

"I've been tied to a man who ended up being ten times worse than I could have imagined him to be and survived. If I can do it once, I can do it again."

Griffin stopped and grabbed her arm, pulling her around to face him. "I mean it, Ava. Are you sure you want to do this?"

She stared at him momentarily, noticing the lines on his forehead. He hadn't questioned her in such a way since one night a few years ago when the mine was attacked. After helping a few injured men, she'd loaded her guns and taken off on her horse, only to be stopped about a mile from the mine by Griffin, who had come riding after her. She hadn't thought about what she was doing, hadn't considered that she was riding after a group of men with guns alone.

She looked at him much like she had that day, but this time, she had a different answer to whether or not she wanted to do what she thought she wanted to do. "Yes," she finally said.

"All right. Fine. Let's find some men to work the mines. Let's just try to find ones with experience first."

They passed what looked like the Pipers Opera House in Virginia City, and just like in the tiny Comstock town, flickering light and canary tunes whispered from the many arched windows as they passed. Gold-painted, framed advertisements of barely dressed women with feather boas around their shoulders were plastered along the outside walls of the three-story building. Some tantalized from the images with cigarette sticks in their hands and pistols holstered around their thighs, while others teased as they held a bottle of liquor in one hand and a shot glass in the other.

"Are you hungry?" Griffin asked.

"A bit, but let's get this over with first."

Different from this afternoon, cigar smoke billowed throughout the saloon as they entered; the haze clouded Ava's vision until her eyes adjusted to the darkness. Groups of men filled every table, and with their hands full of poker cards or glasses of whiskey, they concentrated either on the distractions in front of them or the woman perched atop a piano, singing a song and fanning herself with her lace-covered fan. Her huge chest threatened to burst from her dress with each deep breath she inhaled to hold the high pitch of her tune.

Griffin and Ava made their way to the bar, ignoring how numerous conversations silenced as the soft clanks of their spurs rattled by them. More and more men began to peer over their choice of entertainment, staring at the newcomers with piqued interest and studying them curiously.

Noticing an uncomfortable hardness through Griffin's stiff movements, Ava bumped her shoulder into his. "You really should relax. You look like you're either planning to commit a crime or hiding from a crime you already committed."

He snorted, tucking his chin slightly. A soft smile crossed his lips, and he relaxed a bit. He leaned back against the bar and folded his arms across his chest as he faced the room.

"Good evening, Miss Adams," a voice said behind her. She

turned to see the bartender from this afternoon approaching her. His thick frame shifted from side to side with his short, choppy gait. "I wasn't expecting you until later."

"I've learned over the years that the time of day—or night—you choose makes a difference."

The bartender furrowed his brow. "How?"

"Usually, those looking to hire a few men make the mistake of coming in too late. They think a drunk man is easier to hire since he will say yes to anything—especially lower wages. What they find, however, is that in the morning, half the men don't even remember saying yes to the job."

Out of the corner of her eye, Ava caught Griffin's smile as he glanced down at the floor. He knew she always loved to correct people when they were wrong.

She called it a gift of hers.

Others called it her annoying habit.

The bartender stared at her for a long moment before he turned and walked off.

"He'll be thinking about that one all night; I just know it," she said.

Griffin laughed. "You know, I don't think there's a day that goes by that I don't wonder why your mouth hasn't gotten you in trouble."

"I hate to admit it, but I wonder that a lot myself." She looked around the room, scanning it for any men who piqued her senses. A few of them returned her gaze, and she pushed off the bar, heading toward the table in the corner where they sat, playing cards with one she immediately didn't like.

It didn't matter.

She didn't have to hire him.

It was the others she wanted to talk to.

"Good evening, gentlemen. May I join your game?" she asked, approaching the table.

The one she didn't care for locked his gaze on her and rolled a toothpick from one side of his mouth to the other. Annoyance cloaked his shoulders. His scruffy red beard, in dire need of a trim, covered half his round face, and he scrutinized her, hesitating before he answered.

"I suppose you can. If you can keep up." He shifted his weight, and from the window's light, she caught the faint pearl line of a scar on his face running down from his forehead to his jaw. The deep line darkened with dirt and discolored his eye with an opal color instead of the blue hue of the other one.

"Oh, I can more than keep up."

Her rump slid into the seat between two men who were more her taste and across from Scar Face while Griffin took his stance right behind her chair. His hands rested on the back, gripping the wood.

"Your partner seems a bit tense," Scar Face said.

Ignoring the man's candor, she smiled. "I could say the same about everyone sitting at this table. Relax, gentlemen; I'm only here to enjoy a few games. What is the worst that could happen? You guys make a little money off me?"

While the three she wanted to talk to laughed, Scar Face didn't. He only focused on her more as he shuffled the cards and tossed them around the table. His wrist flicked with jerked movement.

She scooped up the worn pieces of thick paper, flipping them over to study the suit and face value of each one. The other three men and the thin one did the same, discarding a couple of cards for new ones—their eyes and lips just as emotionless as hers, even though she stared down at a royal flush of hearts.

"Do you want any cards?" Scar Face asked her.

"No. But I will start the bid."

Following her lead, they tossed their own money in, upping the bid each time. Round and round, they continued, and the pile of money in the middle of the table grew. With each pass, the question remained on their minds—who would continue, and who would fold? After throwing down another few dollar bills, she leaned back in her chair. Even with the cards in her hand, her heart thumped. She'd seen men clash and explode over poker games before. Men didn't take too kindly to losing, and by the look of Scar Face, he mirrored a stick of dynamite with a short fuse.

"I fold," one of the younger ones said.

The other two agreed, mirroring the first one's movement. With all three of them out, Ava inhaled a deep breath and raised her bet even more. Scarface's lips tightened. His eyes slit like a snake, and he threw in his own cards, leaving her to collect her winnings.

"I think you've played this game before," the first to fold said. He laughed and looked at the other two, who joined his mirth.

"I haven't seen anyone beat Mick in a long time. Either you're one good player or nothing but a lucky lady," another one said. He glanced from Ava to Scar Face. "Don't worry, Mick. I'm sure you will win your money back."

Mick didn't say a word nor look at the other men. He stared at Ava, removing the toothpick from his lips and tossing it onto the table. He reached into his coat pocket, yanking out a cigar, which he lit and puffed on.

"So... what brings a woman like yourself to Deer Creek?" he asked.

"I'm just passing through. I work for Mr. Miller and am heading to Featherstone Valley in the morning to manage his mining company."

"Mr. Miller hired a woman to run his mines?" The first of the three men who spoke before glanced around the table. His mouth gaped.

"Brad, if I haven't told you to hush today, then take this as your first warning," Mick growled, causing Brad to cower in his chair. Mick turned his attention back to Ava, taking another few puffs on his cigar. Smoke billowed over his head.

She both loved and hated the smell of the robust tobacco.

Cigars weren't like cigarettes. There was a hearty earthiness to them.

"Yeah, Brad, shut it," the second man said, laughing.

Brad smacked him in the back of the head. "You shut up, Trey."

Trey retaliated with a smack of his own, and the two started into a war that lasted a few seconds before Mick slammed his fist down on the table.

The two men froze and then sat in their chairs with their shoulders hunched. The third hunched his shoulders, too, even though he hadn't gotten into trouble. He hadn't done anything but sit there watching the whole scene at the table, just like Griffin.

"So, Mr. Miller hired you, huh?" Mick looked back at Ava. "I heard Mr. Miller hired a man named Mr. Adams from Tonopah to head up his mines. At least, that was the rumor around town."

"There is no *Mr.* Adams in Tonopah. Just me. So, I guess the rumor isn't true, then." Ava raised one eyebrow. Mick's lips twitched, but he didn't say anything, and as the air shifted around them, she continued, glancing at the three men, Trey, Brad, and the unnamed one sitting to Trey's left. "I need men who are interested in working in the mine."

Griffin shifted his weight behind her.

Mick watched him before moving his gaze to the three men. "Don't even think about it," he said to them. "You're needed on the farm. Old Man Perry needs you to watch them hogs and cows."

Brad furrowed his brow, and his face flushed a bright shade of red. "But I don't want to work on the farm anymore. And Old Man Perry doesn't pay a living wage. We're going to starve if we keep working there." He lifted his hand as though he thought

Mick would argue, and he wanted to stop him. "I don't care what you say, Mick. I can't work on that farm anymore." Brad turned to Ava without even an inhaled breath. "What kind of experience are you looking for, ma'am?"

"Depends on what you did on that farm?"

"Well, I'm in charge of the pigs and cows. I don't have much experience finding gold, but I can shovel manure better than anyone else working in that barn, and I got the strength to haul as much as you need out of the mines." He glanced at Trey and the other one. "We're loyal, hard-working men, too. We'll do anything and everything you ask of us."

"If that's true, then be here tomorrow morning to leave for Featherstone—"

Before she could finish her sentence, the three jumped and rushed toward the door. Brad shouted that they would be there as they left the saloon. Their screams of excitement could be heard as they ran down the street.

The commotion of them leaving caused a stir of attention around the saloon, and several men stood from their seats and made their way over to Ava's table. Each of them asked about the job, and while most were asking about work for themselves, one man approached, shaking his head.

"I got a job on the railroad that I'm not lookin' to leave, but ya can have my boy," he said. Leaner in build, his dirt-stained clothes stank of cigarettes, booze, and sweat. His blond hair, so thick with grease from a lack of washing, framed his face in chunks. The hint of dishonesty about him caused her to pause. His brow furrowed. He drew in a long puff off his cigarette and exhaled the smoke. "Don't know if he'd make it as a muckman, but he's a good hand with the horses; trains them up real nice." He looked over his shoulder and snapped his fingers. His voice rose to a shout over the loudness around them. "Get over here, boy."

From the corner of the saloon, a skinny, young lad jumped

to his feet. His face was swollen, and a bluish, purple-tinted mark dwelled under one of his eyes; the colors gleamed against his pale face.

"Yes, Pa?" The boy's voice squeaked with a high pitch as he cowered away from his father. His body trembled.

Concern hitched in Ava's chest. She knew the evidence of abuse, and the boy showed all the signs. "How old is he?"

"He turned ten just last month. Sometimes he takes to not listenin' to orders, but usually, a couple of whippins' on his backside does the trick. He's scrawny for his age, but he's as strong as a mule."

And from his black eye, I'd say he's been worked pretty hard.

"Go get your belongings, boy. I found ya some work."

"Yes, Pa."

"Ten isn't old enough to work in the mines."

"But he's old enough to work the horses. Trust me. He'll work hard for ya."

She opened her mouth, but Griffin grabbed her shoulder, squeezing it before she could say anything.

"Are you sure you wish to send him away?" he asked the father, watching the boy flee the saloon as though someone chased him. "Won't you and your wife miss him?"

"Nah, I shoulda got rid of him a year ago when I had the chance. I ain't gonna make that mistake again."

He waved his hand toward Ava. His nonchalance regarding his flesh and blood churned in her stomach, and she desired nothing more than to punch him in the face. She glanced at Griffin, and the two shared a silent moment, both thinking the same thing—ten wasn't old enough, but there was no way they were leaving this town without that boy.

As quickly as he had vanished, the boy returned, running through the saloon with a sack slung over his shoulder. His lungs heaved from his haste, and as he reached the table, his father grabbed his shoulders, halting him.

"Now, ya listen to me, and ya listen good. You had better do a good job for these folks because if ya don't and they try to send ya back, we aren't takin' ya. Do you understand? Ya can't ever come back home."

"Yes, Pa." The boy nodded, glancing at Griffin, who moved over to his side and placed his hands on the boy's shoulders. The boy almost looked relieved, and the father walked away without uttering another word.

Mick let out a groan and shuffled the cards. "Enough of all this! Get away from my table!" He shouted at the men near the table and waved his arms. "You can talk to her once I win my money back!"

Although Ava didn't want to play another round, she stayed in her seat, nodding to Griffin, who motioned for the few remaining men standing around, wanting to ask about the job, to follow him outside. She turned her attention back to Mick and folded her arms across her chest.

"Are you sure you want to play another game?" she asked the older man.

He met her gaze as he dealt the cards, saying nothing. She shrugged and flipped her cards over; a full house stared back at her. She tossed a few coins in the middle of the table, matching and raising his bid several times. Beads of sweat formed on his forehead, and his eyes fluttered from her, to his cards, and to the pile of money building between them.

"Are you ready to show me your cards?" he asked, clicking his tongue.

"Are you ready for me to show you my cards?"

His eyes narrowed, and he set his cards on the table.

"Two pairs. That's a nice hand," she said. "It's a shame it's not nice enough."

She laid her winning hand down just as she had the first time. Mick stood and shoved the table. She leaped from her seat as the table flipped over on its side from his force. Cards, dollar bills, and silver coins all floated in the air briefly before they scattered on the floor. The crash was so loud it silenced everyone in the saloon. Mick yanked his pistol from the holster around his waist, pointing it in her face as he stepped toward her.

"Was that necessary?" she asked.

Her question seemed to catch him off guard, and he blinked a few times while jerking his head back. "You cheated," he accused.

"I did not."

"No woman is that lucky." He stepped closer to her until the barrel of his gun tapped her nose. The smell of steel and powder made her cough.

"People don't need luck when they are that good."

Before her words resonated in his mind, she lunged forward, clasping the gun in her hand and twisting his wrist until he let go. He cried out while she spun the weapon in her hand and pointed it in his face faster than he knew what had happened. With another swift movement, she bashed the handle into the side of his head, hard enough to knock him silly but not hard enough to knock him out completely. He fell to the ground, moaning in pain as he struggled to roll over onto his side. He shook his head like a dog shakes water from its coat, but the movement was too much for him, and he lay flat on his back.

She stepped one leg over his body and bent down until her face was inches from his. She dropped the gun on the floor, letting it bounce next to his head.

"And I am that good at everything," she whispered.

TWELVE

CRAIG

The air was thick with pine scent and the earthy aroma of freshly turned soil as Craig surveyed the potential site at Rattlesnake Mountain. The midday sun filtered through the dense canopy of tree branches, casting dappled patterns of light and shadow across the forest floor. His men were busy unloading equipment from the wagons; the clatter of metal and the hum of voices created a symphony of activity.

He had arrived back in Featherstone Valley late last night, and after a long morning of back-breaking work to get the crusher to Rattlesnake Mountain, his body was growing tired. He hurt all over, especially in muscles he didn't know he had.

"Let's get those wheelbarrows over here!" Craig called out, his voice cutting through the din. The group of men hustled to move the heavy wooden carts into position. Nearby, others were stacking buckets and lanterns, the essential tools of their trade.

Wyatt approached with a confident stride and a smile on his face. If Craig didn't like the boy so much, he would have punched him. No one should be this cheery right now.

"We're making good progress, boss," the young man said.

"The crusher's set up, and all the other supplies are neatly organized."

Craig nodded, his gaze shifting to the machine sitting in the clearing. It'd taken so much to get it here, and now that it sat, waiting to start its job, it suddenly looked small. His brow furrowed as he looked over the belts, gears, and heavy steel jaws.

"All we need to do is get to work," Wyatt continued. "Speaking of which, when is the meeting with Mayor Duncan and Mr. Miller?"

"This afternoon. I should leave here soon. I just wanted to check out everything before I go."

"Well, I've got it all under control. You don't have to worry."

Although Craig nodded, his mind raced, firing off different questions—some he hadn't thought of until now. "Let's go over the supplies list one more time. I want to make sure we have everything we need before I head back to town. That way, if we missed something, I can get it while there."

Wyatt pulled out a clipboard and began reading off the inventory. "Wheelbarrows, check. Buckets, check. Lanterns, check. Shovels, picks, dynamite... all here."

Craig listened, mentally ticking off each item. "Good. And the men? They know their tasks?"

Wyatt nodded. "I've briefed them all. They know what's expected. We're ready to start as soon as you give the word."

Craig looked around at the men, now gathered in small groups, talking and preparing for the work ahead.

"Alright," Craig said, a note of determination in his voice. "Keep them focused and on task. I need to head back to town for a meeting with Mr. Miller and Mayor Duncan. Make sure everything runs smoothly while I'm gone."

Wyatt gave a mock salute. "You got it, boss. We'll keep things moving."

Craig gave a final nod before turning to leave. The forest

seemed to close around him as he walked away from the bustling camp, and the sounds of preparation faded behind him. He felt a pang of unease not only for leaving his men but also for the meeting he was headed off to.

It was no secret that Mr. Miller proved an untrustworthy foe. Evil and conniving, there wasn't anything that man wouldn't do to come out on top. Craig had heard the stories his men had told one another over the years, stories of how Mr. Miller ran his businesses and the things allowed in the saloons. Things like fixed poker games, drunken gun fights, and even one of his women found dead in her room. He had been so focused on getting the saloon settled down that he told the sheriff he didn't even want to press charges or even find the criminal responsible and had disposed of the woman's body in the hog barn on the other side of town.

A knot twisted in Craig's stomach.

He didn't want to think about the story then, and he didn't want to think about it now. Nor did he want to consider why the mayor had involved such a man in his business deals.

∽

WYATT

After Mr. Harrison left, Wyatt turned to the men, clearing his throat and deepening his voice. "Alright, listen up! This contest will start soon, and we want everything in its place. You two," he pointed to Tom and Huck, "check the dynamite storage. We need it secure and away from the main camp."

The two burly men nodded and set off to their task. Wyatt turned to another group, led by one of his best friends—and possibly his only friend—Reed Hall. "Reed, you and your team must ensure the wheelbarrows and buckets are ready. We'll need them as soon as we start digging. Check over the equipment, too. I don't want any busted handles or wheels slowing us down."

Reed nodded, barking orders to a few men around him. A couple of them groaned, pointing out that the task had already been done twice before, but after Reed pressed the issue, threatening them a little, they soon trotted off to do what they were told. Reed made his way toward Wyatt, running his hands through his hair.

"Hey, Wyatt. May I ask you something?" Reed asked.

"What is it?"

A crease formed on Reed's forehead, and he glanced over one shoulder and then the other before leaning toward Wyatt and lowering his voice. "Well, a few of the men have been wondering about that crusher." He hooked his thumb over his shoulder, and the two glanced toward the machine. "None of us know how to use it."

While that same thought had crossed Wyatt's mind, he wasn't about to make that known. Instead, he shrugged and waved his hand as though to brush Reed's concern away. "It doesn't matter that we don't. Mr. Harrison does, and he'll show everyone how it's done. I'm not worried, and you shouldn't be either."

"It's not me that's worried. It's some of the others."

"Well, then just tell them not to worry."

"So, you think it's safe?"

"Of course, it's safe. Mr. Harrison wouldn't have purchased it and brought it up here if it wasn't. That would be ridiculous."

"Yeah. I suppose you're right." Reed nudged Wyatt in the shoulder. "Hey, are you still planning on coming by the house for supper tonight? Rebecca planned to go to the mercantile today and get us a roast."

Wyatt nodded. "I was still planning on it if the invitation is still open."

"Rebecca's cousin, Emily, will be visiting, too. She arrives in town on the afternoon stage. But she won't be a bother. She might even give you someone else to talk to."

A slight groan inched through Wyatt's chest. "This doesn't by chance happen to be the same cousin Rebecca has been trying to get me to meet for the last year, does it?"

Reed's eyes widened, and he cleared his throat. "I... I'm not sure. Maybe. But what does it matter if it is?" Reed nudged Wyatt again, letting out an awkward chuckle.

"It does kind of matter." Wyatt rolled his eyes. "I've told her a hundred times already that I don't want to be set up with her cousin."

"Well, this isn't a setup. Her cousin is just in town for a visit... I think she's just staying for a week or two." Reed paused, patting Wyatt on the shoulder. "If you want, I can talk to Rebecca before you come over and make sure she knows not to push the issue of you and Emily getting to know one another."

"You don't have to do that. I can tell her myself."

"So, we'll see you around supper time?"

"Yeah. I'll be there."

"Sounds good." Reed patted Wyatt on his shoulder once more before trotting off to finish the rest of his work.

Reluctance swirled in Wyatt's mind. Of course, he was looking forward to dinner with friends and even savoring the thought of Rebecca's home-cooked roast. Their home was a refuge when he needed silence, a place where he could unwind and forget about the mounting pressures of his new job, the high-stakes contest for Rattlesnake Mountain, and the nagging pressures from his mother to find a lovely young woman. But now, knowing that there could be a possible setup...

That was another story.

And one that reminded him of an evening at home with his mother.

He rolled his eyes just thinking about how she mentioned him finding a wife just last night.

Oh, what would she say if she found out about Rebecca's cousin?

He almost shuddered at the thought of what she would say. Sure, he couldn't deny he was curious about Emily—Rebecca had been talking her up for months—but Wyatt's plate was already full. The new job demanded his undivided attention, and now, with the contest looming, he needed to focus on helping Mr. Harrison win. Distractions were the last thing he needed, and a potential setup with Emily felt like exactly that: a distraction.

He let out a deep sigh, shaking off his worries. "Alright, let's get back to work! We've got a mountain to conquer." As the men resumed their tasks, Wyatt's determination hardened. Whatever happened tonight, he would deal with it. But for now, his focus was on the job at hand, ensuring they were ready for the challenges ahead.

∽

CRAIG

By the time Craig returned to town, the sun had moved lower in the sky, casting long shadows and bathing the town in a warm golden light. He walked briskly through the streets, headed toward the mayor's office with a pace that ignored the hustle and bustle of the townsfolk meandering about their day, running errands, or chatting with friends. A few children, finished with school, ran around the streets, chasing one another while they screamed and played.

The town had a timeless charm, with its old wooden buildings and sidewalks. Craig made his way toward the Mayor's office with nothing but the agreement and contest on his mind.

As he approached the Mayor's office, a carriage pulled up in front of the building. The horses threw their heads and swished their tails as the driver stopped them. Craig's eyes narrowed as Mr. Miller stepped down from the carriage with a smug look.

"Mr. Harrison. Lovely day, isn't it?" Mr. Miller asked.

"I suppose it is, Mr. Miller," Craig said, his voice carrying a hint of challenge. While he never wanted to be rude to anyone, even the likes of the man standing in front of him, the less he had to say to Mr. Miller, the better.

The two men exchanged a long look before turning and walking up the steps to the Mayor's office together. Craig reached for the door first and held it open as Mr. Miller crossed the threshold. Their boots thumped on the dark hardwood floors, and as Craig shut the door behind them, the slight afternoon breeze flew through the opened windows, making the long sheer curtains flutter.

∽

Mayor Duncan stood from behind the large desk. The dark cherry piece of furniture dominated the room and was flanked by two high-backed chairs upholstered in rich leather. Craig remembered how the set had been the talk of the town when it arrived last summer, and for a moment, he thought about what Prudence Chatterton would have said about it had she been writing her articles back then.

Mayor Duncan moved around the desk. His big belly strained against his waistcoat as he shook both men's hands.

"Good afternoon, Mr. Miller and Mr. Harrison. Please have a seat." His voice was jovial—a little too much for Craig's taste.

This wasn't a meeting among friends or men who wished to do business with one another.

After motioning toward the two chairs, he returned to his seat and drew his chair toward the desk, reaching for a small pile of papers. His face flushed with a slight shade of pink from his exertion in greeting them.

Craig and Mr. Miller took their places in the chairs opposite the Mayor's desk. Craig leaned forward slightly; his eyes were fixed on the mayor.

"Thank you both for meeting with me today to finalize the details of the bet. I have all the paperwork finished, and I hope you both can agree to what I think is a fair compromise."

"We're here to finalize the agreement for the contest," Craig said, cutting straight to the point.

Mayor Duncan nodded, shuffling through his papers. "Yes, yes, of course. I've reviewed both of your proposals and believe we've reached a fair compromise."

Mr. Miller leaned back in his chair, and his expression relaxed in such a way that made Craig want to smack him in the back of the head. "I'm sure whatever you've decided will be more than fair, Mayor Duncan."

Craig glanced at Mr. Miller, slightly snorting under his breath. *If the mayor were fair, he would have sold me the property after receiving my first offer.* He turned his attention back to the mayor. "Let's hear this fair compromise."

Mayor Duncan cleared his throat. His gaze dropped to the papers. "Both teams will be working in the same area on Rattlesnake Mountain. We want to avoid blasting the mountain in too many places, as it could weaken the structure and pose a danger to everyone involved."

Craig frowned. "That's a stupid condition. It could lead to cheating. There's no way to ensure both teams are playing fair if we're all in the same area."

Mr. Miller's calm demeanor didn't waver. "I don't see a problem with it, Mr. Harrison. If anything, it will keep things interesting."

Craig clenched his fists, his frustration simmering just below the surface. "Interesting? This isn't a game, Mr. Miller."

"I realize that, which is why I agree with Mayor Duncan that blasting the mountain in too many places could weaken part of it, putting lives at risk." Mr. Miller cocked his head to the side. "Or do you not agree with that?"

"You know I do. Out of all three of us in this room, I have the most experience."

"Then you agree."

"I agree it's better for the mountain. I'm afraid I have to disagree that it's better for the bet. How are you going to ensure there isn't cheating?"

Mayor Duncan nodded. "Both teams will be monitored, and any signs of cheating or unsafe practices will result in disqualification."

Craig wasn't convinced. "And who will be doing the monitoring? How do we know they won't be biased?"

Mayor Duncan looked slightly flustered. "We have a neutral party lined up for that—experienced miners who have no stake in this contest."

Craig's eyes narrowed. "And we trust these so-called neutral parties?"

Mr. Miller chuckled, the sound grating on Craig's nerves. "You worry too much, Craig. I've already agreed to the terms. Perhaps you should, too."

Craig glared at him. "Easy for you to say. You probably think you have the upper hand."

Mr. Miller's smile widened. "I know I do."

"Yeah? How?"

"Well, it just so happens that I've hired one of the best in the mining business."

Craig's jaw tightened. "I'm the best in the business."

"That's quite a statement to make."

"I've mined more land than you'll ever know, from California to the Klondike. I know what I'm doing." Craig straightened his shoulders, and every muscle in his body clenched.

The two men stared at each other, neither wanting to look away.

Mayor Duncan cleared his throat again. "Gentlemen, please. Let's focus on the task at hand. We need to finalize these details so we can move forward."

Craig took a deep breath, forcing himself to calm down. "Fine. Let's get this over with."

Mayor Duncan began outlining the specific rules and conditions of the contest, his voice a steady drone as he read from his notes. "And remember," Mayor Duncan concluded, "the goal is to extract as much valuable ore as possible within the allotted time. Safety is paramount, and any violations will be dealt with swiftly."

Craig nodded, though his mind was still occupied with the thought of Mr. Miller's mysterious expert. He needed to stay focused and ensure his team had every advantage possible.

Mr. Miller stood, smoothing his coat lapel. "Thank you, Mayor. I'm sure this will be a fair and exciting contest."

Craig stood as well, his eyes fixed on Mr. Miller. "You can count on me to play fair. Just make sure your men do the same."

Mr. Miller's smile never wavered. "Of course, Mr. Harrison. I wouldn't think of having them do anything but remain fair and just. May the best team win."

After Craig and Mr. Miller read the contract, they picked up a pen and signed their names. Seeing his name etched on the line weighed on Craig's shoulders. This was it. This was the deciding factor in him staying in Featherstone Valley or being forced to leave at the end of it.

Once the men were finished, the mayor added his own signature with a flourish, sealing the agreement.

"Well, that's that," Mayor Duncan said, smiling broadly. "I look forward to seeing the results of your efforts. Best of luck to both of you."

Craig nodded curtly, then turned for the door. The mayor and Mr. Miller followed him outside, and the three stopped on the porch of the mayor's office. The sun had lowered even more in the sky, casting long shadows across the street.

The sound of horses' hooves drew their attention, and as Craig glanced toward the animals, his breath caught in his throat. A small group of riders was making its way into town, led by a man and a woman—a woman he would recognize anywhere.

She was the same one he had seen in the restaurant in Butte; her striking features and confident demeanor were unforgettable.

His brow furrowed. His pulse quickened—questions fired in his mind.

What was she doing here?

Miss Adams dismounted gracefully. Dressed in the pair of pants he'd seen at the train station, the dress from dinner was long gone. Her eyes scanned the town before landing on Craig, and she sucked in a breath. A flicker of recognition seemed to hit her in the chest, and she approached with a hesitant smile.

"Ah, Miss Adams. Your timing is perfect." Mr. Miller stepped forward, a broad grin spread on his lips.

Craig's stomach twisted, knowing the pair knew each other.

Was she the expert Mr. Miller had mentioned? And if she was, had she known when they were having dinner? He retraced what he could remember of their conversation, but so many parts of that night now blurred in his mind.

"Mr. Harrison?" Mr. Miller's smooth voice jerked Craig's attention. "I'd like you to meet Miss Ava Adams. She's a miner from the deserts of Nevada. She'll be working as my head foreman."

Craig's heart thumped even more as he stared at the woman he thought he'd never see again. "Hello again," he said.

"Good evening."

"Again?" Mr. Miller glanced between the two, mostly keeping his gaze on Miss Adams. "Have you two already met?"

"We were at the same restaurant in Butte the other night."

"Ah. I see." Mr. Miller focused on Craig. "I didn't know you were in Butte."

"I was picking up a piece of machinery."

"Well, I suppose it's fortunate you already know each other." Mr. Miller checked his watch. "I should be heading back to Deer Creek before it gets dark. Miss Adams, you and your men should find a room for the night at the inn across town. Mayor Duncan will see you find your way to Rattlesnake Mountain in the morning." He glanced at the mayor. "Won't you?"

"Of course. I can show them the way."

Mr. Miller turned toward his wagon, but Ava stopped him. "Mr. Miller, what about the supplies the men and I need for the mine?"

He smiled. "I would not worry about that. All the supplies you need are being delivered to the mine site as we speak, including something... special that I think you'll like."

"What is that?"

"You will see. Good day, Miss Adams. I trust you know how important this bet is."

"Yes, sir."

Before anyone else could say another word, Mr. Miller strode across the porch and climbed back into his carriage. Everyone around them watched as he left, and as the carriage's wheels rolled down the street, Miss Adams turned to Craig.

"I look forward to working together," she said.

"We aren't. You work for that man. I work for me." Although he tried to keep his voice low and without anger, he failed. His words had a slight growl that he wasn't proud of but didn't try to curtail either.

Just what in the world was going on?

"Oh. Well, then, I suppose I will look forward to starting on the mountain."

He inhaled a deep breath, letting the air fill his lungs. He turned and stormed off, muttering the last word under his breath. "Likewise."

THIRTEEN

AVA

"So... your evening out in Butte was just a nice dinner, huh?" Griffin's question wasn't a question. It was more of a statement that hung between him and Ava as they walked away from the mayor's office. Benjamin trailed behind them with his little, choppy footsteps.

While she knew her friend would have questions, it didn't mean she liked it.

"And you didn't think telling me you had dinner with a man was important enough?"

"No, I didn't think it was important." Her mind was fuzzy, and her thoughts swirled with confusion and frustration. Of course, this was his town, and seeing him wasn't a shock. But the whole situation had taken a turn she hadn't seen coming.

"So, you didn't think it was important to tell me that you had dinner with a man who owns another mining company you are now competing against?"

"I didn't know who he was when we had dinner." A growl whispered through her voice. Knocked off balance, she tried to shake off the unsettling twist in her stomach. She glanced around the town, focusing on the buildings she could see lining the main street. The mercantile and the livery caught her eye, with horses standing lazily outside, their tails swishing at flies. The men broke off and headed toward the stables with not only their horses but Griffin's, Benjamin's, and Ava's, with orders to see to their water and feed after finding them a stall to stay in.

The town was quiet, starkly contrasting with the bustling mining towns of Tonopah, Virginia City, and Truckee. This was partly because hordes of men weren't meandering through the streets looking for enjoyment at the local saloon, dance hall, or brothel. She glanced around even more, noticing that none of those places even existed in this town.

Griffin fell into step beside her, casting a glance her way. "So, you just decided to have dinner with a random stranger that night?"

"That's not how it went." She closed her eyes, taking a few breaths. "He was at one table, and I was at another when we both overheard the waiter talking about a problem with a couple needing a table and not having one. Both of us had an extra seat, and we thought it would be helpful to share a table so the couple waiting could get a table. I didn't know who he was when he sat down."

"And he didn't mention anything about what he did for a living?"

"He did. But he told me he was from Featherstone Valley, and since we were headed to Deer Creek, I didn't think anything of it."

"Until Mr. Miller mentioned we were headed to Featherstone Valley."

Griffin had finished the sentence she hadn't wanted to say. Her jaw clenched. "He was just a miner with whom I had dinner. He's nothing more."

Griffin raised an eyebrow, clearly not convinced. "You seemed pretty shaken up for it to be 'nothing more,'" he pressed, his tone gentle but insistent.

Ava shot him a warning glance. "I told you, it's nothing. Let's just get to the inn."

Griffin studied her, then spoke again, his voice softer. "You know, you can talk to me about it. If there's something more going on and if he made an impression—"

"There's nothing to talk about, Griffin. And there's nothing more going on. The only impression that man made was that he made me realize that I could have a nice dinner with someone and never think of them again."

Griffin fell silent, and although she could sense the questions firing off in his mind—questions he wanted to ask—he said nothing. They continued walking in silence. The sound of their boots crunching against the dirt road and Benjamin humming behind them were the only things breaking the quiet.

Ava forced herself to focus on the town again, noting the bank and several houses lining the streets. Smoke rose from the chimneys, billowing above the town and giving the sky a slight haze. The last thing she noticed was a church resting among a grove of trees in the distance, and its bright white paint almost looked orange in the sunset settling over the town.

This really is a different little town.

Continuing down the street, Ava, Griffin, and Benjamin approached the inn, crossing the porch and through the front door. Scents of supper cooking filled the air in the foyer, and after Griffin hit the bell on the desk, a voice called out.

"Just one moment, please," a woman said from the other room.

Ava turned a few circles, looking around the room. A cozy feeling wrapped around her as though she'd stepped into a home and not an inn, and she inhaled a deep breath, closing her eyes as every inch of her body relaxed.

There is something different about this whole town.

"May I just say one more thing?" Griffin's voice broke the silence and calm.

"Do you have to?" She opened her eyes, staring at him.

As they neared the inn, Griffin spoke up again, his tone more insistent. "Ava, I just want to understand. If there's something between you and Mr. Harrison—"

"There isn't," Ava snapped, her frustration boiling over. She'd been so calm in the last few moments, and he'd ruined it with more stupid words. "Leave it at that."

"But—"

"I said leave it."

Griffin sighed. "Alright, fine. But if you ever want to talk about it..."

"I know. I know. You're here to listen." She closed her eyes again, inhaling several breaths.

Footsteps thumped against the floor, and as Ava glanced toward the entryway into another room, an older woman entered the foyer. A smile spread on her face, and she wiped her hands with the apron tied around her waist as she walked over to the desk in the corner.

"Sorry for the wait," she said. "I was right in the middle of chopping an onion, and I wanted to get it in the skillet before I stepped away. How may I help you two?" She glanced between them.

"We are here for a couple of rooms," Ava said, making her way toward the desk, too.

"Oh, all right. I can help you with that. My name is Mrs. Sarah Holden. Welcome to my inn."

"Thank you. I'm Ava Adams, and this is my partner, Griffin Baker, and his... ward, Benjamin."

Griffin nodded and tipped his hat but remained several feet from the desk. Benjamin stood close by Griffin with his head tucked toward his chest. He didn't even look up when Ava said his name.

"So, you need two rooms?" Mrs. Holden asked.

"Well, we have some men with us. They are employees of

Mr. Miller. They will need rooms, too. But it's just for tonight. Unlike my partner and me, they will camp on the mountain. I don't know how many you have available, but I'm sure they can sleep two or three in a room. I'll let you figure out when they arrive from getting the horses settled at the livery."

"Oh. You're here to work for Mr. Miller." Mrs. Holden's smile vanished, and her tone changed. No longer cheery, Ava suddenly wondered if the woman was about to kick them out.

"Yes."

"Both of you?"

Ava nodded.

Mrs. Holden stared at her, blinking. "So, you are a miner?"

Ah. There it is. Ava smiled, letting out a slight chuckle. "Yes, I am. I'm Mr. Miller's new head foreman."

"Well, that's... that's nice to hear. My husband was the head foreman for Mr. Harrison's mining company until he passed."

"I'm so sorry for your loss."

"Thank you. It was a long time ago." She paused, furrowing her brow and blinking a few more times. "It's also nice to know that Mr. Miller hired a woman for a job other than..." She let her voice trail off.

"Other than what?"

Mrs. Holden waved her hand in front of her face. "Oh, it doesn't matter." She focused on a book in front of her and clicked her tongue as she checked the list of names she had written down. "Let me see. I don't know if I'll have enough rooms depending on how many men there are. But we will make it work, however we have to. It's just for one night, too, so it will be fine." She offered another smile. However, there was a difference to it, as though she only did so to hopefully smooth over any questions Ava and Griffin might have.

The pair exchanged glances again as she turned to grab a couple of keys hanging on a rack on the wall.

"Just follow me, and I'll show you to your rooms," she said.

"Dinner should be ready in an hour. The dining room is right there. You're more than welcome to come down whenever you wish. I serve until well into the evening."

∼

Ava lay on the bed, staring out the window of her hotel room. The light had changed over the hour she'd been there, casting shadows that moved across the floor through the curtains. She glanced up at the ceiling, trying to sort through the tangled mess of thoughts swirling in her mind.

Since leaving the restaurant, she had replayed that night with Mr. Harrison so many times, but it wasn't until the last hour that the thoughts troubled her so much. She replayed the conversations; however, there was nothing he had lied about. Nor was there any chance he could have known who she was.

At least, she didn't think so.

A knock thumped on her door, and as she opened it, Griffin leaned against the doorframe with his arms crossed. "Are you hungry?"

"Yeah."

Griffin stepped to the side, motioning her down the hallway toward the staircase. "After you."

"Where is Benjamin?" she asked.

"He fell asleep. But not before he asked if he could eat supper in the bed." Griffin chuckled and rubbed his chin. "Poor boy. I do believe today was the first time in his life he'd ever seen a bed. He told me that if he didn't sleep in the barn, he was outside or on the floor near the fireplace in the living room."

"I would say that I can't believe parents would treat their child that way, but then again, nothing surprises me when it comes to that."

"Well, I can't make up for his past, but hopefully, I can change his future."

"And you will." She paused, cocking her head to the side. "Did you want to wake him so he can eat?"

"I'll take him up a plate when I'm done. He's exhausted, and I want him to get some sleep."

Ava's stomach growled as she descended the staircase and made her way into the dining room. The scents of beef stew and cornbread called out to her, distracting her as her gaze whispered across the room, landing on a familiar face. She halted so fast that Griffin, who was walking behind her, ran into her, knocking her off a step.

"Why did you stop?" he asked. His brow furrowed, but before she could answer, he noticed what she was staring at. "Oh. Do you want to go back upstairs and come back down later?"

"No. There's no need for that." She straightened her shoulders, ignoring how, when she walked into the room and saw Mr. Harrison, he froze, too. The whole scene reminded her of the night of their dinner and how he had looked at her with genuine interest. She had felt a connection with him, a rare spark in her world.

She'd been so foolish.

"Are you sure you'll be able to just brush him off?" Griffin asked.

She looked over at him, her chin touching her shoulder. Annoyance bubbled in her chest. "Do you not think I can?"

Griffin shrugged. "It just seems odd. Like, what are the chances of you meeting him in another town, and now you're both here? Doesn't that sound like fate?"

"Fate?" Ava scoffed and rolled her eyes. "I don't believe in fate. I believe in hard work and determination. That's what gets you places."

"So, that's it? You won't even consider that sometimes things happen for a reason? Do you really believe you can just pretend like nothing happened?"

"Watch me."

She wiggled her shoulders, brushing her hair as she walked through the dining room and sat at a table in the corner. Although she didn't look in Mr. Harrison's direction, she sensed his eyes fixed on her. Griffin followed close behind her, taking the seat across from her. He raised one eyebrow, giving her a look she knew all too well. And one she hated.

"What is it?" she asked him.

"I just don't understand why you're trying to avoid the issue."

"I'm not avoiding anything. I'm focusing on what matters."

He stared at her, then leaned back in his chair. "Fine. If that's how you want to play it, then do it. Just... don't shut yourself off to something completely."

"I'm not. Dinner was nothing. We talked, we ate, and we went our separate ways."

Griffin smirked. "It must have been some dinner for you to still think about it."

Ava shook her head, a small smile tugging at her lips. "You're impossible, do you know that?"

Griffin chuckled. "I try."

"Do me a favor and try less."

∽

Although Ava kept her gaze tightly on either her supper or her company, the sense of Mr. Harrison's gaze haunted her throughout her meal. Surely, he wasn't out-and-out staring at her the entire time. But out of the corner of her eye, she could see his head move in her direction, and each time she caught his movement, her heart thumped harder. She adjusted her seat, turning slightly away from him to distract herself.

As she did that, Griffin did the opposite, turning toward Mr. Harrison and glancing in his direction.

"What are you doing?" she asked him.

"I'm not doing anything."

"Yes, you are."

"No. I'm just sitting here enjoying the last few bites of my dinner." He paused, glancing at Mr. Harrison again. "And when I'm done, I'm going to go upstairs to my room and get a good night's rest." He cocked his head to the side, shoving the last bit of his slice of cornbread into his mouth. He smiled as he chewed, and he lifted his hands above the table, wiping them so the crumbs would fall onto his plate.

"You really know how to get under my skin. You know that, don't you?"

"Yeah," he sighed. "It's a gift." He paused again, then stood from his seat. "And on that note, I'm going to head upstairs with some supper for Benjamin."

"Are you seriously going to leave me in this dining room alone?"

He winked. "Goodnight, Ava. Sleep well."

Before she could say a word, Griffin left the dining room, heading to the kitchen to ask about a plate for the boy. Ava closed her eyes, inhaling a few deep breaths. She glanced down at her not-yet-empty bowl of stew and plate of cornbread. Of course, she could leave and return to her room. But it wasn't that simple, especially with her stomach telling her it wasn't finished.

I'll be fine. I'll finish my meal and return to my room. I'll be fine.

She set her spoon on the plate and grabbed a slice of cornbread. Movement flickered in the corner of one eye, and she braced herself, praying the movement came from someone other than the one she feared it came from.

"Excuse me, Miss Adams?" a voice said, familiar in tone.

She glanced up. "Good evening, Mr. Harrison."

"Good evening. May I join you?" He motioned toward the chair Griffin just vacated.

"Um. I suppose. But I was going to return to my room soon."

"I promise I won't keep you." He sat, exhaling a slight breath. "I have to admit that I was pretty shocked to see you this afternoon." He paused, his eyes narrowed. "You didn't seem as shocked to see me, though."

"Well, it was easy for me. I knew I was coming here. I figured it was inevitable that we would run into each other."

His brow furrowed. "If you knew when we had dinner in Butte, why didn't you say anything?"

Ava bristled at the accusatory tone in his voice. "I didn't know then," she snapped. "I was headed to Deer Creek, where I believed the job was."

"How can I believe that? How do I know Mr. Miller didn't hire you to spy on me and that you knew who I was the minute I sat at your table? You were rather eager to have me join you."

Her eyes widened, and anger pulsed through her veins. "I was not eager! And I did not know who you were! And I am no spy. How do I know you didn't know who I was and that you weren't spying on me?"

"Why would I need to spy on you? I could win this bet in my sleep. I don't need to know anything about you. It would make more sense if you were spying on me."

"This is all just a misunderstanding."

Craig shook his head. "A misunderstanding?" he repeated, his tone laced with disbelief. "There is no misunderstanding. You knew who I was. Period. End of story."

"I didn't!" Her voice growled.

"You can't think I trust you. You knew I was a miner. You must have known there was a chance we would cross paths again."

"For the last time, I had no idea. But even if I had, what difference would it make? We had one dinner. That's it."

Mr. Harrison's jaw clenched. Accused of a crime, tautness built through his chest while words seemed to swim in the waters of his blue eyes. His lips twitched, and his brow furrowed as though he was thinking of different excuses to lie at her feet. Which untruth would he use? Would he create an elaborate story or deny it?

"It makes a difference now that I know you work for Mr. Sidney Miller."

"I don't understand."

"Let's just say the man has a reputation for cheating and ruthless tactics."

Ava's stomach twisted. "I didn't know that when I took the job. I just needed the work."

"Well, now you know."

"I'm not sure about the man you know, but Mr. Miller has only shown me that he wants to win a mountain to mine for gold. Just like any other man in this country." She leaned forward in her chair, resting her elbows on the table. "I didn't come here to fight with you. I came here for a job. I will do that job, and no one will stop me—including you."

Disappointment whispered across Mr. Harrison's face. "Then you weren't the woman I thought you were in Butte."

Tears prickled at the corners of her eyes, but she refused to let them fall. "That thought goes both ways, Mr. Harrison."

FOURTEEN

WYATT

Wyatt strolled down the dusty street with Reed at his side. It'd been a long day preparing the mine site at Rattlesnake Mountain, but luckily, they'd gotten everything done.

"I can't wait for supper," Reed said, exhaling. "I swear I can already taste it."

"I'm hungry myself. I didn't pack much for lunch, and my stomach has growled for the last hour." Although Wyatt was looking forward to supper, a slight itch of anticipation and reluctance itched through his skin. Of course, he looked forward to an evening meal with friends, but the thoughts of meeting Rebecca's cousin, Emily, weighed heavily on his shoulders. It wasn't out of disdain at the chance of meeting her but a simple desire to avoid new social interactions—especially when this social interaction had unspoken expectations.

From all accounts, Emily was, according to his friends, considered a pleasant young woman. Or at least that was the impression he got. Rebecca had spoken highly of her, and Reed had given his subtle nod of approval. Yet, Wyatt found himself wishing he could avoid the encounter altogether. Socializing wasn't his strong suit, especially with someone new. With that, he also never wanted to be rude. Rebecca and Reed had done so much for him; the least he could do was meet her cousin with some semblance of politeness.

He couldn't bring shame to his family name by acting otherwise.

His parents would tan his hide if they found out he'd been anything but cordial to the young woman. Wyatt's mother was like any other mother in town, dreaming of the day her children would find love and marry. And it was a fact she made known every chance she got. Of course, Wyatt wanted those things, too. He wanted the warmth of a loving home, a devoted wife's companionship, and children's laughter. Yet, he wasn't sure if he was ready for it all.

Shaking the thoughts from his mind, he continued down the street through town, and as he passed the inn, a carriage rolled by him and clattered to a stop. Wyatt slowed his pace, curiosity momentarily overcoming his preoccupation. The tall and slender driver jumped down, fetching several bags from the back and setting them on the inn's porch before he made his way to the carriage and opened the door. A smile spread across his lips under his trimmed beard, and as he tipped his hat, a woman's leg popped out from inside the carriage.

Although Reed kept walking, Wyatt halted, staring at the purple-heeled shoe and the woman's leg attached to it. The sun glinted off her ivory skin. The rest of the woman's body followed, and she stepped out of the carriage as if in slow motion. A parasol hid her upper body from his view.

Finally noticing Wyatt wasn't with him, Reed stopped and turned around. He threw his arms up as though silently asking what was wrong, and when Wyatt didn't answer, Reed walked back to his friend.

"Why did you stop?"

Wyatt inhaled a deep breath, shaking his head. His curiosity piqued, and he cocked his head to the side.

Reed moved his hand in front of Wyatt's face. "Wyatt? Wyatt?"

"What?"

"Why did you stop?"

"I just... just let me see something."

"What?" Reed turned, glancing in the direction Wyatt stared. "Ah. I think I know what it is." He moved to stand next to Wyatt and folded his arms across his chest. He said nothing else.

After helping the woman out of the carriage, the driver shut the door, tipping his hat again. "Your luggage is on the porch, ma'am," the driver said to the young woman, pointing to the bags on the porch. "Have a nice evening."

"Aren't you going to take them inside and up to my room?" she asked.

"My apologies, ma'am, but I don't have time."

"You don't have time? But aren't you paid to have the time?"

He shook his head and tipped his hat at her. Before she could say anything, he climbed back into the carriage and tapped the horses' rumps. The carriage rolled down the street, creating a slight dust cloud around her.

The woman turned toward the carriage as it rolled away in Wyatt's direction. She shouted several words Wyatt couldn't hear, and as her gaze found him, his breath caught in his throat, and time seemed to stand still. Wyatt stood rooted to the spot, his earlier thoughts forgotten. She was young, perhaps his age, and her long, golden blonde hair cascaded in soft waves around her shoulders. Her beauty was undeniable, and her presence commanded the space around her as if she were an actress stepping onto a stage.

"Excuse me," she said to him and Reed, waving in their direction. Reed's eyes widened, and he spun on his heel and strode off, muttering under his breath about knowing what the woman was about to ask and wanting no part in any of it. Wyatt ignored his friend, not even looking in his direction as he left.

The woman walked toward Wyatt, glancing after Reed but then shaking her head as though she, too, ignored the man who walked away. "Can you help me?" she asked Wyatt.

"Me?" He pointed at his chest, and although it seemed like a logical question, he regretted it as soon as the word left his lips. What a dumb thing to ask.

"No. I'm talking to the invisible man behind you." She rolled her eyes. "Yes, you. Can you help me?"

He walked toward her, trying to ignore how he'd just made a fool of himself. He needed to turn this meeting around. Like yesterday. "Of course, I can help you. What do you need?"

"My driver seems to have forgotten who pays him his wages and has left my luggage on the porch instead of taking it into the inn. Can you get my bags for me and take them inside?"

The woman's gaze remained steady. Her blue eyes held his with an intensity that made his heart skip a beat. All thought left his head.

"Did you understand what I asked?" she asked, snapping her fingers in front of his face. "Hello?"

Wyatt finally tore his distraction away, feeling a flush creep up his neck. He shook his head. He wasn't one to be easily rattled, but this woman had managed to do just that with a single look. He cleared his throat, hoping to dispel the awkwardness in the air.

"Of course. Let me just grab your bags," he said.

Before she could say another word or he could humiliate himself further, he dashed toward the porch, grabbing her bags by the handles. His arms strained under their weight.

Exactly how much had this woman packed?

He struggled to the inn's door, ignoring how the bags were banging into his shins. Surely, they would be black and blue after this. The young woman followed behind him, moving past him with a slightly annoyed *humph* sound under her breath as they entered the foyer. She made her way to the desk, tapping on the bell. Impatience seemed to spread through her, and she shifted her weight from one foot to the other.

While they waited, Wyatt fought the urge to attempt any small talk. His courage was lacking.

"Good evening," a voice said behind them. Wyatt turned as Mrs. Holden entered the foyer. She glanced between them. "Oh! Mr. Cooper. I didn't realize it was you. Are you looking for Mr. Harrison?"

Wyatt shook his head and pointed toward the young woman. "No, Mrs. Holden. I'm just helping this nice lady with her bags since the carriage driver wouldn't bring them in."

"Well, isn't that nice of you?" She then turned her attention to the young woman. "Good evening. How may I help you?"

"Good evening," the young woman said. "My name is Elizabeth Claremore. I believe I have a reservation."

"Ah, yes. Miss Claremore, I was told you would be arriving today." Mrs. Holden made her way over to her desk and fetched a book from one of the drawers. She set it on top of the desk, scanning the pages with her finger until she found what she seemed to be looking for. "All right, Miss Claremore, I have you in my biggest room, and I see that the check-out date is unknown at this time." Mrs. Holden glanced at the young woman and raised an eyebrow as though to stress her question. "Is that correct?"

Miss Claremore shrugged. "Yes. That was what I was told."

"Perfect. Well, welcome to the Featherstone Valley Inn." Mrs. Holden wrote a few words in her book, speaking again while she still looked down at the book. "Have you eaten supper yet?"

"I have not."

"I'm serving now in the dining room, and I can save you a table while you get settled."

"Could I have my meals delivered to my room instead? If you don't mind."

Mrs. Holden smiled. "I don't mind at all. I can bring up supper after you're settled."

"Thank you. I'd rather not come downstairs for anything."

"I understand." A flicker of hesitation inched through Mrs. Holden's movements, catching Wyatt's attention.

Did she know the young woman? And who told Miss Holden she'd be arriving today?

After Mrs. Holden finished writing her notes in the book, she closed it and grabbed a key from the rack behind the desk. "Right this way." The two moved toward the stairs, and Miss Claremore glanced at Wyatt and then at the bags at his feet.

"Would you mind?" she asked.

"Not at all." He grabbed the bags' handles once more and followed behind them.

∼

Wyatt crossed the porch, stopping at the first stair as he looked upon the street. He inhaled deeply, replaying the last ten minutes or so in his mind. It was a whirlwind of thoughts and questions. Exactly who was that young woman? And what was she doing in Featherstone Valley? How had Mrs. Holden known she was coming? Did she have family here? Friends?

He yearned to know more about her.

"Finally," a voice said behind him.

He spun to see Reed leaning against the side of the inn with his arms folded. "I thought perhaps that young woman had taken you to her room and devoured you."

"What are you even talking about?" Wyatt chuckled, shaking his head. "She just needed help taking her bags inside."

"Just taking them inside, huh? Is that all you did? Because you were gone quite a long time just to have taken her bags inside."

"Well, no, that's not all I did. I did also help her take them upstairs to her room. But what is so wrong with that? She is a lady, and she needed help."

Reed laughed, shaking his head again. "Miss Elizabeth Claremore is no lady, I assure you."

"How do you know her name?"

"Everyone who lives in Deer Creek or has traveled to Deer Creek knows who Miss Claremore is."

"I don't understand what that means."

Reed laughed again and patted Wyatt on his back as he motioned for them to leave. "It's probably better if you don't. Come on. Rebecca is waiting for us at the house."

∼

Although Wyatt had tried to broach the subject of Miss Claremore a couple more times with Reed as they walked to Reed and Rebecca's house, Reed stayed tight-lipped, just shaking his head and uttering, 'I'll tell you later' each time.

It wasn't until they reached the porch that Reed had finally had enough and exhaled, pausing with his hand on the doorknob. "She's just known around Deer Creek."

"Yes, I figured that out. But how is she known?"

"Let me put it to you this way... you know of Mr. Sidney Miller, right?"

"Yeah."

"And you know the type of businesses he owns, right?"

"Yeah."

"Well..." Reed shrugged, then cocked his head to the side, raising one eyebrow.

Wyatt stared at his friend momentarily, waiting for Reed to elaborate on his thought. He didn't. "I don't understand. Are you saying she works for Mr. Miller in one of the brothels?"

"Yeah." Reed nodded and blinked several times.

"But I don't understand how that can be. She's... she's a lovely young woman."

"And that means?"

"Such a lovely young woman couldn't be one of *those* types of women."

"I know you want to think that, but it's true."

A hint of anger bubbled in his chest. "And how would you know? Just what are you up to when you go to Deer Creek for Mr. Harrison? Don't tell me you're visiting those types of places. It would break Rebecca's heart."

"No." Reed held up his hands, shaking his head. His eyes widened. "No. I'm not. I swear. I don't even walk near those places. But the women walk around during the day, and if you're there enough, you hear things."

Questions swirled around Wyatt's mind, and his stomach twisted. Surely, Reed was wrong about such a lovely woman. Surely, Miss Claremore wasn't... wasn't... *that* type of woman. The encounter with her at the inn lingered in his mind, and he couldn't help but replay the interaction over and over. There was something captivating about her, and he found himself drawn to her.

Reed had to be wrong. He just had to.

"But that makes no sense. Why would she be in Featherstone Valley? He doesn't have a business here."

Reed shrugged and then pointed at Wyatt's chest. "Yet."

"That would be foolish beyond foolish. The town will never approve of him opening a brothel. I think you have the wrong woman."

"If you want to tell yourself that, I can't stop you. But I'm not wrong, Wyatt. You should forget about her. She's nothing but trouble, mark my words."

Wyatt shook his head, exhaling as he moved past Reed. He grabbed the doorknob and twisted it so the door popped open before his friend could stop him.

The scent of roast beef, potatoes, and carrots wafted through the air, and although Wyatt's stomach growled, the thought of eating suddenly didn't sit well with him. Reed followed close behind him, and before Wyatt could say anything, Reed called out to his wife.

"Rebecca? We're home."

Rebecca appeared from the kitchen, wiping her hands on a dish towel. Her face lit up with a smile when she saw them. "Hey, darling. You're just in time. Supper's almost ready."

Wyatt and Reed removed their hats and hung them on the pegs by the door. The inside of the house was cozy, with wooden floors and simple furnishings, and the walls were adorned with framed photographs and embroidery, each telling a story of family and love.

Reed walked over to Rebecca and kissed her on the cheek. "Smells amazing, darling. You've outdone yourself."

Rebecca blushed. "Thank you, Reed. I hope you're both hungry."

"Starving. It's been a long day."

"I'm sorry, darling. Did you finish all the work you needed so you can start the work on the new mountain?"

"We did."

"That's good." She pointed toward the couch and patted the patchwork quilt draped over the back. "Have a seat while I get the table set."

"Are you sure you don't want any help?" Reed asked.

She opened her mouth, but something seemed to stop her, and she cocked one eyebrow. "Would you mind if I asked you to set the table?" She smiled and widened her eyes as she tilted her head toward the kitchen behind her.

Reed's brow furrowed, then he blinked and nodded. "Oh, yeah. I can set the table. No problem."

"Great. Thank you." She turned her attention to Wyatt, motioning toward the couch once more. "You can have a seat if you like. I'll let you know when supper is ready."

She vanished back into the kitchen while Wyatt took his seat. Reed followed his wife, and the sounds of plates clanking echoed through the house. A fire popped and cracked in the fireplace, and as Wyatt stared at the flames, thoughts of what Reed had said about Miss Claremore replayed in his mind.

Surely, he was mistaken. Surely, he had the wrong woman.

While he knew only a little about the women who worked in brothels, what he did know was enough to tell him that his parents wouldn't be too keen on him bringing home a woman like that. His mother would probably drop dead from the shock and horror of it all.

Someone cleared their throat next to him, and he flinched before looking up to find a young woman standing next to him.

"I'm sorry. I didn't mean to startle you," she said, handing him a glass of water. A slight smile inched across her heart-shaped face, and she tucked her chocolate hair behind one ear. "Rebecca said I should bring this to you."

Guilt prickled through Wyatt's chest. He'd almost forgotten about meeting Emily in the whirlwind that had been the last hour. "Oh. Thank you for the water."

"You're welcome. You must be Wyatt. My name is Emily. I'm Rebecca's cousin, and I've heard a lot about you."

Wyatt laughed. "It's nice to meet you. I can only imagine what they've said. I hope they haven't exaggerated too much."

She smiled. "Oh, I'm sure they haven't."

Wyatt opened his mouth to disagree, but Rebecca's voice echoed through the house. "Dinner is ready!"

Emily and Wyatt nodded and headed into the other room, where Reed and Rebecca were setting the finishing touches to the meal and table. They moved around one another, exchanging smiles and glances as though they knew exactly what the other was thinking. It was just another one of those silent conversations they were both so good at.

"Everything smells wonderful, sweetheart," Reed said to his wife. He kissed her on the cheek, then helped her into her chair, scooting it toward the table before helping Emily with her chair.

"Thank you. But I can't take all the credit. Emily helped more than I could have asked for. In fact, this meal is mostly hers." Rebecca looked at Wyatt. "Emily is an amazing cook."

"I really didn't do that much." Emily's face flushed a bright shade of pink, and she dropped her gaze to the table.

"Don't lie. You did more than I did."

Reed shoved a bite into his mouth, closing his eyes. "Well, whoever did what, it doesn't matter. Both of you have outdone yourselves."

As his friend continued to enjoy bite after bite, Wyatt took his own bite, closing his eyes as the savory meat hit his tongue.

"I could eat this every night," Reed continued, motioning toward Wyatt with his elbow. "This is so much better than the beans and cornbread we had nightly up on Old Bear."

"Old Bear?" Emily glanced between the two, raising one eyebrow.

"It's the old mountain where the mines were." Rebecca took her own bite, and after she finished chewing and swallowing, she grabbed her water, sipping a few gulps before she set the glass down. "Now that they've moved to a mountain closer to town, I get to enjoy having my husband home every night." She reached over and clutched her husband's hand. The two smiled at one another.

A hint of longing and jealousy flickered through Wyatt's body.

"I'm happy that I'll be home, too. But I gotta say, if you keep cooking meals like this, I will be too lazy and big to get through the tunnels."

At the mention of the tunnels, Rebecca's body shook as though she got a chill. Her smile vanished, replaced with an almost disgusted look. "I hate that word."

"Which one? Tunnels?"

"Yes. Don't say it again. It makes me nervous just thinking about the word, much less you going underground in them. I wish you didn't have to work in the mines."

"I wish I didn't have to either. But it's what I have to do for now. We don't always get to work the job we want. Sometimes, we have to just do what we can."

Do what we can.

Reed's words lingered in Wyatt's mind. What if what he said about Miss Claremore was true, only it wasn't what she wanted to do? What if it was the only thing she could do? What if she was only doing what she could to survive?

The memory of Miss Claremore's piercing blue eyes sent his pulse thumping. Her beauty and mysterious aura surrounded her like a magnet, drawing his thoughts back to her again and again. Even though she hadn't said much to him, he could almost hear her voice.

Heat spread through his body, moistening his skin with a thin layer of sweat and suddenly making his collar itchy. He stretched the material for relief, but it didn't work.

He had to get some fresh air.

"Excuse me," he said abruptly, standing from his chair. "I need to step outside for a moment."

Before anyone could say anything, he strode for the door, opening it and shutting it behind him as he exhaled.

The cool evening air hit him, and he leaned against the porch railing and looked out toward the inn. The distant lantern and candlelight in the windows of each room flickered, and as the crickets chirped in the weeds at his feet, Wyatt couldn't shake the questions repeating in his mind. He didn't know if or how he'd see Miss Claremore again, but he knew he had to try.

He just had to.

FIFTEEN

SARAH

The early morning sunlight filtered through the lace curtains, casting a warm, golden hue across the inn's kitchen. The aroma of sizzling bacon and freshly cracked eggs filled the air, mingling with the scent of the fresh coffee brewing on the counter.

She looked out the window as birds fluttered from tree to tree, chirping and whistling songs as they greeted the morning. A smile inched across her lips, and she inhaled, moving over to the stove. Bacon sizzled in a skillet, and she turned over the strips of meat before grabbing a wooden spoon and pushing chopped potatoes around another skillet to brown the sides. She cut off a chunk of butter, tossing it in with the potatoes and watching it melt. The rich, creamy scent wafted around her.

The kitchen door opened, and Jack rushed inside. A smile beamed across his face. "Sarah! Sarah! Look what Mr. Lockhart delivered this morning. He said it came in early this morning and knew I would want to see it immediately."

"What is it?" She moved over to the pastor, wiping her hands on her apron. He held a letter in one hand and a photograph in the other.

"It's a letter from Patrick and Julia and then a picture of them with Henry." Jack showed her the picture of the young couple standing beside one another with a tiny infant in Julia's arms. It was his first official photograph. Or at least that was what Patrick said in his letter.

"Oh, my, that is wonderful." She stared at the picture. "It seems like it was just yesterday they left. But I know it's not. Look at how much Henry has grown in just those few weeks. I wish we weren't missing it."

"I know. Me too. I miss them."

They both looked at the photograph, pointing out the different things that attracted their attention.

"He looks so much like you. I noticed it when he visited you, but there is something about the printed image that makes it stand out. I'm curious to see your other son, Kit."

"Yeah, seeing him after all these years would be nice."

"Have you written him yet?"

Jack shook his head. "Not yet. Patrick said he would talk to him and write me what was said just in case Kit doesn't want to hear from me. I don't want to force him."

"Well, I think that's exceptionally kind of you to think about his feelings like that." She laid her hand on his shoulder and leaned in, kissing his cheek.

"I don't know that I would give myself that much credit. Just because I won't contact him doesn't mean I don't want to."

"I know."

Jack took another deep breath while looking at the photograph. "But I am happy to hear from Patrick. He says in his letter that they have plans to return for another visit, but he's not sure when."

"Well, that's something we can look forward to." She patted Jack on the shoulder and moved around him, reaching for a tray on the top shelf of a nearby cabinet. She set it on the counter and wiped off the top.

Jack furrowed his brow, motioning toward the tray. "What is that for?"

"A new guest." Sarah exhaled, fetching a plate from the cabinet. She spooned a heaping pile of scrambled eggs onto the plate before taking a fork and stabbing a couple of slices of bacon. She laid those next to the eggs, then added a spoonful of fried potatoes to the other corner of the plate. "She's a young lady who wishes to eat her meals in her room."

"She isn't coming down to the dining room?"

Sarah shook her head. "No. Given who she is, though, I honestly don't blame her."

"Who is she?"

"She works for Mr. Sidney Miller. She's his special guest and is staying here for an undisclosed amount of time."

"What do you mean special guest?"

"She's one of the women who works in his brothel in Deer Creek."

Jack's brow furrowed again. He opened his mouth but waited a second before speaking. "Are you saying she's a... a..."

"A woman of questionable morals?" Sarah finished his sentence. "Yes, that's exactly who she is."

"So there's a... well, you know the word, staying at the inn?"

Sarah nodded. "She's actually a nice young woman. Pretty, too. If I were to meet her on the street, I would think she was just a married woman out for a stroll in town. She's graceful and eloquent and seems... proper by all accounts. I don't understand why she would work for Mr. Miller."

Jack shrugged. "Sometimes we have to make difficult choices, and sometimes life makes them for us. Perhaps she doesn't want to work for him, but she must."

"Lord, I hope that's not the case. I can't imagine a young woman like her being forced into that situation. It would just break my heart." Sarah finished arranging the food on the plate and set it on the tray along with a set of silverware and a glass of water. She finished the breakfast tray with a folded napkin before grabbing a blueberry muffin she'd made last night. She placed the muffin on a smaller plate and set it in the other corner of the tray across from the glass of water. "Can you get more bacon in the pan while I take this to her room?" Sarah asked Jack.

"Of course. I don't have to be at the church until this afternoon." He watched as she moved around him, but before she could grab the tray, he reached for it. "Do you want me to take the tray up to her? Perhaps I could introduce myself and talk to her a little bit. Maybe even invite her to service this coming Sunday."

Sarah smiled, cocking her head to the side. She softened her voice. "As lovely as that sounds, perhaps we should let her settle in before approaching her. Perhaps in a few days, you could introduce yourself."

"Yeah, you're right. I don't want to overwhelm her."

Sarah smiled again and grabbed the tray, leaving the kitchen. As she neared the stairs, Miss Adams, Mr. Baker, and the small boy traveling with them were headed toward the dining room.

"Good morning," she said to the three of them. "I'll be back in a moment and get your breakfast."

∽

AVA

Ava shoveled the last bite of potatoes into her mouth and glanced out the window as she chewed. Across the table, Griffin sipped his coffee, and Benjamin happily hummed while eating the stack of pancakes Mrs. Holden had made especially for him. The scent of maple wafted around the table from the syrup.

Griffin chuckled and shook his head as he read the morning newspaper.

"What's so funny?" Ava asked.

"You're famous."

"Famous? What are you talking about?"

He folded the newspaper and tossed it down onto the table in front of her. She read the headline. "A new face in town: mystery and miner's grit. What is this?"

He shrugged. "I don't know. Apparently, this Prudence Chatterton, whoever that is, has taken it upon herself to write an article about you." He chuckled again. "She seemed quite taken with your attire."

"My attire?" Ava furrowed her brow, and she ignored Griffin's laughter as she read the rest of the article.

GOOD MORNING, ESTEEMED READERS OF FEATHERSTONE VALLEY! PRUDENCE CHATTERTON HERE, READY TO SERVE ANOTHER DOSE OF THE LATEST GOSSIP SEASONED WITH A DASH OF MYSTERY THAT HAS RECENTLY STIRRED OUR QUAINT TOWN.

THIS WEEK, THE STREETS OF FEATHERSTONE HAVE BEEN ABUZZ WITH THE ARRIVAL OF A MOST UNCONVENTIONAL LADY. YES, DEAR READERS, A MYSTERIOUS WOMAN HAS COME TO TOWN, AND SHE'S NOT JUST ANY ORDINARY VISITOR. WHILE SHE SEEMS TO HAVE CONNECTIONS WITH MR. SIDNEY MILLER, INFAMOUS FOR HIS LESS-THAN-REPUTABLE ESTABLISHMENTS IN DEER CREEK, ONE CAN TELL AT FIRST GLANCE THAT SHE IS FAR FROM BEING ONE OF HIS USUAL ASSOCIATES. WHY, YOU ASK?

WELL, THE LADY WEARS PANTS! AND NOT JUST ANY PANTS, BUT THOSE BEFITTING A MINER OR A FRONTIERSWOMAN, STRIDING ALONGSIDE THE RUGGED SOULS THAT DELVE INTO THE EARTH'S DEPTHS.

OUR NEW ARRIVAL HAS BEEN SPOTTED MINGLING WITH THE MINERS,

and it appears she's quite at home in their dusty, boisterous company. Yet, what's most intriguing is her apparent feud with Mr. Craig Harrison, owner of the Harrison Gold Mining Company. Observations around town reveal a frosty tension between the two, marked by cold shoulders and occasional spats that make bystanders pause and ponder.

The plot thickens as not only has this daring woman graced our town with her bold presence, but she is also accompanied by a man and a young boy. From what your diligent Prudence has gathered, the trio does not seem to fit the typical mold of a family. They are not partners, nor does she appear to be the boy's mother. Could they be siblings, or is there another twist to their tale?

While names and exact relations remain elusive at this juncture, rest assured that I am on the case. This woman's bold demeanor and unusual attire have set tongues wagging and minds wondering about her past and her intentions here in Featherstone Valley.

As always, I will keep my ear to the ground and my pen ready to disclose any developments. Who is this mysterious woman in pants? What brings her to our town? And what will come of her confrontations with Mr. Harrison? Stay tuned, dear readers, as I vow to uncover the truth behind this enigmatic new resident.

Until we meet again through these pages, may your days be filled with curiosity and your conversations rich with speculation. Featherstone Valley is never short of surprises, and neither is your devoted chronicler.

"Is this a joke?" Ava asked, pointing at the newspaper.

Griffin shrugged. "I don't know, but it's funny." He grabbed his cup of coffee and took a sip. "So, what's the plan for today?"

"I suppose we will head to the mayor's office after we're done. He's supposed to escort us to the mountain and show us around." She rolled her eyes. "I hope he doesn't get us lost."

Griffin snorted. "I was thinking the same thing yesterday. He doesn't seem like the type to go traipsing around a mountain, does he?"

"Not in the slightest."

Griffin exhaled a slight groan and leaned forward, resting his elbows on the table. His shoulders hunched. "It will be interesting to see what these men we hired know. I hope we didn't make a bad choice in hiring some of them. Mining a mountain is hard enough without adding someone who doesn't know what they are doing. It's not safe."

Ava shrugged. "Nothing we can do about it now. If we have to train them, then we have to train them. Do you know where they are?"

"Down at the livery, getting all the horses ready to leave. They'll meet us at the mayor's office."

She glanced at the boy, still humming while he shoveled bites of pancakes into his mouth. "What do you want to do with him? We can't exactly take him up there with us, and I don't think leaving him here alone is a good idea."

Griffin glanced at the boy, too. His brow furrowed as he leaned back in the chair, letting out another breath. This one held a little more annoyance than the last. "Yeah. You're probably right. I didn't think about that. Unless, of course, Mrs. Holden doesn't mind. Do you think she would?"

"I don't know. I suppose you could ask her."

Griffin frowned again, but before he could say anything else, Mrs. Holden entered the dining room with another plate of pancakes stacked high.

"Here you are, young man." She set the plate in front of

Benjamin, and the boy's eyes widened. He licked his lips, grabbed the plate, and dug in before finishing the one already in front of him. She glanced at Griffin with a slight chuckle. "He certainly has an appetite."

"Yeah, you wouldn't know that looking at him." Griffin folded his arms across his chest, shaking his head. "I don't know what his father did to him, but I don't think I want to know."

"I don't think I would want to know either." She patted Benjamin on the head. "But it doesn't matter now. He's found the home he was meant to have." She paused, then looked back at Griffin. "Have you thought about what you will do with him while you're at the mine?"

"We were just talking about that." Griffin leaned forward again, clasping his hands and resting them on the table. "I don't think he should go with us, but I don't think I should leave him here either."

"Well, of course, he's more than welcome to stay here with me. I promise not to give him too many chores."

At the mention of work, Benjamin looked at Griffin. His eyes widened, and his breath quickened.

Sensing that was a word the boy feared, Mrs. Holden bent closer to him. "Don't worry. When I talk about chores, I mean fun stuff like playing with the cows and chickens." She brushed her finger on the tip of his nose, and his body softened. She straightened up. "However, as much as I would like the company, he'd probably benefit more from some schooling. We have a schoolhouse here and a fine teacher named Miss Evans. She's wonderful with the children."

Griffin raised an eyebrow and glanced at Ava. "There's an idea."

Ava nodded. "He would benefit from it."

"Yes, he would." Griffin touched Benjamin's shoulder, gaining his attention from the stack of pancakes. Clearly, the boy had learned early on to ignore when adults spoke about him. Ava didn't want to think about the conversations he'd probably heard in his lifetime.

The thought sent a shudder down her spine.

"What do you think?" Griffin asked the boy. "Do you want to go to school while I work at the mines?"

Benjamin shrugged. "I've never been to school before. Is it fun?"

Sarah grabbed the back of the chair next to Ava and slid it around so she could sit next to Benjamin. "I think it's a fun place."

"But what do I do there?"

"Well, you will get to learn new things."

"Like what things?"

"Do you know how to read and write?"

"A little. Pa said there was no need for me to fuss around with school. I wasn't going to amount to much anyway."

"Then you will learn to read and write, add and subtract numbers, and learn about plants and animals, too."

"I know about animals. Or at least some." The boy scrunched his face. "It's mostly how to take care of them before we slaughter them and eat them. I know how to do that, too."

Mrs. Holden glanced at Ava and Griffin. "Well, that certainly is good knowledge to have. But I don't think Miss Evans teaches those things. She teaches other things about animals, such as their habitats in the wild. You will also meet all the other boys and girls that live in town."

Benjamin's eyes lit up. "You mean I could make friends?"

Sarah nodded. "But only if you go to school and listen to what Miss Evans says."

"I will. I promise."

"Well, I guess that settles that." Griffin chuckled. "I guess I'm taking him to school."

∽

By the time Griffin had Benjamin ready to leave, Ava had finished breakfast, and the three of them stepped out onto the inn's porch, looking over the street. They made their way down the lane and into the heart of town. A few townsfolk nodded at them with morning greetings, and while Griffin veered to the left and headed toward the church and schoolhouse, Ava went to the right, headed toward the mayor's office.

The sun had risen higher in the sky, and although there was a slight chill in the air for an early March morning, the rays warmed the back of her neck. The first night in the quaint little town had been interesting, to say the least. Devoid of the noise she was used to, she found her room at the inn almost a little too quiet. There was no ruckus like that of Tonopah or even Virginia City. Men didn't wander the streets in the middle of the night, singing to the moon about women they once loved and lost, and there certainly weren't any gunfights about winning or losing hands at poker.

Ava glanced around the town, wondering if anything exciting ever happened, and as she rounded the corner of the mayor's office, she came face to face with Mr. Harrison.

They both halted in their tracks.

"What are you doing here?" she asked.

His brow furrowed, and his head jerked. "Not that it's any of your business, but the mayor asked me to be at his office this morning so I can head up to the mine with you two. My men are already up there."

"Up there? Doing what?"

"Getting the supplies in order."

"Ah." She turned away from Mr. Harrison and folded her arms across her chest as she looked out at the town once more.

"Where is your friend?" Mr. Harrison asked.

"He's taking his... the young boy he adopted... he's taking him to school." She paused. The less she said, the better, but she also had a question just sitting on her tongue, burning a hole as it begged to be uttered. "Why are you outside and not in the mayor's office? You aren't waiting for me, are you?"

"Nah. The mayor is picking up Mr. Lockhart's wagon at the livery to take it to the mine."

"Aren't we just riding our horses?"

"You and I are. But he doesn't ride."

Her head whipped toward Mr. Harrison. "I beg your pardon?"

"The mayor doesn't ride horses."

"But... why?"

"Because he doesn't know how."

Laughter burst from Ava's lips, and she covered her mouth to stop herself. She cleared her throat. "I... I shouldn't have done that."

"Nah, it's fine. Everyone in town laughs at that man daily. He's always making stupid decisions." Mr. Harrison paused. "Kind of like the one when he decided to entertain Mr. Miller's offer for Rattlesnake Mountain and decline all of mine, creating the need for this silly bet." Although Mr. Harrison had only moments before let his voice soften, his tone hardened again by the time he finished his sentence.

"I know nothing about any of it."

"If that's the stance you wish to continue to take, then by all means take it. But you should know I still don't believe you."

"It doesn't matter to me. I know the truth."

He turned his body toward her and opened his mouth. Before he could say a word, however, a boy ran into him, knocking him off balance as the boy ran. Without so much as a glance toward Mr. Harrison, the young lad darted off, blending into a pack of rowdy children roughhousing as they made their way down the sidewalk.

A mother holding an infant wrapped tight in a blanket weaved through the townsfolk after the young boy. "Miles!" she shouted. "Miles, slow down. You have to wait for me." With her words ignored, a forlorn look shadowed her eyes, and hopelessness hunched her shoulders. Her attempt to secure her son failed, leaving the tired-looking mother with barely the energy to wipe her sweaty brow as she watched the boys from a distance either shove each other or pull a girl's pigtails, causing shrill screams to burst from pouted lips. "Miles! Do not pull your sister's hair. I said to wait for me. Do not cross the road without me."

Hooves pounded the ground in the distance. The loud thumps vibrated through the soles of Ava's boots, up through her legs, and into her chest. She spun around as a wagon hurtled around the corner of a building and down the street. The horses galloped at a dead run, their pace fast and thunderous, and their reins dragged on the ground. Out of control and missing their coachman, they headed toward the cluster of children frozen in panic.

"Run!" the mother shouted. As if to snap out of it, all but one —her son—mistakenly dashed for the side of the road instead. She lunged for him but stopped herself after just a few steps. Her fear overtook her as she held her infant in her arms. "Miles, don't!"

The boy skidded to a stop, and in realizing his error, he turned and scurried back toward his mother in a split-second decision that was about to cost him his life.

Ava's hand slapped against her mouth as she screamed. Mr. Harrison charged out into the middle of the horses' paths. His arms wrapped around the boy, and his forward momentum suspended both in the air. Their bodies landed with a thud in the dirt as the horses ran by, their hooves inches from Mr. Harrison's legs.

A haze of dust clouded the air, blinding Ava as she sprinted toward them, lying on the street. They coughed and sputtered on the grit and grime, their faces, hair, and clothes covered in the thick brown powder, but neither appeared injured. Several men jumped on nearby horses and rode off after the out-of-control wagon. Their shouts echoed as everyone in the area ran after them or into the street to help Mr. Harrison and the boy.

"Miles! Miles!" The mother's knees hit the ground next to her son. Tears streamed down her cheeks. "Oh, my Lord, please be all right. Please, please, please." She moved the infant into one arm and scooped the boy into the other, squeezing him tight. "Please be all right."

"Yes, Mama. I'm fine. I'm so sorry. I'm sorry," the boy whispered. His voice cracked with every word.

"Oh, thank the Lord. Thank the Lord." She looked at Mr. Harrison, reaching out for his arm. "Thank you. Thank you for saving his life."

"You're welcome, Mrs. Fields." Mr. Harrison exhaled a few deep breaths and rose to his feet, dusting off his pants before he patted the boy on the head. "You all right?"

"Yes, sir."

"All right. Get out of the street now. You're going to be late for school."

"I'm sorry, sir."

"It's all right. Just listen to your mother from now on."

"I will."

As the mother and her children left the scene, the people around them began to disperse, and the men who had gone after the wagon returned, walking the horses back through town. Their lungs heaved, and the animals danced around as if they could still bolt in fear at any moment.

Mr. Harrison took the reins from one of the men and made his way back to the front of the mayor's office, dusting off his clothes as he walked with a slight limp. He tied the reins around the hitching post, bent over, and took several deep breaths.

"Are you sure you're all right?" Ava asked him as she stood next to him.

"Yeah. I'm fine. My heart's pounding pretty good, though."

"I bet it is. It was lucky you were here to save the boy."

Mr. Harrison shrugged. "I didn't think his parents would want to bury their boy today. I know what it's like to lose a parent; I can't imagine what it's like to lose a child. I wouldn't wish such pain on anyone."

Ava sucked in a breath. For a tiny moment, she caught a glimpse of the caring man she'd met in the restaurant miles away. Had she been wrong about him?

She opened her mouth but stopped as the mayor ran toward them. His enormous belly swung back and forth with his movement, and by the time he reached them, his lungs seemed to beg for breath.

"Oh, thank goodness. You caught them." He brushed his hand across his forehead.

"What are you talking about?" Mr. Harrison asked.

"I was just leaving the livery with this wagon when something spooked the horses, and they took off."

"This is yours?" Mr. Harrison straightened up. "These horses just ran through town and almost killed a boy."

"It's not like I let them go on purpose." Even through his stifled breaths, annoyance bubbled through the mayor's words. "They spooked. What was I supposed to do?"

"Why were you leading them?"

"I wasn't. I was in the wagon. I fell out when they bolted." Upon his admission, the mayor dropped his gaze to the ground. His shoulders hunched, and Ava pressed her lips together to keep from laughing again.

Exactly how did this man become mayor?

While Ava continued to fight laughter, Mr. Harrison grabbed the bridge of his nose. "Can we just head to the mine now? It's getting late in the morning." He threw the reins onto the buckboard and climbed into the wagon. A growl whispered through his tone.

"We have to wait for Griffin," Ava said, resting her hands on her hips. She glanced over her shoulder as her hired men rode down the street toward her, ponying her and Griffin's horses. "He should be along shortly."

Mr. Harrison closed his eyes. "Fine. We'll leave when he gets here."

SIXTEEN

GRIFFIN

THOSE WHO GIVE TO THE POOR WILL LACK NOTHING, BUT THOSE WHO CLOSE THEIR EYES TO THEM RECEIVE MANY CURSES. *PROVERBS 28:27*

Griffin had never been a man who attended church. He hadn't grown up that way. His parents never took him, nor did they talk about it in their evening conversations around the dinner table. He had, at times, passed by a church in his travels, and in those moments, he couldn't deny that curiosity piqued inside him.

He always squashed it, though.

Never believing, and still didn't, that it was for him.

With that said, however, he also wasn't a stranger to a few different Bible verses—sayings that he'd overheard men in the mines repeat to themselves in an hour of need or to each other when it seemed like no other words could bring them the comfort they sought.

And it was in those verses that one of them always seemed to stick out to him: Those who give to the poor will lack nothing, but those who close their eyes to them receive many curses. *Proverbs 28:27*

It was a verse men would utter when one forgot a coat or a lunch. It was also a verse used when one would complain they didn't have enough money to buy their family supplies for the week. Following the words, he would see these men giving the ones in need what they lacked—a blanket, a coat, food, and, a few times, even cash from their own pockets.

He never really understood the whole meaning—at least not until he saw one man give away half his wages to another so the latter man's children wouldn't go to bed hungry. Looking down at Benjamin walking beside him, the reality slapped Griffin in the face. Of course, he had always thought of himself as a good man, a kind man, one who would do anything for a friend in need.

But a stranger?

He hadn't ever done anything for a stranger before.

Not until he saw this skinny child meandering through the saloon toward him with the look of the weight of the world on his shoulders. Battered and bruised, anyone questioning that this boy had seen things he should never have seen would have been a fool.

And Griffin wanted to make sure he never saw anything he shouldn't ever again.

"Mr. Baker, do you think I will like school?" Benjamin asked, breaking Griffin's thoughts.

He nodded and cleared his throat. "I do. You'll learn a lot from your teacher, which will be good."

"Why is it good to learn a lot from a teacher?"

"Men with an education are more successful in life."

"Are you successful?"

Griffin opened his mouth but paused for a second. "Well, I... I guess I'd like to think so. But my parents probably wouldn't say the same. They wanted me to go to college and become a doctor." Griffin chuckled, remembering all the times his father would broach the subject. He also remembered when he told them he was leaving San Francisco for the deserts and gold mines of Nevada.

It was that day they disowned him.

Benjamin stared at the ground with his brow furrowed. "Well, I hope I like school because it would make me sad if I didn't."

"Don't worry about that. I'm sure you will." Griffin patted the boy on the shoulder, repeating the verse in his mind. A slightly more understanding flickered in his heart.

Now, it made more sense.

⁓

A woman stood outside the church, ringing a bell as the pair approached. Other children ran past them, and she greeted them one by one with a broad grin that illuminated her entire face, catching Griffin off guard.

"Do you think that is the teacher?" Benjamin asked Griffin.

Griffin nodded, although a slight part of him wondered if he should. Weren't teachers always older women with graying hair they kept up in a bun? That was all his experiences with teachers. When did the school district start hiring pretty young women? He definitely would have done better with his schooling if he had a teacher like her.

"Good morning," she said to Griffin, glancing between him and the boy. "And who might you two be?"

"Mr. Griffin Baker." He held out his hand to shake hers. "This is Benjamin."

The teacher smiled another grin and knelt so she was face to face with Benjamin. "Well, hello, Benjamin. My name is Miss Evans, and I'm the teacher here in Featherstone Valley. Are you here to join us for school today?"

"Yes, Ma'am."

Benjamin nodded shyly, hiding slightly behind Griffin's leg. Griffin gave the boy a reassuring pat on his shoulder before stepping out of the boy's way. "I'm afraid he hasn't had much in the way of schooling before now. I don't know if he knows how to read or write."

"That's all right. School is where you learn those things." She rose back to her feet, turning her attention to Griffin. "Don't worry. Even if your son can't read or write, it won't take him long to catch up."

"He's not my son."

"Oh. I'm sorry for assuming."

"You don't have to apologize. Surely, it's an easy assumption to make." Griffin chuckled, hoping to ease the embarrassed flush in her cheeks. "Honestly, I suppose in a way he is now my son. I took him in when his father didn't want him anymore."

"Wow. That's..." Her shoulders softened, and she cocked her head to the side. "I was just studying Mark in the Bible. Whoever welcomes one of these little children in my name welcomes me; and whoever welcomes me does not welcome me but the one who sent me."

"I beg your pardon?"

She snorted a slight laugh and tucked her chocolate hair behind her ears. "It's a Bible verse. *Mark 9:36-37*, He took a little child whom he placed among them. Taking the child in his arms, he said to them, "Whoever welcomes one of these little children in my name welcomes me; and whoever welcomes me does not welcome me but the one who sent me."

Warmth spread through Griffin's neck. "Oh. Right. I knew that." He cleared his throat, letting his gaze dance around as he suddenly wanted to beat himself silly for not memorizing the entire Bible each year of his life. "Well, I should get back to the mayor's office. We're heading up to the mine this morning." He hooked his thumb over his shoulder. "Do you think you can take him to the inn after school? I'm not sure when I'll return from work."

"Of course. I'd be happy to."

Griffin couldn't help but notice how her smile lit up her whole face. "Thank you, Miss Evans. I appreciate it." His stomach twisted as he walked away from the school. For the first time in his life, he had met a woman who had stolen not only his thoughts but the breath from his lungs.

∾

AVA

The mountains of Montana were nothing like the mountains of Nevada. While Nevada had a mix of pine trees with vast spaces of sagebrush and barren rock, Montana was all forest. At least, that was the land around Featherstone Valley. Dense and tall, the trees shaded the trails, making the air cooler as all the employees of the two mining companies headed to Rattlesnake Mountain.

The sun was already high, casting long shadows between the branches while the breeze fluttered the needles. They reached a clearing in the trees, and Mr. Harrison stopped the wagon and climbed down after setting the brake.

Ava glanced at Griffin, and the two dismounted their horses, spinning in a few circles as they looked at the landscape around them. They exchanged glances before Ava moved toward a tall, thick rock section stretching toward the sky. She made her way toward the slab, running her fingers along the grooves and colors of the rock.

"What are you thinking?" Griffin asked, stepping up next to her. He looked toward the sky, too, inhaling a deep breath.

"It's batholith."

"What's that?"

"A huge rock that goes deep underground. It's made of granite."

"Can we mine it?"

"Yeah, as long as we have the right tools." She glanced around and found a pile of supplies tucked between two trees. She walked toward it, studying all the equipment Mr. Miller's men had stacked. Buckets, axes, ropes, and wheelbarrows sat in rows, waiting to be used.

Out of everything she saw, one thing stood out: a machine sitting under two trees, waiting to be turned on. She'd heard about rock crushers before but had never seen one.

She stepped back, looking over the mountain again.

"Miss Adams?" the mayor beckoned. He strode toward her, unbalanced on the rough terrain, while he tried to keep his dress shoes from getting too dirty. "May I have a moment of your time? I wanted to go over some things with you and Mr. Harrison."

She made her way over to the two men, ignoring the smug look on Mr. Harrison's face.

"Different than you imagined?" he said as she approached.

She cocked her head to the side. "Different, yes. Harder, no."

He shrugged. "There's still time to quit, you know."

"And why would I do that?"

"All right, you two, that's enough." The mayor moved between them. "Although this is a competition, you must work together on some things. I will not allow you to risk a collapse due to unsafe work conditions."

Mr. Harrison and Ava exchanged glances, and even though she didn't want to agree, she had to. She didn't want those things either.

"He's right, you know," she said to Mr. Harrison.

His eyes narrowed. "Fine. My team will blast an opening, and we will fork the mine. I'll take one direction; you take the other. That way, we minimize the risk and can still focus on our own work."

Although Ava's annoyance bubbled, she nodded. "I will agree with that."

They returned to their teams, instructing their men to step away and prepare for the blast. She'd opened up a few mines in her years, and as with all of them, the pulse of excitement drowned out any fear or hesitation. There was something about blasting open the side of a mountain that she couldn't describe. Perhaps it was because it mirrored how she had been forced to live.

Control over her own life had never been a concept she'd lived with. There was little of it for a child left at an orphanage without so much as a blanket to call their own. Everything from what she wore to what she ate, from the lessons she learned in school to how she acted and what she said, was dictated by the sisters at the home.

It wasn't until she left that she made any choice of her own, and much like a stick of dynamite set in the perfect position, once she lit her fuse, the control was surrendered to the forces of nature and chemistry. The raw power unleashed by an explosion was both terrifying and exhilarating. It reminded her that no matter how much she tried to steer her own course, there were always moments when chaos would take over, and she would have to navigate through the aftermath. It was in those moments of chaos, where the outcome was uncertain, that she felt most alive.

The workers carefully placed the sticks of dynamite in strategic positions, ensuring the blast would create a manageable opening. Once the dynamite was in place, the men ran the line to the plunger and connected the wires, telling one another every step to ensure everything was done as it was supposed to.

As they stepped away from the plunger, Mr. Harrison

approached the wooden box, rechecking their work. "All right, men. We're ready. You know what that means."

All his men surrounded him in a circle, and with their hands clasped at their waists in front of them, they bowed their heads.

"What are you doing, Mr. Harrison?" Ava asked. She glanced at Griffin, who looked at her and shrugged as though to say he didn't know either.

"We are saying a prayer, Miss Adams."

She cocked her head to the side. "A prayer?"

"Yes, and you're welcome to join us." He motioned for them to join his men, and while the men she had hired to work for her rushed to the circle, she and Griffin hesitated.

"Are you going to..." Griffin pointed toward the men without finishing his sentence.

"I don't know. Are you?"

"Yeah," he nodded. "I want to."

"You want to?"

"Yes, I do. We are living in a different town, and I have Benjamin now. It's time to think of something bigger than myself."

Before she could say a word to him, he strode off, joining the men in the circle.

Her stomach twisted. She was never proud of the choice to turn her face away from the Bible. But it was also easier for her to push God away than live knowing how He felt about her. Sister Gretchen's words prickled in her ears. "You are nothing but a vile sinner, Ava Adams, and God will never love you."

Ava tucked her chin toward her chest, closing her eyes tight against the voice in her head.

"Lord," Mr. Harrison began. "We humbly come to You today to ask for Your protection as we undertake the tasks for today. Please guide our hands and our hearts and keep us safe from harm. Let this blast be clean and effective, and may every man...

and woman here return to their families and loved ones unharmed. Amen."

"Amen," the workers echoed, lifting their heads.

Mr. Harrison clapped his hands and then rubbed them together. A broad grin spread across his face, and he had an odd bounce to his step. He seemed to love this job just as much as Ava did. "All right, men. Let's get to work. Everyone clear!"

The anticipation hung in the air, thick and heavy. As Mr. Harrison shoved the plunger down with a loud boom, the dynamite detonated, sending a plume of dust and debris into the air. When the dust settled, a large opening was visible, leading into the heart of the mountain.

The first of many blasts was finished.

As the men dispersed, barking orders at one another to get the needed supplies and to start digging, Mr. Harrison made his way to Ava. He came up beside her, glancing at her.

"Well, Miss Adams, are you ready to get to work?"

"I've never been more ready for anything in my life."

"So, you still think you're up for this?"

"I wouldn't be here if I wasn't."

He turned his shoulders toward her. For a second, it seemed like he would outstretch his hand to shake hers. He didn't, though. Instead, he kept his hands to himself, lowering his voice as he furrowed his brow. "May the best miner win."

She squared her shoulders, matching his stance. "Don't worry, Mr. Harrison, I intend to."

SEVENTEEN

AVA

A week of blasting, digging, and building scaffolding had turned the mountain from an untouched site to a mine that hummed with the hustle of men moving more dirt out of the hole than any other mountain Ava had ever mined.

Over the last few days, more and more weatherworn tents had popped up, and the makeshift camp for the men staying at the mine at night was scattered through the trees, along with the iron rails now lying on the forest floor. They had been built for the trolley cars and stretched outward several feet from the tunnel's opening. A few of the bars skewed off, looking disjointed and out of sorts as though something struck them by mistake or shoved them out of the way for one reason or another. Whatever their placement was, each one was laid to move rock from the depths of the mine and haul in the needed lumber to build the scaffolding. A few looked as though the sun had beaten them and were rusted in some places; the orange lightened the metal with a bright pigment.

Two mules were hitched to a wagon next to the mine shaft, and they slept while the men worked around them. Their long ears twisted in all directions as though listening to the shouts from one man to another, even from their sleepy haze. At total peace, however, their eyes were closed, and their tails swished at the flies bugging them.

Ava stood outside the shaft opening, studying the map they'd made from the short shafts they'd dug out. While Mr. Harrison's team had gone to the left of the main shaft, her team had gone to the right, and there had been issues with the rock that she hadn't liked. It wasn't that the walls were unstable; there was something else about them that she hadn't seen before, and she'd been studying every detail over the last week, trying to figure out a way around the problem. Any more digging and blasting, and she knew the shaft would come down on all of them.

A loud rumble echoed from the mine, and within seconds, a chorus of frantic yelling came from the shaft. Dust billowed out as men ran from the entrance, both her team and Mr. Harrison's. Their fear was etched on their faces while dirt clung to their sweaty brows. She darted toward her men.

"What happened?"

"It's going to collapse!" Brad shouted. He bent over, took several deep breaths, and coughed.

"Where is Griffin?"

"He's coming." Brad waved his hand at her and stumbled away several feet, coughing and spitting with every step. The rest of the men followed, and they headed toward the creek as Ava dashed for the entrance; Mr. Harrison, Mr. Cooper, and Griffin came outside. Covered in dirt, they coughed and sputtered, gasping for fresh air.

"Are you three all right?" she asked them.

Griffin knelt on the ground, wiping his face, while Mr. Harrison rushed to the water bucket. He dunked his hands in the water, scooping up what he could and splashing his face to wash off the dirt. His right-hand man, Mr. Cooper, followed him, gasping for breath while waiting for his boss to finish. He splashed his face and remained on his knees, wrapping his arms around himself.

"What happened?" she asked Griffin.

He shook his head. "It's not going to hold. It's unstable."

"What's unstable?"

"The whole mountain!" Griffin stumbled to his feet and went to the water bucket, splashing his face, too. "The scaffolding isn't holding. I don't know why."

Mr. Harrison glanced at Mr. Cooper, and they nodded as though they were having a silent conversation.

Annoyance tickled through Ava's chest, and as she was about to ask why they were over on her side of the camp, Mr. Harrison spoke. "My side is just as bad." He wiped his face one last time and rolled onto his backside, sitting in the dirt. "I've never seen anything like it."

"Sharing secrets, are you now, Mr. Harrison?" she asked.

"The fact that I just came running out of the mine covered in dirt and gasping for breath hardly means that I'm keeping secrets. I think you can pretty much guess what's happening in there. Anyone can figure that out."

"The wall on the outside is solid rock." She glanced at the mountain.

"But it's not solid rock on the inside. At least not where we've blasted," Mr. Harrison said.

He and Mr. Cooper looked at Griffin, and the three men shook their heads.

"Are you thinking what I'm thinking?" Griffin asked Mr. Harrison.

The latter nodded. "I think so."

"And what are you both thinking?" Ava rested her hands on her hips.

"Blasting two shafts at once is causing problems," Mr. Harrison said.

"And they are problems making the whole mountain unsafe

for everyone. The walls are weaker, and we can't keep digging until we fix the problem." Griffin wiped his face.

"So what are you suggesting? Do we mine on different days? You get the morning, and I get the evening?" She paused, her agitation growing. "How am I supposed to know this just isn't a ruse to get me to stop mining this mountain so you can win?"

"Because I'm telling you, I think the same thing." Griffin coughed a few times to clear his lungs. "We are facing the same problem, and we haven't gone down deep. We could go down further if we had a different scaffolding system to support blasts in other shafts."

Ava's team returned from the river and rested on boulders scattered around the opening. Dirt caked their careworn faces so much that Ava barely recognized them. A few gulped from canteens of water while others splashed themselves instead. Two of them stood as they approached, shaking their heads as though deeply troubled.

"Brad? Trey? Are you two all right?" Griffin asked, worry evident in his voice.

"The thing darn near collapsed on us again," Brad coughed through his words, dust puffing from his clothes. His voice rasped, betraying his exhaustion. "I hated working with the animals, but at least they never tried to kill me. Well, I suppose a bull or two tried, but I don't know if I'm cut out for this job."

While Brad rested his hands on his hips and shook his head, Trey stared at the ground with a faraway look of fear and the relief of having survived.

Without another word, Ava strode toward the mouth of the mineshaft, grabbing a lantern as she entered. Griffin and Mr. Harrison chased after her, fetching lanterns to illuminate the pathway through the tunnel.

Coolness swept across Ava's skin, and her lamp's flame flickered against the mine's dirt and rock guts. Dampened from the lack of sun deep below the earth, the wooden boards reinforcing the walls and ceiling held a musty scent, and the stench of mold closed in on her.

They traveled deeper through the mineshaft. Blackness and coldness surrounded them as their heavy breaths intensified, panting harder and harder with every few yards.

Coming upon the cavern, Ava ran her fingers along the wall and over the quartz they'd uncovered the day before. Rough to the touch, it glistened in the light of their oil lamps. She waited until Griffin slid up beside her.

"All the sulphurate silver must be separated before you run the gold through the rocker. If you don't, the machine will clog."

"Yeah, I know. But that's not the problem. We know. You see this..." Griffin pointed to another line along the vein. "While we can easily excavate this, the ore and earth around it are soft and weak. If we start digging it out, this wall will cave in on us."

The three of them continued to stare at the wall.

"That's the problem we're running into, too," Mr. Harrison finally said, breaking the silence.

"More secrets, Mr. Harrison?"

"There's more to this than this bet, Miss Adams. Stuff like this... it's about the safety of the men working in these shafts."

Although she wanted to disagree, she couldn't. He was right. This was more than just a bet between the two companies. This was about making the job safe for her team. She nodded. "You're right."

He moved around her, glancing at Griffin as he wiped the sweat from his brow and ignored the dust floating around them. "I thought surely we could support the wall first, but that won't hold with the blasting and the weight of it all. Although your scaffolding looks slightly different, it has the same concept. I've never had any issues with my scaffolding until now. I'm not sure why they aren't working this time. But I don't want to lose any men or gold over this, so I've got to find a way to fix it before I can dig anymore out."

"What if we added some timber for support here and here?" Griffin traced the lines of the T-frame.

"How does the wall cave in as you are digging?" Mr. Harrison asked, ignoring the conversation. He lifted his lantern and squinted as he studied the angles of the rock and boards.

"There's never any one direction except for down. It just all collapses in on itself," Griffin answered.

"Yeah, that's how our side moves, too." With a slight *humph* noise on his lips, Mr. Harrison continued his examination, grazing the palms of his hands along the wall. His eyebrows furrowed together with each crack and crevice. "There's something we are missing." He paused, clicking his tongue. "Do you have a section that has collapsed? Even if it's just a little bit?"

Griffin nodded and motioned them to follow him to Ava's side of the mountain, where her team had blasted the day before. Each little sound they made ricocheted around them, and as they inched down another short corridor, they came upon a few piles of debris still lying scattered in the dirt. Mr. Harrison began to snoop around the broken boards and fallen rocks, shifting rocks that tumbled and rolled a few inches.

"It's different but the same." He sighed. "If that makes any sense."

"It does." Ava groaned as she placed her hands on top of her head and spun in a few circles. "I guess there's nothing to do but try to figure it out."

"Honestly, I wonder if it's the fact that we're both in here that's the cause of it."

"Mines fork, Mr. Harrison, and they do so several times. There is never just one shaft. This mountain isn't that weak. We just have to figure it out."

"We?" He rested his hands on his hips, glancing at her. "Tell me, Miss Adams. What happens when one of us figures out what to do before the others?"

She stared at him, knowing the underlying question he didn't ask even though he wanted to—what happens if one of them finds the solution? Do they share the information with the competition or keep it to themselves to advance and win the bet? In all fairness, it was a question she had wanted to ask, too, and although she would have asked it, she hadn't been quick enough. "Then I should hope *we* do what is best for the miners."

∼

The sun had arched over the sky, painting the few clouds Ava could see through the trees with pink, purple, and blue colors. She rode next to Griffin, counting the horse's rhythmic steps as they crushed through the fallen pine needles, pine cones, and dead branches. A cool evening breeze blew through her hair, whispering across her skin and drying what little sweat was left of the day.

It had been a long day.

And if she didn't find a solution to their problem, it would turn into a long ride back to Nevada after Mr. Miller fired her.

Griffin exhaled a deep breath, glancing at the clouds through the trees. "The problem with the walls is more serious than I thought."

Ava nodded. "Yeah."

"So, what do you think we'll do about it?"

She shifted in the saddle, pausing as the leather squeaked. "I don't know. Yet. We need to find a solution, though."

"Do you mean we as in the three of us or we as in you and me?"

"I haven't figured that out yet."

They rode in silence for a few moments; the horses walked the narrow path through the trees. Each time she'd asked herself that same question today, she'd shoved it from her mind. She wanted to do what was best for the men. She also wanted to make sure she kept her job.

Griffin finally broke the silence, his tone more serious. "Do you think you can trust Mr. Harrison?"

"What does it matter if I do or if I don't?"

"I think it matters greatly."

"Not when I don't have much of a choice."

"You do have a choice, Ava. We can work to solve this problem together, you and me, just like we have always tackled anything that has stood in our way."

Ava glanced at her friend, her brow furrowing. Trust hadn't always been easy for her. That's what happens when one is abandoned by their parents and kicked out of the orphanage when they are too old. There had been only one person in this world she could trust, and he was riding the horse next to hers.

She'd learned long ago that strangers were a different story—an unopened book that was a risk to open, and more often than not, she was left regretting she'd even turned a page. Mr. Harrison certainly didn't seem the terrible type; however, he was still new, untested in her eyes, and trusting him felt akin to stepping off a cliff into the unknown, hoping there would be something to catch her fall.

"I'm sure you'll figure out something," Griffin said. "You always do. Come to think of it; you always get the best ideas when you take a long ride just by yourself. Why don't you do that tomorrow morning? Clear your head."

"That does sound like a good idea. Maybe it would help."

"I'm sure it would."

∽

CRAIG

Isaiah 41:10, So do not fear, for I am with you; do not be dismayed, for I am your God. I will strengthen you and help you; I will uphold you with my righteous right hand.

Craig sat alone in the dining room at the inn, repeating the verse in his mind. The distraction of his thoughts drowned the low hum of conversations and clinking cutlery around him as he looked at all his drawings spread across the table. Each was a different take on the scaffolding problem they faced in the mine, and he'd worked on them since leaving the mine this afternoon.

He leaned back in his chair, absently tapping his pencil against the table, his mind racing with possibilities and worries. None of what he'd come up with seemed to be a good fit, and by the looks of the papers, he was running out of ideas.

"I've got to think of something. Why is this so hard?" He threw the pencil down as he muttered under his breath. It rolled across the table, and before he could grab it, it fell off the table, bouncing on the floor several times.

He bent down to pick it up, but another hand grabbed it instead.

"Good evening, Mr. Harrison," Pastor Boone said.

"Good evening, Pastor Boone."

"You sure are working hard tonight, aren't you? What is all this?" He handed Craig the pencil, and Craig answered as he took it.

"Plans for new scaffolding for the mine, or ideas for plans. I'm not sure. None of them are working out to be what I want."

"Are you having trouble with the mine?"

Craig nodded. "We're having trouble with our scaffolding holding up to the pressure. It's nothing to warrant stopping the project, and we haven't had any injuries. However, the current setup isn't holding, and it's putting the men at risk."

Pastor Boone picked up one of the sketches and examined it

closely. "I see. And you're trying to come up with a better design?"

"Yes," Craig replied, leaning forward. "The problem is that the ore and earth around the gold are too soft. If we start digging, the walls cave in. We need to support the walls better, but adding more boards to the existing frame hasn't worked."

Pastor Boone nodded thoughtfully. "That does sound like a serious issue. And what about Mr. Miller's team? The one led by the woman from Nevada. What was her name again?"

"Ava Adams." Craig ignored how her name tingled against his lips and fluttered in his chest. "She's having similar problems."

"So, you two have discussed the matter, then?" An odd smile spread across Pastor Boone's face, making Craig chuckle.

"I don't know where you're trying to go with that question, Pastor Boone. But we have discussed it, and she is also working on a solution."

"I'm not trying to go anywhere. It was a mere question. Nothing more." Pastor Boone shrugged and looked over the plans again.

As much as Craig wanted to say the seeds hadn't just been planted in his mind, he couldn't. Of course, truth be told, it wasn't just the pastor's words that had brought Miss Adams to the forefront of his mind. He had thought about it more times than he wanted to admit since leaving the mine this afternoon.

Working with Miss Adams today had gone surprisingly well. For the first time since she arrived in Featherstone Valley, they had managed to set aside their differences and focus on the task at hand, and he now understood why she was so highly regarded in Nevada. She was sharp, determined, and undeniably skilled. Her gumption made her a force to be reckoned with. If that wasn't enough to make him nervous, knowing she'd also found such a rich vein when his own discovery paled in comparison, he couldn't shake the worry that her find could overshadow his efforts.

And win Mr. Miller the mountain.

Pastor Boone stared at him, then cocked his head to the side. "Why do I get the feeling it's not just the scaffolding problem that's on your mind?"

"Because you're a smart man."

The pastor laughed. "I suppose it's the ranger still in me."

"I didn't know you were a Texas Ranger. That explains a lot."

"Yeah, I guess it does." He pointed toward the chair as though to ask to sit, and after Craig nodded, Pastor Boone sat. "So, what else is troubling you?"

"It's a lot of things, honestly. If I lose this bet..." Unable to finish his sentence, he let his voice trail off.

"What will happen if you lose the bet?"

"There will be nothing left for me in Featherstone Valley, and I'll have to leave."

"Ah. Well, that does seem like an immense problem. Having to leave the town you were born in can put quite the damper on one's life."

"I wasn't born here. I was born back east. I moved out to California before going up to the Klondike. I only moved here a few years ago."

"Oh, so you started over before when it was time to move on to the next chapter God called you to?"

Craig opened his mouth but shut it without a word. He smiled, knowing where the pastor was going with his question. "Yes, I've started over, and yes, I overcame the obstacles that came along the way. But I don't want to leave Featherstone Valley. This is the first place I've felt like it's home."

"I can understand that. Believe me."

"I don't want to leave."

"Then don't."

"If I lose, I have to."

"You sound as though you already know the outcome of this competition, and you're planning on losing."

"I don't know it." Craig paused and rested his elbows on the table. He took a deep breath, exhaling slowly. "Miss Adams is... better than I anticipated. I'm worried she will figure out this scaffolding problem, and she won't share what she finds."

"So, you don't trust her?"

"I don't know her. She had the chance to tell me who she was and who she was working for when I met her in Butte, but she didn't."

"Then it sounds like you do know; you just don't want to admit it."

Craig shrugged. "I want to."

"I believe that. And we are called to. Two are better than one because they have a good reward for their toil. For if they fall, one will lift his fellow. But woe to him who is alone when he falls and has not another to lift him up! *Ecclesiastes 4:9-10.*"

Craig let out a slight snort. "Iron sharpens iron, and one man sharpens another. *Proverbs 27:17.*"

"Exactly. We need to have wisdom in our relationships, whether they are with one we are married to or even our friends and family. But we also cannot push people away just to protect ourselves. God never intended us to be alone, no matter how much we may think we are meant to be or we think it's better for others that we do."

"But what if I trust her, and she betrays that trust? After all, she does work for Mr. Miller. How can anyone trust someone who associates themselves with a man like that?"

"Well, all I can say with that is it's not my place to judge. That is for God to do." Pastor Boone smiled. "And as for her betraying your trust... that would be when forgiveness comes in."

"Of course." Craig chuckled, and the pastor did, too.

"Forgiveness isn't the hardest thing we have to do—trust me.

It's even harder when the person we have to forgive is ourselves. But we are called to do it, just as we are called to trust."

"I know."

Pastor Boone stood from his chair and heaved a sigh. "You know what I've always found helpful when I needed to figure out something?"

"What is that?"

"Someplace where there are no distractions. Some of the best problem solvers in this world are a mountain, a horse, and a saddle."

Craig chuckled again. "I've had that very same thought a time or two."

"Then I trust you know what to do?"

Craig nodded. "Yeah. I do."

EIGHTEEN

AVA

The dawn sky began to lighten with bright orange, red, and yellow as the sun started peering over the horizon. The rays cast shadows on the pine-needle-covered ground, and flickers of light danced around the trunks and branches.

Mile after mile, Ava rode her horse up and down the mountain trails. The trek worked her horse into a frothy lather, the sweat dripping from his chest. His lungs heaved, and she brought him to a halt under the shade of a tree and climbed out of the saddle.

She closed her eyes, inhaling the rich pine scent of the forest around her. Birds chirped from the different branches, and a creek echoed in the distance. She rubbed her backside, ignoring the hint of soreness as she clutched the reins and walked the horse toward the sound of the water. After several more yards, they came into a clearing near the water's edge. The creek pooled in a few places, and her horse took a long drink before sighing.

"Decided to take a ride to clear your thoughts, too, huh?" a voice asked behind her.

She spun to see Craig riding toward the creek. A half-smile inched across his lips. "Something like that," she said.

"How long have you been out here?"

"Longer than I want to admit."

"Yeah, me too."

He snorted a slight laugh and pulled his horse to a halt, throwing his leg over the saddle to dismount. His smirk vanished as he attempted to sit down, and his rump hit the rock. His breath hissed through his teeth.

Laughter burst from Ava's chest, and he glared at her from the corner of his eye.

"I'm sorry," she said. "But I only laugh because I'm still standing for that reason. I don't trust my legs."

"I don't understand it. I ride all the time."

"I know. I do, too."

"I suppose it's not for as long as I have this morning." He paused, taking a deep breath. "It's been nice, though. I forgot what it was like to get out in the mountains and clear my mind."

"Yeah, me too."

"I love the smell of the pine trees, too. It reminds me of the Klondike."

"How long has it been since you left?"

"About two years."

"Do you miss it?" She pointed toward the space on the rock next to him, and he shifted his seat, scooting over slightly so she could sit. The hardness of the granite scraped against her pants and the palms of her hands.

"Not really." He dropped his gaze to the ground, letting a far-off look drift through his eyes. "Well, I suppose I do, and I don't. The gold was nice. The summers were nice—except for the bugs. But the cold wasn't. Nor was dealing with other men and living in fear they would slit your throat in the middle of the night."

"Yeah, that wouldn't be something I would miss."

"And don't get me started on the pack horses."

"Pack horses? Really?"

"Oh yeah, those animals were horrible to deal with. I mostly used mine for packhorses. More often than not, they weren't broke for much else other than carrying crates of supplies. I can't tell you how many times those animals brought nothing but trouble. They spooked at everything and could cripple a man with just one kick."

"It sounds like they were just scared."

"Oh, there isn't a doubt they were. Men shipped them up to Canada without care or concern for how they were treated or whether or not they were wild or young. I felt bad for them; more died on the trail than made it up to Dawson City, and their bodies were just left to rot wherever they collapsed. I always tried to do better with them. I tried to treat them better. Tame them. Teach them, even if they were horrible to handle. But I know that treating the ones I owned better couldn't compensate for all the others' suffering."

A far-off look fixed in his eyes as he watched their two horses graze on patches of nearby grass. Their tails swished, and their heads shook at the gnats buzzing around while they ripped the vegetation from the roots and tried to chew with the bits in their mouths.

"What was it like up there?" she asked. "I read stories in the newspapers, but the journalists never seemed to ask the questions I wanted to know the most."

"Cold." He laughed. "Cold and breathtaking. I don't think I'll ever forget it as long as I live. The mountains were as high as the clouds and capped in snow even in summer. The forests were thick with pine and as tall as the eye could see. They could block out the sun in some parts, darkening the ground as though it was night. You would think nothing could grow, and yet, even without the light, the moss grew everywhere, right down to the deep crevices of the bark, so lush and green it blinded you."

"It sounds amazing."

"It was." His once broad grin faded. "However, it's vicious all at the same time. A pack of wolves or a hungry bear could attack and kill a man; sometimes, they'd even start eating before their victim was dead. People could freeze to death in a matter of hours, or they could fall and break a leg, dying a painful death of starvation or thirst if they were alone. I knew several men who died from scurvy and even more who died in the occasional mudslide."

Once again, his eyes glazed over as though he was reliving a memory, and he paused. "I lost a couple of friends in one. We'd been traveling from Dyea for several days when we arrived at Sheep Camp. Tired and worn out, I don't think I ate dinner before falling asleep. The mud came roaring through early in the morning, waking everyone up, the sound so loud it drowned out the screams of every man, woman, and even a few children. People, supplies, and even horses were all swept away and buried under rocks and mud. By the time it stopped, I'd lost everything."

Ava kicked a tiny rock. It rolled several inches before knocking against another one. No matter the cause of death—freezing temperatures, animal attacks, broken limbs, or gunshot wounds—pain was still pain, and she hated the thought of someone having to face it.

"Mining is a tough business," she whispered.

"It wasn't just the mining. It was the land—both magnificent and brutal. You could almost feel the gold underneath the granite just calling your name, yet the land hid from you, teasing until you started to wonder if it was worth searching for it."

"I know that feeling."

"Sometimes, it felt like the land didn't want you to succeed. Instead, it wanted to make your life hard, make you search deep inside yourself to see how badly you wanted it."

"Is that why you left? You didn't want it?"

"Not that part of it." He cleared his throat.

"So what part do you want?"

"Just a place I can call my own, I guess. I found it in Featherstone Valley. I love this town, and I don't want to leave."

"It is a nice little town, from what I've seen so far."

They both looked out over the horizon. Two eagles flew over their heads and cawed at one another as they circled the creek before landing near the water and the horses. It was as though the birds either desired to investigate the horses or wondered if Ava and Mr. Harrison had any food. Disappointed in their derisory findings, they spread their wings, flapping them with fervor to pick up their heavy bodies from the ground.

"So, Miss Adams, now that I've told you all about me, what's your story?" He broke off a few blades of tall grass beside him, letting them fall from the palm of his hand.

She shifted her weight, resting her elbows on her knees. Although the question was innocent, the meaning behind the words beat against her secrets; powerless to stop them, they began to chip away at the wall she'd built around her heart. Dust from the boards fluttered down through her soul as the nails wiggled loose, some falling to the ground, rusted and weakened like the scaffolding of an old mine.

The young girl part of her screamed for him to leave her clandestine world for her and her alone. A world she could feel safe in, knowing no one knew her strife or knew her pain. A world full of hardships for someone so young and naïve she made choices an older woman wouldn't make—the plight of the embarrassing fool.

On the other side of her, along with his question, a woman waged war against the wall she built up, screaming words of honesty, daring her to free herself from the confines of the world she had desperately clung to for more years than she cared to say aloud. Who cares about the actions of a foolish child? Wasn't that the lot in life? Making mistakes in front of others so the mistake makers could see the errors of their ways and rebuild upon the lessons learned?

Which is what she'd done.

Long gone were the days of eating from a dumpster. Long gone were the days of living life as a penniless girl on the brink of fleeing to the whorehouse so she could have a hot meal for the night. The life she'd created with the hard work of her own two hands came from the tarnish in her past.

Ava cleared her throat. "There isn't much to say about my life."

"Surely that isn't true."

She shrugged. "No, it is. I grew up in an orphanage in Virginia City and left there to start working in the mines when I got too old to stay. That's pretty much it."

"That's it? It can't be everything."

"It's enough."

He shook his head. "I'm not buying it. There's got to be so much more than just that."

Ava bit her lip. Just how was she supposed to tell a stranger everything she'd fought her whole life never to tell anyone other than Griffin?

Even Griffin didn't know much of it, and he knew more than anyone else.

"What was life like in the orphanage?"

"It was an orphanage. There were nice teachers and not-so-nice teachers. There were also nice children and not-so-nice children."

"Hurt people tend to hurt others because they think it makes them feel better."

She snorted. "Yeah, they do."

"A few months before I left, a man brought his daughter into the orphanage. His wife had died, and he didn't have anyone to care for her while he worked on the railroad. We were about the same age, and I remember hearing her scream for him as he left. I tried to comfort her, but she never allowed anyone near her. As the weeks passed, she befriended a couple of the girls. I always treated her nicely, but she never liked me. I don't know what I did or said, but it didn't matter. One morning, the girl started yelling at me and dumped my porridge in my lap. One of the boys helped me clean up the mess and offered me his bowl."

"And is the he you speak of Griffin Baker?"

"No. I didn't meet Griffin until I moved to Tonopah. The boy was Billy Jack. He still lives between Tonopah and Virginia City, but he's no longer a friend."

"Sounds like he was more than just a friend." Mr. Harrison chuckled.

"For a time, I suppose we were. We were young, and we believed we were in love. One night, we snuck out to the barn just to escape from the other children. Nothing happened; we didn't do anything we weren't supposed to, but that girl who didn't like me caught us sneaking back into our rooms. After she snitched on us, Sister Helen locked me in the basement room to await my punishment for the next morning—a whipping of sixty lashes to my backside. Billy Jack broke the door in the middle of the night. We fled and never looked back."

"But you stayed in Virginia City. Didn't you worry about them catching you?"

"We only ventured out from our hiding place at night when we knew Sister Katherine and Sister Helen were asleep. We didn't have the money to go anywhere else, and neither of us knew how to do anything. We were sixteen. It was no matter, though; we knew they never left the confines of the orphanage.

"We would sleep during the day and then head for the saloons at night. I'd put on a fancy dress Billy Jack got from one of the dancehall girls who didn't want it anymore and distract the drunken men while Billy Jack stole their wallets." Ava snorted a giggle through her nose, but her smile faded as the guilty memories haunted her still. "I'm not proud of my actions. I was young and foolish and hungry and broke."

"We all make mistakes. No one is immune."

"I've told myself that so many times. But it's still something that weighs on me."

"Have you prayed about it?"

She snorted. "No. Why would I?"

"I think the better question would be, why wouldn't you?"

"I'm not... that's not... me. I don't do that."

"Perhaps you should. Perhaps it would help."

"I don't think it would." Her stomach twisted with the thoughts of church, pastors, confessing sins. The sisters in the orphanage forced all that upon her when she was a child, using God's words to reprimand and punish her if she did anything wrong in their eyes. She had had enough of that as a child; she didn't need it as an adult.

She shrugged and shook her head. No matter how much she willed herself to say something, she couldn't.

Mr. Harrison seemed to sense the unease, and he cleared his throat. "So, where did you sleep?"

"In an abandoned shack just outside town, we spent a year there before I befriended Mr. Thompson's daughter and found my job at the Silver Queen Hotel. He and his wife took me in and allowed me to live in the shed behind their home. It wasn't much, but it was better than I had."

"What happened with Billy Jack? Did he stay there, too?"

Ava shook her head again. The painful and bitter memories she'd thrust from her mind so many times now stared her in the face, forcing themselves upon her once more. They laughed and taunted, pointing at her as they danced around, singing songs with lyrics about liars and cheats.

"One night, we were in the Bucket of Blood Saloon," she said. "I had snatched a wallet from a man's blazer when another man grabbed my wrist. As more men around the table noticed the commotion, I feared what would happen to me. Would I go to jail, or would they send me back to the orphanage? Without a word, he dragged me outside, waving off everyone's concern."

"What happened?"

"Billy Jack rushed outside behind us. He attacked Mr. McCoy, but Mr. McCoy's men pounced on him. He couldn't fight them all off, but he got a few good punches in. The next evening, Mr. McCoy offered Billy Jack a job. He liked his grit and thought he needed another strong hand to compel some people who owed him money to pay."

"And did he take the job?"

"He said yes before Mr. McCoy even finished asking him the question." A lump caught in her throat, and she stuttered on her words. "He tortured and killed people for a paycheck, and he loved every minute of it."

Ava dropped her gaze to the ground, focusing on the blades of grass surrounding her shoes. The honesty behind her words slithered down through her as the sorrow and guilt rubbed a hole in her chest, one that, at times, had left her gasping for air. Hoodwinked into a world of browbeating those who owed Mr. McCoy money, Billy Jack followed a path of greed, becoming a man she didn't recognize. They grew apart until she had to abscond from the only man and family she had. She vowed that day never to fall for another man as long as she lived. A vow she'd kept all these years, not because she still loved Billy Jack, but because she loved herself and never wanted to go through that kind of pain again.

"I couldn't stay with him, not after the things he'd done." She tucked a few of her raven locks behind her ears. "While he slept one night, I left. I didn't know where I would go or what I would do. Mr. Thompson found me roaming around about an hour later and brought me to his wife. Billy Jack wasn't too happy about it. But he left me alone... for the most part."

"I'm sorry you faced that," he whispered.

"So am I."

He stared at the ground for several minutes, and his brow furrowed as he finally glanced at her. "Do you know what happened to your parents and why they left you at the orphanage?"

"No, I don't."

"Do you know their names?"

"No, I don't. I overheard Sister Helen telling Sister Katherine that my mother had never told her who my father was." She ripped a few blades of grass, breaking them from their roots and clutching them in her fingers. "Sister Helen also said she never left her name because she didn't wish me to seek her out after I had grown."

"She didn't want you to look for her?"

"That is what Sister Helen said. I have no idea if she was lying. It wouldn't surprise me knowing her, but she could be telling the truth."

"But you are your mother's daughter."

A chuckle snorted through Ava's nose. "A daughter she never wanted."

"Well, she certainly missed out on knowing a good person."

She smiled, inhaling a breath as she rose to her feet. "I should get back to town. Griffin and I have a lot of work to do." She turned toward her horse, thinking about the mine and the scaffolding. The shapes flashed through her memory, landing on one she'd built a few years ago for a troublesome shaft in Tonopah. Before she took a step, the thought hit her like an out-of-control train. She spun back around. "I know what to do."

"About what?"

"The scaffolding problem. I know how to fix it."

"How?"

She knelt in the dirt and grabbed a stick, using it like a pencil in the sand. "Adding more boards to the scaffolding frame won't solve our problem. It will just add more work and waste lumber, and our men will still face cave-ins." She brushed her fingers against her forehead and started drawing in the dirt with the other. "I did this design a few years ago. I can't believe I didn't think of it before. The scaffolding design we use has two vertical posts on either side of the excavation area, capped by the horizontal board, which won't support the digging. The ore is too heavy, and it won't hold it."

"So, what do you think we should do?" He pushed off the rock and knelt beside her. His body was close to hers, and she could smell the cologne he had been wearing when they met in Butte. She'd loved the scent before, and smelling it again made her stomach flutter.

She closed her eyes for a second, shaking her head as she opened them. "Well, as the men remove the ore, replace it with timber on either side into the wall, thus creating a lattice support. Refill the void space with waste rock, rebuilding the side of the shaft as we dig out the vein. Building this way will allow us to safely dig any depth and height without worrying about collapse."

She drew the plans in the dirt, and as Mr. Harrison studied them, his eyes narrowed then widened. "Of course. This has to work," he said.

"It did for me once."

"I believe it will again."

NINETEEN

AVA

Ava sat by the window, finishing her breakfast as she watched the townspeople of Featherstone Valley stroll past the inn. The streets were bustling with activity, and the residents were dressed in their Sunday best, making their way to church. Women in elegant dresses and bonnets, men in neatly pressed suits and hats, and children scampering in their finest clothes. Guilt prickled in her chest, and she couldn't help but think about the words Mr. Harrison said yesterday about praying.

God doesn't want to hear my prayers any more than He wants me to step inside His church.

She sipped her coffee, and her gaze followed a young couple walking hand in hand. Their laughter drifted slightly through the glass, and a pang of longing tugged at her heart.

Just stop.

She pushed the chair away from the table and rose to her feet, making her way to the staircase just as Griffin and Benjamin descended the steps from the second floor. They were both dressed nicely. Not quite the suits and hats of the men walking through the streets, but still, for the Griffin she knew, he looked cleaned up with a crisp white shirt and a dark chocolate vest. Benjamin also appeared to have new clothes and a red bowtie tied around his neck. His hair was brushed and slicked back, and he smiled when he saw Ava.

"Good morning, Miss Adams," the boy said.

"Morning, Griffin. Benjamin," Ava greeted, a smile tugging at her lips at seeing them. "Where are you two headed off to looking so dapper?"

"We're going to church," Benjamin announced.

Ava stopped in her tracks. She looked at Griffin, frozen, blinking. "You're going where?"

Griffin smiled and shrugged. "I told Benjamin I would take him to church this morning."

"But why?"

"He wants to go, and, well... truth be told, I kind of want to go, too."

Ava chuckled, thinking he was joking. "And since when did you become the church-going type?"

Griffin's expression remained serious, and he nodded. "I told you I have to start considering things outside myself. I think it's important for Benjamin to have some structure, and going to church is a good place to start."

"Plus, I think he has a crush on my teacher," Benjamin said, giggling.

"That is not why we are going, son," Griffin whipped his head toward the boy. "And how many times do I have to tell you I don't have a crush on her? I like her as your teacher. That's it."

"You talk about her all the time."

"No, I don't. I ask how your day was and what happened in school, but that's my job. I'm supposed to ask those questions."

"And you talk to her a lot when you pick me up."

"Again, I'm supposed to talk to her so I can know how you're doing in school." Griffin sighed and glanced at Ava. "He's doing a fine job, by the way."

"That's good."

"And I know what you're thinking. I don't like his teacher in that way."

"If you say so." Although she wanted to disagree with him, she didn't. She'd known him far too long not to be able to see the glimmer in his eye as he was trying to deny it.

Griffin ignored the look on his face as he adjusted Benjamin's collar, giving the boy a reassuring pat on the shoulder. "You should come, too, Ava."

"Me? No."

"Yes, you should. It would be good for you."

Ava's smile faltered, and she furrowed her brow. "It's been a long time since I've been to church. I'm not sure I belong there."

Griffin's gaze softened, and he stepped closer, lowering his voice. "I don't know if I agree with that. From what I've seen around the mine and this town, that's not anyone's opinion but yours, and it's wrong to have. Everyone belongs at church, even the likes of both of us."

Ava nodded, but doing so did little to convince her. "You two should get going before you are both late. You can't walk into church late." She patted Benjamin on the shoulder. "Have fun."

Griffin gave her a half smile, and although she half expected him to argue further, he didn't. Instead, he motioned for Benjamin to follow him through the inn's front door, shutting it behind them.

A tug wrestled with another tingling of guilt in her chest, and she stared after them, the sound of the door closing echoing in her mind. The slight curiosity in attending church certainly piqued her interest, but however long the thoughts flickered in her mind, the fear of rejection squashed them. What would people think of her? And worse, knowing what He did about her, what would God think of her?

"Good morning, Miss Adams," a voice said behind her. As Ava turned, Mrs. Holden let the kitchen door shut behind her.

"Good morning, Mrs. Holden. You look nice."

"Thank you. Are you coming to church with us today?"

Ava hesitated, glancing back at the front door. "No, I don't think I am."

"Well, that's a shame. Any reason why?"

"I just... I don't think I should."

Mrs. Holden snorted a slight laugh. "Everyone should, Miss Adams."

"But I'm... I've done... things."

"Church is not just for the righteous. Jesus loves the broken and the wounded just as much. Those who believe they are less deserving of Him are perhaps the most deserving of Him. It is said in *Psalm 51:16-17*, You do not delight in sacrifice, or I would bring it; you do not take pleasure in burnt offerings. My sacrifice, O God, is a broken spirit; a broken and contrite heart you, God, will not despise."

"I'm not sure what that means."

"Well, it is a hard but beautiful truth. Sacrifices and offerings without the right spirit and heart are meaningless. They won't get you anywhere. Being broken is easy, but admitting you're broken... that is where it is hard. Acknowledging what you've done wrong, feeling remorse, and surrendering it all to God—that's the real challenge. Once you do that, God does the rest. He receives you and heals you, no matter what. The transformation that follows is truly supernatural and beautiful. It's something you can't accomplish apart from your Creator. He wants you to give up the fight, be broken and repentant before Him, and let Him help you. Let Him make you new."

"But I don't know how to do that."

Mrs. Holden winked. "Well, a good way to start is by attending church."

Ava bit her bottom lip, glancing at the front door once more. Fear still inched through her thoughts, but a louder voice called out when she thought about them—one that told her not to listen to the fear and doubt. *Just breathe*, the voice whispered. *Just go.* "Will you wait while I change my clothes?" she asked.

Mrs. Holden smiled again. "I would be more than happy to."

∼

God doesn't love young women like you, Ava.
Sister Gretchen's words repeated in Ava's mind the whole way to the church. The sound of the bells grew louder as they rang, and each toll vibrated in her chest. She climbed the stairs behind Mrs. Holden and entered the church. Warm light streamed through the stained glass windows, casting colorful patterns on the wooden pews.

As soon as they stepped inside, a moist layer of sweat glistened on Ava's palms. Her breath quickened, and the walls suddenly seemed to close around her. Mrs. Holden continued down the aisle, waving at a few people who greeted her and nodding to others as she passed them. Ava's heart pounded as the woman took a seat near the front.

There's no way I'm sitting in front with everyone watching.

She scanned the room, spotting Griffin and Benjamin beside a young woman close to the front. Griffin saw her, too, and motioned for her to join them. However, the thought of walking through the whole church to get to the pew and skirt by everyone sitting in the pew to get to the seat caused her to shake her head.

That's not happening either.

The weight of imaginary eyes on her, scrutinizing her every move, pounded down upon her. Her mind raced with thoughts that fired in every direction.

This was a mistake.

Run.

Go.

Now.

She spun on her heel to leave, but before she reached the door, a hand reached out and grabbed her wrist, stopping her. She spun back around, ready to pull away, but stopped when she saw it was Mr. Harrison who had caught her.

He gave her a reassuring smile and motioned to an empty seat next to him at the back of the church. "Sit with me," he whispered.

Ava hesitated, then nodded, moving around him to take the seat. A slightly exhaled breath escaped her lips.

"That was a disaster," she whispered.

"But it could have been worse."

~

"Good morning, everyone." Pastor Boone's voice carried over the few conversations throughout the church, and the room grew silent. Everyone turned their attention toward him, choosing to listen instead of continuing whatever had been on their minds so much they wanted to share it with those around them. "It's wonderful to see you all here today. I hope you've had a blessed week. I know I have, and for that, I'm always thankful."

He paused, looking at the faces around the room. "It's never easy deciding what I want to preach about each week. Not because I don't know what I want to say. It's quite the opposite. Far too many times, I have too much I want to talk about. My list of sermons is about a mile long at this point, and it's never easy to choose. Well, rarely. Today it was.

"I've been thinking a lot lately about our struggles and how we use our faith in God to overcome them."

Ava shifted slightly in her seat. She knew all too well about the struggles in life, and the idea of using faith to overcome them was both intriguing and daunting.

"Life is full of challenges, isn't it?" Pastor Boone continued. "We all face hardships, whether they be financial difficulties, health issues, or personal conflicts. These struggles can often feel overwhelming, and it's easy to feel lost and alone in the midst of them. Although we feel this way, we are never truly alone. God is always with us, even in our darkest moments and even when we have made mistakes. He is there to guide us, to comfort us, and to give us strength. When we trust Him, we can find the courage to face our challenges head-on."

A weight pressed on Ava's chest. She'd always felt alone, even when she wasn't. Forever burdened with a bitter battle within herself, the struggles were hers and hers alone.

But were they?

Was the pastor right?

Was God watching over her, ready to offer guidance and support instead of judgment to the point where He hated her?

"One of the most important things we can do in times of struggle is to turn to God in prayer," Pastor Boone continued. "Prayer is so powerful. It allows us to connect with God, to share our burdens with Him, and to seek His guidance. When we pray, we open our hearts to God's love and wisdom and allow Him to work in our lives. He wants to work in our lives. No matter what we've done. No matter how we feel about ourselves."

Ava cocked her head to the side. The God that Pastor Boone spoke of was not the God that Sister Gretchen spoke of.

Are there two different Gods?

"With that said," the pastor continued, "let us remember to be mindful, however, with our prayers. Prayers are not just about asking for help. It's also about listening. It's about taking the time to quiet our minds and our hearts and to listen for God's voice. Sometimes, the answers we seek are not what we expect. Sometimes, God's plan for us is different from our own.

But when we trust in His wisdom and love, we can find peace, even amid our struggles."

Ava's mind drifted to her prayers as a little girl—words to God that were often filled with desperation and confusion. She used to pray for guidance, strength, and a way out of the darkness surrounding her. She hadn't ever thought about how, not selfish, that wasn't the word, but they'd been all about her getting something she wanted. It was always about her, her, her.

She always asked.

She never listened.

Perhaps Sister Gretchen was the one who spoke the truth.

This is all so confusing.

Ava glanced around the church, studying the sides of the faces she could see. None of them looked as lost as she felt.

But, of course, why would they?

I'm the only one in here who didn't belong.

"I know that some of you are facing great difficulties right now. You may feel like you have nowhere to turn. But I want to remind you that God is with you. He sees your struggles, and He cares deeply for you. He wants to help you, to heal you, and to bring you peace. Turn to Him. We must be willing to let go. We must surrender our struggles to God and trust His plan for our lives. It is not always easy. It requires faith and courage. But when we do, we open ourselves up to the possibility of transformation. We allow God's love and grace to work in and through us."

Ava felt tears prick at the corners of her eyes.

Ava's mind wandered back to her conversation with Mrs. Holden earlier that morning. The inn owner had spoken about being broken and contrite before God, about admitting and surrendering her faults to Him.

Was this what she meant? Was she just saying it differently?

It had been a difficult concept to grasp, and although Ava

knew that holding on to her fears and struggles only kept her trapped, letting go was far more terrifying.

Pastor Boone's voice rose slightly, filled with encouragement. "I urge you all to take a moment today to reflect on your own struggles. Consider your challenges and ask yourself if you have truly surrendered them to God. Have you sought His guidance and His strength? Have you opened your heart to His love and His wisdom? If not, I encourage you to do so. Take that step of faith, and trust that God is with you, ready to help you and to bring you through your difficulties."

He paused, allowing his words to sink in. "Let us pray together."

The congregation bowed their heads. Ava's heart pounded, and she tucked her chin into her chest. She hadn't done this in years, and she fidgeted with her hands as Pastor Boone led everyone around her in prayer.

"Dear Heavenly Father," Pastor Boone began, his voice gentle yet firm, "we come before You today with humble hearts. We acknowledge our struggles and our fears, and we seek Your guidance and Your strength. Help us to trust in Your plan for our lives, to find peace in Your love, and to draw strength from our faith in You. May we support one another as a community, lifting each other in times of need. May we always remember that we are never alone, for You are with us, now and always. Amen."

"Amen," the congregation echoed, their voices a soft murmur in the stillness of the church.

Ava lifted her head as people stood and began meandering from their seats into the aisle, words of how much they loved the message this morning echoing on their lips.

"I'm glad you came," Mr. Harrison said beside her. He paused to wait for her to say something, but when she only smiled—it was all she could think to do—he continued. "But I guess the question is, are you glad you came?"

"I am. It was... different."

His brow furrowed, and he cocked his head to the side. "What do you mean different?"

"The sisters at the orphanage... they just made God sound different."

"Different as in?"

"As in that He was more often than not angry with us and more resolved to punish us and not love us when we did wrong."

"Ah. So, kind of like a scare tactic to keep children in line?"

She nodded, letting out a slight chuckle. "I'm starting to wonder if it wasn't more about that."

"Well, perhaps we should discuss it over lunch?"

"Lunch?"

"At the inn." He stood and offered his hand for her to take. "Would you care to join me?"

A tiny flicker of hope fluttered in her chest. There was nothing she wanted more.

TWENTY

AVA

The early morning sun had arched in the sky in the hour they'd been inside the church. A gentle breeze whispered against the heat of the rays, cooling Ava's skin slightly as she and Mr. Harrison made their way down the road back toward the inn.

Thoughts and questions fired in her mind in all directions, and although they all begged for answers, she didn't have one for any of them. Confusion plagued her with a feeling that twisted in her stomach.

"I hope I didn't make a mistake by stopping you," Mr. Harrison said. He cleared his throat as she glanced at him.

"You didn't, Mr. Harrison. If I wanted to leave, I would have done so even after you grabbed my arm."

"You can call me Craig if you like. I mean, I think we are past having to be proper all the time, don't you?"

"Yeah, I suppose we are. Well, Craig, since we are using first names, you can call me Ava if you want."

"I do." The words slipped from his lips quickly, and his volume made her flinch. He cleared his throat a second time and lowered his voice. "Want to, I mean." He paused. "I was hoping I would run into you today. I thought about those scaffolding plans all night and hardly got any sleep. I even got out of bed and drew a few pattern ideas I want to try."

"That's good. I told Griffin, and he thinks they will work, too. Catching the look on his face, I think he was disappointed he didn't think of it."

"I have to say I agree with him. It's a good idea." Craig paused again, clicking his tongue. "Have you... have you spoken to Mr. Miller about it? Or about the problems you've been having?"

"No, I haven't. I'm not sure I want to unless he asks. I think the less he knows, the better."

"You're probably right." Craig snorted a laugh, motioning toward the opening in the fence leading to the inn's front porch. "After you."

She made her way along the cobbled footpath and up the porch stairs. Her shoes clicked on the wooden boards, and as she reached for the doorknob, Craig darted around her.

"Let me get the door for you." He grabbed the knob and twisted it. The door popped open, and the two stepped inside. Warmth from the fireplace in the study welcomed them, and they made their way into the dining room. It was empty, and they chose a table near the window. "It will take a few moments for Mrs. Holden to return. But I do know where she keeps her glasses and pitchers of water. Shall I fetch you a glass?"

"Yes, please."

∼

By the time he returned with a couple of glasses of water, Mrs. Holden and Pastor Boone had returned to the inn from church and greeted them in the dining room.

"I'll be right back with your lunch," Mrs. Holden said to them as she trotted off to the kitchen.

"I don't want to be a bother," Ava said as the woman vanished behind the kitchen door. "I'm not in a hurry to eat." She looked at Craig, who shrugged.

Pastor Boone shook his head, chuckling. "I don't think anyone could ever be a bother to that woman. She would saw herself in half if it helped someone else." The pastor glanced at both of them but then focused on Ava. "On another note, I was pleasantly surprised to see you in church this morning, Miss Adams. I hope the sermon was helpful."

The smile on his face nearly gutted her more than his question. While her answer sat on the tip of her tongue, she hesitated, allowing the fear of appearing weak or ignorant to gnaw at her until she almost couldn't take it anymore. Her heart thumped, and her palms began to sweat. She clenched her hands into fists to keep them from trembling. The thought of admitting her lack of understanding made her cheeks flush with shame, and the more she thought about being honest with the pastor, the more the words seemed to lodge in her throat, refusing to come out. She wanted to tell him the truth, to confess her confusion and seek his guidance, but she was also torn between the desire for clarity, the fear of judgment, and a tangled web of self-doubt.

"It did. I enjoyed it immensely," she finally said.

He raised one eyebrow. "Are you sure? Because you looked rather confused throughout the whole thing."

Heat warmed the back of Ava's neck, and she dropped her gaze to the table, trying to ignore the flush in her cheeks.

"I think... I'm unsure what to make of it all. It was different from what I've always been told."

"What do you mean?" Pastor Boone asked. His brow slightly furrowed, then relaxed.

"Well, the sisters at the orphanage always told us children that God only loved the righteous and those who did not sin. He was also quick to punish and slow to forgive when we made mistakes. But some of what you said today contradicted that, and it confused me."

Pastor Boone nodded thoughtfully. "I understand, and I can imagine it must have been difficult to listen to the sermon this morning, hearing my teachings. I'm not sure I understand where the sisters of the orphanage came across their beliefs. None of the teachings I've ever encountered are focused in such a way."

"So, it's not typical?"

"No. It's not."

Not only did her lungs exhale a deep breath, but her whole body seemed to revel in the news. It was as though a door to a new world unlocked and clicked, opening before her eyes. She didn't know what to make of it, and that fact both scared her and excited her.

"The goal of worship is not punishment for what we do wrong, so we wrong no more. The meaning of worship is getting to God, following Jesus, and asking for help, confessing those feelings to Him, and receiving His truth."

Ava looked at him, intrigued. "What do you mean by His truth?"

Pastor Boone smiled gently. "The truth is that we are worthy because He counted us worthy through the death of our Savior, Jesus. When I came to understand that truth and allowed it to wash away feelings of unworthiness, I felt such strength and gratitude. It's not about what we do to feel or become worthy; it's about what we've already been given through Him."

"But I've done so many things wrong. How can I be worthy?"

"Ah. Well." He pointed toward the seat beside her. "May I?"

"Of course."

He exhaled as he took the seat, scooting it up to the table. "Until you've been broken before God, you might believe that what you do counts toward your worthiness and God's acceptance of you," Pastor Boone said. "This can also lead people to believe that they've done too many things wrong to be accepted and redeemed by God. Both are lies."

Ava's eyes widened, and she nodded slowly. "I've always been told I needed to earn His love and that I wasn't good enough."

Pastor Boone looked at her, and his eyes were full of compassion. "God loves you too much to leave you whole in yourself. He wants you broken before Him so He can restore you back to wholeness in Christ. If you desire that, He will allow you to be broken. It's a hard truth, but it's necessary."

Ava's gaze danced around the room. "Brokenness... sounds painful."

"It is." Pastor Boone nodded. "God will allow fire and pain to break you so He may restore you. Once you've been broken to the point where your faith is tested, but you hold on and don't give in, then He will build you back up and restore you. That's when your faith is proven."

Ava looked down, her voice barely a whisper. "I've been at a breaking point when I felt like I couldn't go on. But I never leaned into faith to save me. I only leaned into myself. I used my determination to get me through."

Pastor Boone brushed his shoulder into hers, making her smile. "And yet you're here. You have the curiosity. Continue down that path, and God can restore you. Your wholeness has nothing to do with you and everything to do with Jesus. It's all because of Him."

She shrugged. "So, what do I do now?"

"You surrender," Pastor Boone said simply. "You allow yourself to be broken and repentant before Him. Let God make you new. When you've been restored by your Savior, there's truly no other way you want to live."

"I'm still confused over it all."

"It's all right. You will learn." Pastor Boone patted her shoulder. "Nothing compares to experiencing the power of Jesus transforming you. But it's something your heart must desire on its own."

Ava smiled and nodded. "Thank you for your help, Pastor Boone."

"Anytime," he replied warmly. "Remember, regardless of your actions, God wants you more than you could imagine. Never believe anyone who says otherwise. Look up *I Peter 1:6-7*, and if you can, commit it to memory. In all this you greatly rejoice, though now for a little while you may have had to suffer grief in all kinds of trials. These have come so that the proven genuineness of your faith—of greater worth than gold, which perishes even though refined by fire—may result in praise, glory, and honor when Jesus Christ is revealed."

TWENTY-ONE

⁂

SIDNEY

Sidney's carriage rolled to a stop in front of the inn, and the horses snorted and threw their heads as he climbed out. It was as though they could sense their master's foul mood and played accordingly. His boots crunched against the dirt as he surveyed the inn's quaint front porch, and a wreath of sprigs hung on the door.

"Frills," he muttered under his breath.

He fetched his hat from the carriage, and after sliding it down on his head, he grabbed his walking stick. The end thumped against the staircase and porch as he approached the front door.

If the wreath wasn't bad enough, the inn's foyer, with tables, chairs, flowers, and a rug, felt like a sweet toothache that wouldn't go away. None of the décor was needed to run a business.

"More frills," he scoffed.

Of course, that was the cornerstone of this annoying little town. It was the sort of place that embodied everything he despised about Featherstone Valley—a town full of goodie-

goodie fools who hadn't yet learned that power and profit ruled the world. He couldn't wait to get his hands on it and turn it into what he knew it could be: another town like Deer Creek, bustling with men all willing to fork over their hard-earned money to the likes of him for one reason or another. Liquor, women, a winning poker hand, it didn't matter.

Sidney straightened his coat and tapped on the bell on the desk. The tiny ding echoed in the room, soon followed by footsteps.

"Good afternoon, Mr. Miller," Mrs. Holden said. She held two glasses of water, one in each hand. "How may I help you this afternoon?"

"Fetch Miss Claremore, please. I need to see her immediately," he ordered, not bothering with pleasantries.

The woman blinked at him. "I beg your pardon?"

"Miss Claremore. The woman I made the reservation for. I'm assuming she is here."

"Yes, she is. She arrived the afternoon you said she would."

"Good. Fetch her." He spun in a half circle. "Where is your study?"

She pointed toward a room across the foyer.

"Ah. Good. Fetch her. I need to speak with her."

"Do you not wish to go to her room?"

He grabbed the bridge of his nose. What was with all the questions?

"No. I don't. I wish to speak with her in the study." He furrowed his brow.

Mrs. Holden's face tightened slightly. "Miss Claremore doesn't often come down, Mr. Miller. She—"

"She will come down when I tell her to," Sidney growled through his words and pointed his finger in the inn owner's face. "Now go and get her."

"I'm in the middle of serving lunch to my guests."

"I don't care. It won't take you long to run upstairs and knock on her door."

"Good afternoon, Mr. Miller," a voice said behind him. Sidney glanced over his shoulder as Pastor Boone walked toward them from the dining room. He outstretched his hand.

Of course, etiquette told him he should be cordial. Not only was this a respected man in town, but a pastor nonetheless—not that it made much of a difference. He didn't care about a man of the cloth. Not one bit. Etiquette aside, however, Sidney didn't care.

He looked at the pastor's hand, then at Mrs. Holden. "I'll be in the study. Tell her not to keep me waiting."

Before either of them could say another word, he strode off toward the study.

His mind raced back to the mountain and the bet. It had been over a week of digging, with no significant strikes reported. The thought of losing the mountain and his plans for total control of Featherstone Valley tightened his chest with anger. Everyone who stood in his way, who even thought of underestimating him, would regret it bitterly.

As he turned toward the study, his gaze drifted across the dining room, and he froze. There, sitting at a table together, were Miss Adams and Mr. Harrison. They were deep in conversation, and a smile played on both their lips. Sidney's blood boiled. Rumors had been circulating that Mr. Harrison and Adams might be working together, but seeing it with his own eyes ignited a new rage. It was a slap in the face, and he headed for them, knowing he couldn't afford to ignore the threat they posed.

Miss Adams was about to feel his wrath. She might have been useful to him once, but her alliance with Mr. Harrison made her an enemy. Sidney clenched his fists, imagining how he could make her regret her betrayal. His mind churned with plans, each more ruthless than the last. If he didn't win the mountain, everyone would regret it. The stakes were too high, and the potential gains too significant for him to accept failure. Sidney envisioned the future—salons, brothels, and establishments that turned a real profit. He could already hear the jingle of coins and the hum of a thriving business empire expanding under his control. Losing the mountain to Mr. Harrison would not only be a blow to his plans but a direct challenge to his authority. And challenges had a way of being crushed under Sidney Miller's boot.

He moved closer to the dining room, his eyes narrowing as he fixed his gaze on Miss Adams. She looked comfortable, at ease even, in Mr. Harrison's presence. It was infuriating. She had been an asset, someone he had hired against his better judgment because of her reputation, and now she was sitting with his enemy, potentially plotting against him. His jaw tightened, and he felt a surge of anger.

"Miss Adams, Mr. Harrison," he greeted them with a forced smile that didn't reach his eyes. "Fancy seeing the two of you here... together."

Miss Adams looked up, her eyes widening in surprise. "Mr. Miller, what brings you to the inn?"

"I could ask the same of you," he replied smoothly, shifting his gaze between her and Mr. Harrison. "But I guess the answer is clear." He paused. "Tell me, do you frequently meet with your competition?"

Her brow furrowed. "No."

"Oh. Well, I suppose that's good to know," Sidney said, his tone dripping with sarcasm. "Here, I was beginning to think that you were associating with the competition. Perhaps you were discussing recent developments about the mountain that I should be aware of. Or perhaps you were simply plotting against me."

Miss Adams shifted uncomfortably, as though her confidence wavered under Sidney's intense stare. She glanced at Mr. Harrison. "We were just talking about the progress. Or lack thereof."

Sidney's smile widened, though his eyes remained hard. "I have to say I'm rather surprised I haven't received any written updates on the progress—or lack thereof."

"Mining is a slow process, Mr. Miller. It takes time to do it right."

"Time is a luxury we don't all have," Sidney said. "Especially when there's so much at stake. I must warn you, there's been talk around, of course, but it's been quite disappointing that I haven't heard from you."

"There's been nothing to report. We are having scaffolding issues, but I think I have worked through the problem."

"Ah. With Mr. Harrison's help, I assume?"

"I hate to disappoint you, Mr. Miller," Mr. Harrison said. He leaned back in his chair. "But whatever you're thinking is going on... you're wrong. Miss Adams and I are not here together. I approached her table, and she respectfully asked me to leave. I was just about to when you walked into the dining room."

"And why did you approach her table?"

"I, too, am having scaffolding issues, so I came over to get an idea of what she's doing. You would be happy to know she's keeping a tight lip on her plans, though."

Sidney cocked his head to the side. A slight smirk spread across his face. "Are you trying to cheat, Mr. Harrison?"

"Not cheat. I'm just worried about the men's safety... both mine and yours."

"Do you think Miss Adams is not?"

"I am," she said, glancing between the two men. "That is why Mr. Harrison and I were discussing what to do."

Caught trying to lie, Mr. Harrison closed his eyes, groaning slightly.

Sidney studied him, then turned to Miss Adams. "You probably should have just gone with his lie instead of thinking it would be better for you to tell the truth."

"We aren't working together, Mr. Miller. But I have the safety of my men to consider. If I find a better way to build the scaffolding, but Mr. Harrison continues to mine in the manner he has, it will undermine all my attempts to ensure I'm safe."

"Then perhaps your ideas weren't good enough."

"My design will work, and you will have your mountain when I'm finished."

Sidney's voice dropped, low and threatening. "I sincerely hope so, Miss Adams. Because if I find out that anyone is standing in my way to get that mountain, they will regret it. Deeply. Do you understand what I'm saying?"

"Are you threatening me?" she asked, deepening her tone to nearly match his.

He clenched his jaw. "It's a promise. This mountain, this town—they will be mine. And anyone who thinks otherwise will have a problem on their hands."

"I'm not afraid of you, Mr. Miller."

Sidney's smile turned icy, and his mind was already plotting his next move. Miss Adams had made a grave mistake, and if she wasn't careful, she would learn just how ruthless he could be.

"You should be, Miss Adams."

He turned to leave but only made it a few steps when she spoke again. "How do you know I haven't faced men like you before, Mr. Miller? How do you know I haven't faced men worse than you?"

He turned his head slightly, not fully glancing over his shoulder but making sure his voice carried. "No one is like me, Miss Adams. No one."

WYATT

Wyatt followed his parents and sister through the inn's front door, their voices blending with the hum of lunchtime chatter. The lingering scents of roasted meats and freshly baked bread wafted through the air, making his stomach growl. He hadn't had time to enjoy breakfast before church, and by the time they'd reached the inn for lunch, he had planned to order two meals.

"Good afternoon, Mr. and Mrs. Cooper," Mrs. Holden said to his parents as they made their way to the dining room. Standing near the staircase, she smiled and nodded to them, as did Wyatt and his younger sister.

"Good afternoon, Mrs. Holden," Wyatt's mother, Catherine, said, returning the smile. "We're here for lunch, as always, on a Sunday afternoon."

"Of course, Mrs. Cooper," Mrs. Holden replied. "There are several open tables just waiting. Let me show you to one."

Wyatt hesitated near the staircase as the inn owner, his parents, and his sister continued into the dining room. His gaze drifted to the second floor, and his breath caught when he saw the young Miss Claremore descending the stairs in a royal blue dress that clung to her figure as she moved down each step.

Gathering all his courage, he darted toward her, removing his hat as she drew near. "Good afternoon, Miss Claremore," he said.

"Do I know you?"

"The name's Wyatt Cooper—Mr. Wyatt Cooper. I helped you with your luggage when you arrived in Featherstone Valley."

"Oh, yes. Good afternoon, Mr. Cooper." Her blonde hair, resembling spun gold, curled around her shoulders, and her blue eyes sparkled like the sapphire in his mother's pendant. A brief smile touched her lips before she glanced toward the study.

"How have you liked your stay at the inn?" he asked. "It's quite nice, isn't it?"

"Um. Yes, it is nice."

"Have you wandered around the town much? Have you had a chance to see the sights? I mean, I suppose Featherstone Valley doesn't have much by the way of sights to see." He chuckled as he adjusted his tie. "But it's still a great little town."

"I've heard. I've mostly kept to my room."

"Oh. I can understand that. New towns can make a person nervous."

Miss Claremore's eyes darted to the study door again before she answered. "The town is quaint, though. From what I hear from the window."

Wyatt nodded. "I was hoping to see you at church this morning," he said, trying to sound casual. "We have a nice church building near the edge of town and a nice pastor, too."

She laughed, a light, almost mocking sound. "Church? You thought I'd go to church?"

Wyatt frowned, puzzled by her reaction. "Why wouldn't you? Everyone's welcome at church."

Her laughter faded, replaced by a look of surprise. "You're serious?"

"Of course I'm serious," Wyatt said. "It's a nice church, and Pastor Boone... well, he's the best pastor the town has ever had."

She blinked, clearly taken aback. "I... I don't think..."

He stepped closer, his eyes softening. "You should come next Sunday. I think you'd enjoy it."

Miss Claremore bit her lip, and her gaze shifted to the study once more. "I'll think about it." She pointed toward the door to the study behind her. "I have to meet someone. It was nice seeing you, Mr. Cooper."

Wyatt studied her, noting the tension in her posture and how her eyes drifted away from him. As she turned to leave, he moved slightly in front of her. "Is everything alright, Miss Claremore?"

She forced a smile. "Everything is fine. Now, if you'll please excuse me."

Before Wyatt could say anything else, she hurried toward the study. A sense of unease settled in his gut, and he couldn't shake the feeling that something wasn't right. Her hurried steps and the way she kept glancing around like a trapped animal only fueled his concern, and his curiosity urged him to follow her. He tiptoed down the short hallway toward the study. His heart pounded with each step, making the inn's cozy atmosphere suffocating. The cheerful chatter of other guests was a distant hum compared to the loud thumping of his own heartbeat.

He reached the study and peeked through the crack in the door. His breath caught in his throat as he spotted Mr. Sidney Miller rising to his feet from a chair near the hearth. Wyatt's eyes widened, and his pulse quickened; confusion and dread tightened his chest.

"You know I don't like to be kept waiting, Elizabeth," Mr. Miller said to her.

"I'm sorry. I didn't know you were here, and I had to dress."

"Do you think I want excuses?" He moved toward her.

"It's not an excuse. I..." She inhaled, turning her face away from him. Her shoulders hunched, and she looked like she was bracing for something. "My apologies for keeping you waiting."

He released his grip on her, and she moved slightly away from him, cowering even more than she already was.

Wyatt furrowed his brow. While part of him told him to burst into the room and protect Miss Claremore, the other part of him said not to.

At least not yet.

"What have you been doing these last few days in Featherstone Valley?" Mr. Miller asked.

"Nothing. I've stayed in my room, just like you told me. I even have the inn owner bring my meals to the room."

Mr. Miller nodded as he moved around her, circling her in a slow gait as though he was the predator and she was the prey. "And have you spoken to anyone?"

She shook her head. "Just the owner of the inn."

"That's all?"

"Well, there was a young man who helped me with my luggage, but—"

"I told you not to speak to anyone but the inn's owner!" Sidney raised his voice. She cringed, closing her eyes.

Wyatt rushed inside. "What is going on here? Miss Claremore, are you all right?"

Both she and Mr. Miller looked at him. She covered her mouth, shaking her head at Wyatt.

Mr. Miller strode toward him, and the man's advance caused him to step backward out of the study. "This doesn't concern you, young man. Miss Claremore is with me."

Wyatt frowned, his confusion growing. "What do you mean she's with you?"

Sidney's smile widened, but there was no warmth in it. "If you want Miss Claremore's company, you must pay for it just like the rest."

"What do you mean pay for it?"

"Do I have to spell it out for you, boy?"

The realization hit Wyatt like a punch to the gut. His face paled, and he took a step back. "She's a..."

Sidney's grip tightened on Wyatt's arm, his smile never wavering. "That's right. Now, I suggest you leave before I make you."

Wyatt pulled free from Sidney's grasp, his heart pounding. "I'm not leaving until I know you won't hurt her."

Mr. Miller laughed, and then his amusement turned into a

seriousness that made all the hair on Wyatt's neck stand. He wanted to flee, but he couldn't—fleeing was weak.

"I'm all right," Miss Claremore said to him. "I want you to leave." She nodded, glancing at the study door with her eyes and without moving her head.

"It's not right for me," Wyatt said to her.

"Yes, it is. Go."

"You heard the lady," Mr. Miller moved toward Wyatt, who stumbled backward and held his hands up.

"All right, fine. I'll go." He cast one last, pained glance at Miss Claremore, who stood with her gaze locked onto the floor before turning and fleeing the study.

As he stumbled into the inn's foyer, the world spun around him. His parents and sister were still in the dining room, chatting with Mrs. Holden. Wyatt's mind raced, struggling to process what he had just learned. The image of Miss Claremore's haunted eyes stayed with him, and he took a deep breath, trying to steady himself.

"Mr. Cooper?" a voice said behind him.

Wyatt spun to find Pastor Boone standing in the doorway to the dining room. His head was cocked to one side, and one eyebrow was raised.

Wyatt hooked his thumb over his shoulder. "I... I need some air." Not waiting for the pastor's response, he pushed through the inn's doors and rushed into the fresh afternoon air.

Boots thumped on the hardwood floor behind him.

~

"Mr. Cooper? Mr. Cooper?" Although Pastor Boone said his name several times, Wyatt didn't stop until he reached the road. He bent over, taking several deep breaths.

"She's a... a... she works for him... in... one of the brothels."

"Are you talking about Miss Claremore?" Pastor Boone asked.

"Yes."

"Well, then the answer is yes. She works in one of Mr. Miller's brothels."

"But that means that she's..." Wyatt closed his eyes. "But she's... she's too pretty. She's too young. She's too pretty."

Pastor Boone laid his hand on Wyatt's shoulder. "I know it's hard to understand. I, myself, had a hard time with it when I first met her. I thought she was just a young woman visiting a nice little town. Perhaps she was related to one of the families, like a distant cousin."

At the mention of the word 'cousin,' Wyatt thought of Rachel's cousin Emily, who was staying with them for a couple of weeks. "I thought the same thing," he admitted to Pastor Boone. "I never thought she was anything but a lovely young woman visiting."

Pastor Boone patted Wyatt's shoulder again. "Well, to be honest, in her defense, she still is a lovely young woman. She just happens to work in a *certain place*."

"A certain place?" Wyatt snorted. "That's putting it gently, Pastor Boone."

"Would it be better if I quoted *John 8:7*? When they kept on questioning him, he straightened up and said to them, 'Let any one of you who is without sin be the first to throw a stone at her.'" The pastor paused. "Are you going to throw a stone, Mr. Cooper?"

Wyatt shook his head. The shocked tension that had stiffened his shoulders relaxed slightly. "No."

"That's good." The pastor turned to leave but paused, laying his hand on Wyatt's shoulder one last time. "Many people have pasts, Mr. Cooper, and those pasts tend to make their lives look different. If you have not gone through anything so significant that it changes your whole world... then you should consider yourself lucky."

Wyatt listened to the pastor's thumping footsteps as he looked out on the horizon. Questions circled his mind, and as he thought of each one, the image of her face flashed in his memory.

A woman of questionable morals or not, it didn't matter.

His resolve hardened. He would find a way to reach her, to understand her. She was like a book with a missing chapter, and he was determined to read every word.

TWENTY-TWO

SIDNEY

Sidney watched Wyatt flee the study, and a satisfied smirk played on his lips. Turning back to Elizabeth, his expression hardened, and his eyes narrowed. He took a step closer, towering over her, relishing the fear that flickered in her wide eyes.

"It seems you have an admirer," he said.

"Not because of anything I've done or said. I have no interest in him and do not share the same feelings. I don't know him."

"Good. Keep it that way." His eyes narrowed. "You need to be careful now. You wouldn't want to end up like Mindy, would you?"

Elizabeth sucked in a sharp breath, her eyes widening in horror. Her face paled, and she shook her head vehemently. "No, Mr. Miller." Her words were merely breaths on her lips instead of spoken. "I... you don't have anything to worry about."

"Good. Being favored only gets you so far, Elizabeth. You should know this. It's one of the reasons I brought you here and why I don't often share you with other men."

"Why did you bring me here?" she asked. "You sent me here

all by myself. I know no one, and you hardly visit. I don't understand why I'm here."

"You're here because I want you here, and that's all you need to know." He reached for her face, letting his fingers trace along her jawline. She closed her eyes, and while he got the impression it was out of fear, he ignored it, imagining instead that she had done so from the pleasure of his touch. "I've meant to visit more, but plans keep getting in my way."

Her fear was palpable, almost tangible in the air, and Sidney reveled in it. The power he held over her was intoxicating, and he could see the terror reflected in her trembling form.

"I have a meeting with Mayor Duncan, and then I have to return to Deer Creek. But I will be back in Featherstone Valley soon. Perhaps then we can spend some time with one another." He leaned in and brushed his lips against her forehead. "In the meantime, stay in your room. Do not talk to anyone. Do you understand me?"

"Yes, I do."

"Good." With that, he turned on his heel and left the study. His boots echoed ominously against the wooden floorboards, and he crossed the foyer without glancing toward the dining room. He stepped outside, and the bright sunlight blinded him until his eyes adjusted to the light. He walked onto the street, passing Mr. Cooper talking to the pastor. The two stopped talking as he walked by, and they stared at Sidney. While some of him wanted to ignore them, he tipped his hat, smirking as the young man only glared in return.

I suppose the young man has grit, even if it's only enough to make him stupid.

As Sidney made his way to the Mayor's office, his mind shifted back to the mountain and Mr. Harrison—the important things he should be thinking about. Not some mindless young man who believes himself to be a hero to a young woman who lived better than he did. How could Mr. Cooper look at Elizabeth and think she was lacking anything? She'd had the finest since Sidney found her starving in the alleyway behind the saloon, picking through the garbage.

And she loved the life he'd given her.

And if she didn't, she'd be a fool.

∼

Sidney strode through town, letting the thoughts of Elizabeth, Mr. Cooper, Miss Adams, Mr. Harrison, and the bet for Rattlesnake fester in his mind. He'd faced worse opposition before trying to take over a town. It wasn't anything new. But it still didn't mean that he wished for hard. It would be easier if everyone just did what he told them, like they did in Deer Creek. Taking over that town had been about the most straightforward task he'd ever taken on.

And look where the town was now.

The town was a bustling hub of business and tourists. Store owners were making profits, and so was the town. The bank could loan people money for homes, and the town had the money for its needs.

Sure, crime had risen, but what town wasn't without crime? It was no skin off his nose, and if the people didn't like it, they could leave—which, thankfully, most of the ones who were his biggest problems did.

And now it was time to take on another town, raking in more money than he made in Deer Creek. If the people of Featherstone Valley didn't want this progress or think that crime doesn't exist, well, they're darned fools—all of them!

With a groan on his lips, Sidney crossed the porch of the mayor's office. He thought about knocking for a second but decided against the idea and shoved the door open, entering the office without concern for anyone already in there.

Mayor Duncan jumped from his desk and slapped his hand against his chest. "Mr. Miller, you... you surprised me."

"I would be concerned if I hadn't."

The mayor glanced down at his desk covered in papers strewn all over the top. "I wasn't expecting you. Did we have a meeting scheduled?"

"Since when do I need a meeting scheduled?" Sidney cocked his head to the side. "Sit down, Duncan. We need to talk."

The mayor swallowed hard and sank back into his chair. His hands trembled slightly as he fumbled with the papers. Sidney moved to the desk, resting his hands on two of the corners as he leaned over it.

"Things aren't going as planned. Mr. Harrison and Miss Adams both seem to have a scaffolding problem, and instead of dealing with it on their own, they are working together to solve the issue."

"Isn't it good that they figure out for the safety of the two teams?"

"Do you think I want them working together?"

Mayor Duncan shifted uncomfortably, avoiding Sidney's gaze. "I-I don't know. I suppose I didn't think it would be a problem."

"Clearly." Sidney's patience was wearing thin. "And I find that odd, given you know what's at stake here. If Mr. Harrison wins, our entire arrangement falls apart. And you, Duncan, will be left to face the consequences, not only from your town but from me. Trust me, you won't like the ones from me."

The Mayor's face drained of color, and he glanced nervously at the door as if contemplating escape. "Mr. Miller, please, I've done everything possible to ensure this bet tips in your favor. Why do you think I put them in close proximity in the first place? I thought having them together would give you the edge in knowing what Mr. Harrison was doing."

"Well, it seems to have backfired." Sidney's eyes narrowed,

his anger simmering just below the surface. "The question is, what am I going to have to do to fix it?"

Mayor Duncan licked his lips. "I'll think of something. I just have to figure out a way to approach it. My position is delicate. If the people find out about our arrangement, I could lose everything."

Sidney leaned closer, his face inches from the mayor's. The mayor's face turned ashen, his eyes wide with terror. "And if I lose this mountain, Duncan, you will lose more than your position. I'll make sure of it."

The threat hung heavy in the air, and the Mayor's eyes darted around the room as though he was desperate for a way out. "So, what do you want me to do?" he asked, his voice barely above a whisper.

Sidney straightened, a cruel smile curling his lips. "I want you to ensure that Mr. Harrison doesn't win. By any means necessary. I don't care how you do it, but you better make sure it happens."

Mayor Duncan's hands shook as he nodded, the weight of Sidney's words pressing down on him. "I—I don't think I can do that. If he finds gold first... the whole town will ask questions if that happens, and you are named the winner."

"I don't care what questions the town will have," Sidney growled, deepening his voice. "This is your mess, and you need to take care of it. If you don't, I will be forced to, and you don't want that. Trust me."

Mayor Duncan nodded, his hands clutching the edge of his desk as if it were a lifeline. His breath came in short, ragged gasps. "Yes, Mr. Miller. I understand. Although I don't know what I'll do."

"Unfortunately, you decided to play with fire," Sidney said, turning to leave. "It's not my fault if you get burned."

Sidney pushed off the desk and spun on his heel, leaving the office before the mayor could utter a word. The mayor's fear lingered in the air like a foul odor, and as Sidney stepped outside, a cloud settled over him. Deep down, he knew trusting Mayor Duncan to do anything was the most foolish thing to do. That man had the backbone of a house of cards.

He can't be depended on for anything other than messing something up.

If I want something done, I will have to do it myself.

Sidney headed toward his carriage, telling his driver to head back to Deer Creek as he climbed inside.

~

By the time Sidney returned to the saloon, the sun had vanished from the sky. The driver halted the carriage outside the building, and Sidney climbed out, slamming the door before the driver could even jump down.

He strode into the saloon, ignoring all the cheers and screams from the men celebrating at the tables inside. He made his way to the bar, pointing at the bartender.

"Liam. My office. Ten minutes."

As Liam nodded, Sidney continued up the staircase, striding down the hallway to his office. The sounds from the patrons echoed off the walls, making it hard for Sidney to think.

He pushed open the door to his office, and the heavy oak creaked on its hinges as he stepped inside. The quiet of his office was a welcome relief and a stark contrast to the chaos of the saloon below. He shut the door, glancing around the room with its dark wood furniture and shelves lined with books and bottles of fine liquor—collections he'd spent years acquiring. A large desk dominated the space, and behind it, a window overlooked the bustling street below.

He moved to the desk and opened one of the drawers, looking at a stack of papers inside—contracts signed by Mayor

Duncan detailing the loans he'd taken out to hide the fact that he'd used town funds to buy stocks and gamble.

A knock on the door interrupted Sidney's thoughts. "Come in," Sidney called.

The door opened, and Liam stepped inside, angling his burly figure so he could fit through the frame before closing the door quietly behind him.

"You wanted to see me, Boss?" Liam asked, his voice gruff.

Sidney gestured for him to sit. "We have a problem at the mine in Featherstone Valley."

"What kind of problem?"

"It seems that Miss Adams has run into some issues and has taken it upon herself to work with Mr. Harrison to fix them."

"What kind of problems?"

Sidney waved his hand, letting out a sigh. "Something about the scaffolding. I don't know exactly. I'm afraid Mr. Harrison will use this opportunity to gain the upper hand on Miss Adams."

"But if he cheats, then he loses."

"It's not about cheating. It's only about winning, and Mr. Harrison's mining operation is becoming problematic. I need it... disrupted."

Liam raised an eyebrow, the hint of a smile playing on his lips. "What kind of disruption are we talking about?"

"The kind that sends a clear message," Sidney replied, his tone cold and calculated. "Collapses, equipment failures, anything that slows them down and makes them think twice about continuing."

"Aren't they working in the same area? I don't want anything of yours getting damaged in the process."

"You think I care about that? I can replace equipment, and I can replace men. What I can't replace is that mountain if I lose it. Do what you have to. Just make sure that Miss Adams is the first to find the gold. Then deal with whatever."

Liam nodded slowly, a gleam of understanding in his eyes. "Consider it done."

Sidney reached into a drawer and tossed a small pouch of gold nuggets onto the desk. "There's more where that came from. Do a good job, and you'll be well rewarded."

Liam picked up the pouch, feeling the weight of the nuggets before tucking it into his pocket. His smile was all teeth, a predatory grin that matched Sidney's own ruthless ambition. "Don't worry, Mr. Miller. I'll take care of it."

Sidney watched Liam leave, and a dark satisfaction settled in his chest. If Mr. Harrison and Miss Adams thought they could outmaneuver him, they were about to learn the hard way just how ruthless he could be. This town, this mountain, everything in it would be his.

And anyone who stood in his way would be crushed.

TWENTY-THREE

AVA

I Peter 1:6-7, "In all this you greatly rejoice, though now for a little while you may have had to suffer grief in all kinds of trials. These have come so that the proven genuineness of your faith—of greater worth than gold, which perishes even though refined by fire—may result in praise, glory, and honor when Jesus Christ is revealed."

As Pastor Boone had told her, Ava had spent the last two days committing the verse to memory. She still wasn't sure if she understood the deep meaning of it or the conversation they shared, but the once flicker of determination she'd had to learn had now turned into the only goal, aside from finding gold in Rattlesnake Mountain, she'd given herself.

"So, where did you want to go today?" Griffin heaved his saddle on his horse's back, then bent down to grab the cinch, securing it under the horse's belly.

"I don't know. I just need a ride."

"Well, I guess I'll let you lead then." He chuckled, and after finishing the cinch, he grabbed the bridle off the rack and slipped the bit into his horse's mouth.

Ava finished tacking her own horse. Her brow furrowed as she thought of the conversation again. *"You surrender,"* Pastor Boone said simply. *"You allow yourself to be broken and repentant before Him. Let God make you new. When you've been restored by your Savior, there's truly no other way you want to live."*

You surrender.

You surrender.

Just how was I supposed to do that?

She turned toward Griffin, opening her mouth to ask his thoughts. But movement caught her attention from the corner of her eye, and as she glanced toward the stable door, a figure walked toward them.

"Are you two headed up to the mine?" Craig asked.

Griffin shook his head, answering for them. "Nope. We're going for a ride."

"Really?" Craig's gaze danced between the two. "Do you mind having company?"

Although he didn't look at her, instead keeping his attention on the leather strap of the throat latch on the bridle, Ava could feel Griffin's sideways glance.

She could also feel the amusement that spread through his thoughts, and ignoring the smile on his face, she turned toward Craig. "No, we don't mind at all."

"Great. I know the perfect place we can go. And no, it's not the same one." He wiggled his finger at her. "This is a different place."

~

"Well?" Craig sat in the tall grass beside her, grabbing a couple of blades and ripping them from the stems.

"Well, what?" Ava asked.

"Did I not say this place was perfect?" He lifted his hands as if to motion to the whole meadow around them.

"You did. It wasn't like I doubted you, though."

"It's all right. You can admit it if you did." He laughed.

"I did." Griffin raised his hand as he stood a few feet from them in the clearing. He spun in a circle, winking and smiling at the two of them before he walked toward them. "Seriously, though, who owns this place?"

Craig shrugged. "I don't think anyone does."

"Really?" Griffin's brow furrowed. "I wonder who I would talk to about it."

"Are you thinking of buying land here?" Ava asked.

He flashed her a mocking glare. "Maybe. What's it to you?"

She laughed. "I guess I didn't know that you were staying here."

"Just something I was thinking about if we win that bet and have jobs here." He winked again and turned away from them. "I'm going to have a look around."

Ava watched as Griffin meandered away from them, weaving through their three horses, who were knee-deep in the grass on which they were happily grazing. Their tails swished at the gnats fluttering around their ears while the early morning sunlight glimmered across the different strands of their fur, making each one stand out. The only sound apart from them eating was the leaves fluttering in the slight breeze. The rattling sound echoed in the silence of the meadow like a peaceful song no woman could ever sing, even if she'd wished and hoped for it with all her might.

"It is a nice place," she said, trying to ignore Griffin's mention of the bet. She didn't want to think about the unknown future of whether or not they would be staying in Featherstone Valley. "How did you find it?"

"I was just riding around one day and found it. It's one of those places I love to come to, no matter the time of the year. All the leaves turn different colors in the fall, and the snow creates this winter wonderland. It reminds me of a meadow back in the

Klondike." A far-off look washed through his eyes as though he soaked in every second of his time here. A spurred fervor seemed to ignite in him.

"Maybe you should think about buying this place." She laughed.

"You know, I have never thought about it. Huh. Now I wonder why."

"Perhaps it's because owning this place would change the magic of it."

"That's an interesting thought." He turned toward her. "Sounds like you have personal experience with something like that."

"Eh. Sort of. There was a place I knew like that in Tonopah. I could have bought it, but I never did." She closed her eyes, picturing her meadow back home with the lush trees and deep meadow grass cascading in different shades of green. Light and dark, they all drowned out the dull browns and grays of the mountains surrounding the meadow. Like an oasis in the middle of rough terrain, it breathed softness and a sense of tranquility, calming even the most frazzled nerves.

"And you didn't buy it because..."

She shrugged. "I couldn't bring myself to disturb the serenity of it. To bring chaos and strife to such a place by building a home. Once the home was built, it would be calm again, but I couldn't have built it alone, meaning others would have known about it. I didn't want anyone to know about it, and I would have hated myself if I'd shown it to anyone."

"So what if they knew about it? It would have been yours. You could have kept people away."

"True, I suppose. Still, I didn't want to touch it. It was better that I didn't if that makes sense."

"Yeah, it does. And you're right; perhaps that's why I've never asked anyone about buying this land. I don't want to touch it. I don't want to change its magic." He leaned toward her, bumping his shoulder into hers.

"Ha. Ha. Funny."

"I thought it was." He chuckled and reached for a few more blades of grass, ripping them from the stems and tying them in a knot. He held up the knot, releasing the end and watching the grass unfold. "I never got a chance to talk to you about what you thought of church or the lunch with Pastor Boone."

"You mean the lunch that Mr. Miller decided to ambush."

Craig shrugged. "Well, that too. I didn't want to bring it up if you didn't want to discuss that."

"There's nothing to talk about. I won't be intimidated."

"I gathered that about you."

"I did appreciate you trying to cover for me, telling him you approached my table without my permission."

"I had hoped that didn't offend you."

"It didn't. But you also didn't need to lie. I've dealt with men like Mr. Miller before."

"I'm sure you have."

"Just more *lovely* things from my past," she chuckled, tucking some of the loose strands of her ponytail behind her ear.

"Do you care to talk about it?"

She shook her head. "It's nothing. Things I need to forget... or, I suppose, as Pastor Boone said, what I need to let God use to restore me. I'm still unsure what he meant by everything he told me."

Craig rested his elbow on one of his knees and cradled his chin in his palm. He stared at her before speaking. "You've never relied on faith, have you?"

"No." A slight amusement hinted through her voice, making the only word she said more like a laugh. "No, I haven't. I've always relied on myself—my strength, my determination."

"I'm sure that's worked out for you in the past."

"Yes, it has."

"But I'm also sure it's been stressful."

She stopped herself from answering in the matter-of-fact tone she had used before as a weight rested on her chest. The realization that perhaps what she'd thought of as smart—relying on herself—all these years had been instead foolish. "Yes. It has." She paused, inhaling a deep breath. "I don't think I want to do that anymore."

"It's no way to live. That I know."

"You—you used to not live with faith?"

"There was a time when I didn't, yes. When I lived in the Klondike. Church, God, and Jesus weren't words usually spoken in those parts." He snorted a laugh. "Men were too busy getting drunk at the saloons with scantily clad women to be bothered with anything a preacher was trying to say to them. Don't get me wrong, I wasn't one of those men. I never wanted to get mixed up with whiskey and women. That was a one-way ticket to a fortune found and lost instead of just found."

"So what changed?"

"I got trapped in a mine collapse. No one was around, and I was on my own. It took me three days to dig myself out, and I told God on the second day that if He helped me, I would find my faith."

"That was the surrender that Pastor Boone talked about." While he nodded, she shook her head. "I still don't understand the surrender part of it all."

"Complete surrender to God means to have absolute humility. It calls for a heart free from pride, acknowledging that no one is more capable of guiding your life than the One whose ways surpass our own. To surrender yourself completely to God, you must let go of everything."

"But how can we do that?"

"That is the question you will ask yourself every morning you wake up."

"So, it's something you do every day."

Craig nodded. "Yeah. *Proverbs 3:5-6,* Trust in the Lord with all your heart and lean not on your own understanding; in all your ways submit to him, and he will make your paths straight."

"So, I give Him my troubles and have faith in whatever happens?"

Craig didn't nod or shake his head. He simply looked at her and smiled.

She furrowed her brow, thinking about the conversation now and the discussion with Pastor Boone. Although she wanted to say she still didn't understand, the thoughts were shifting into focus. It was just on a much deeper level than she had once believed was possible.

"So, I did understand it; I was just thinking it was harder than it is."

"Pretty much."

She chuckled. "Well, that's good to know."

"Stick with me; I'll teach you everything you need to know."

"Ha. You just want me around so you can steal all my tricks."

"Tricks? And how do you know that I don't prefer working alone? Well, besides with my team."

"To be honest, I can see that in you. I bet you were alone in the Klondike, weren't you?"

He nodded. "Mostly alone. As dangerous as it is, money can change people, and I know enough about broken friendships, hell, even broken marriages, when it came to land rights and finding gold. Two men, heading up the trail with thoughts of partnership, can soon find themselves fighting to the death for what they believe is theirs and theirs alone."

"I suppose the same can be said about any mine around here, too," she mused.

"You seem quite the exception to that, given Mr. Baker's with you."

"He came on his own accord. But I am glad he did. I don't

know how I would have made it here without him. I've always been able to trust him, even from the first day I met him."

"Unfortunately, that can't be said about most men in the Klondike. I never stole any claims as I didn't think it was the right thing to do." He scratched his chin, tilting his head as he chuckled. "I suppose that's part of why I didn't last up there. Men with morals don't belong in the Klondike."

Ava laughed. "Again, the same can be said about down here."

Craig chuckled, too. "I suppose that's true. I knew of a few decent men up there, but there weren't many. One was an Irishman named Flynn O'Neil. He guided people up and down for many years until he met his wife, Cora, and they settled in Dawson City. He was a good man."

As the sun rose a little higher in the sky, Ava watched as the rays flecked across Craig's face. In the few weeks she'd been in Featherstone Valley, he'd gone from the annoying stranger out for the same thing she wanted to a comforting soul she almost felt she'd known her whole life.

"You're a good man," she whispered.

He turned toward her, staring as though her words had knocked his thoughts off balance. A softness hinted through his eyes as he looked at her, and she couldn't deny something had changed between them. It was an essence of something deeper, something that delved into the depths of—dare she say —love.

His gaze stole her breath.

He leaned toward her, and his lips were so close to hers that she could almost feel them on hers. She leaned into him, but before he kissed her, a loud bang echoed through the air.

"What was that?" he said, jerking away from her.

"It was a gunshot."

He blinked, shaking his head. "I know it was a gunshot. But who?"

"Griffin."

They both jumped to their feet, darting off in the direction Griffin had left.

~

By the time they found Griffin, he'd shot a few more shots, and each one had pounded against Ava's fears.

"What on earth are you doing?" she shouted at him.

"There are a few targets over there in the distance. I thought I would get some practice in."

"You nearly scared me to death!" She punched Griffin's arm. "I thought you'd encountered a bear and were in trouble."

"I'm sorry. I just wanted to shoot at the targets a few times. We haven't done it in a while, and I feel a bit rusty." He chuckled.

Ava didn't.

"Oh, come on. We used to go shooting all the time in Tonopah. Don't you miss it?"

"Well, yes, I do. But..." She exhaled through her nose. "Never mind. I'm just glad you're all right."

She turned to Craig, who stood watching them with his head cocked to one side and a broad smile on his face.

"You used to go shooting a lot?" he asked.

"Yeah, I guess."

"She's just downplaying it, Mr. Harrison. Ava's about the best shot I've ever seen."

"Really?" Craig raised one eyebrow. "That's interesting for a woman."

She whipped her head toward him. "I beg your pardon? Are you implying that because I'm a woman, I can't shoot?"

"No, I didn't say that."

"I think you did." She rested her hands on her hips. "All right, Mr. Harrison. How about a little wager?"

"Sounds good to me. You should know I have a lot of experience. Weapons were the difference between life and death up in the Klondike."

"That doesn't mean you have good aim."

"I bet I have better than you." He winked.

Ava's mouth gaped open. "That's quite a bold assumption to make."

A smug smile spread across his lips as he shrugged his shoulders.

"Did you just shrug away my words?" *Oh, now I must prove him wrong.*

"So, what will you give me when I win?" he asked.

She snorted a laugh. "Your confidence does nothing to intimidate me or impress me."

"I didn't think it did, but you didn't answer my question. What will you give me when I win?"

Ava folded her arms across her chest and cocked her head to the side. "I don't know. What will you give me when I win?"

He tapped his lips with one of his index fingers before a broad grin spread across his lips. "Dinner at the inn."

"But I already eat there every day and night."

"Yeah, but if you win, I will pay for the meal. If I win, you pay." He gave her another wink and offered her his hand to shake. "Well, then, Miss Adams, what do you say?"

"I'm not sure you want to do this, Mr. Harrison," Griffin said. "You don't know who you are dealing with."

"I think I'll take my chances. Ava?"

However amusing his conviction was, annoyance began to tickle through Ava's insides, and she grabbed his hand, shaking it. "You have a deal."

"Now," Craig turned toward Griffin. "Where are those targets?"

"They are right over there on that fallen log."

"Ah. I see them. That's a good distance." He looked at Ava. "What do you think? Are you ready?"

"Always."

He chuckled. "Well, then, by all means... ladies first."

With a deep, inhaled breath, Ava pointed her pistol at the first target and fired. She hit every object one by one, knocking them off their pedestals. They flew through the air, landing with thuds in the sand.

"Not bad," Craig said after she finished.

"Your turn."

Her stomach twisted into knots as Craig prepared himself. The flawless lines of his stance set fire to the only chance she had of coming out of this the victorious one—a hope that soon vanished while she watched him hit every mark with his right hand.

"Not bad yourself."

"Yes." His brow furrowed. "Although, I'm wondering how we will determine the winner."

"I have an idea." She pointed at him. "Can you hit them with your left hand?"

His smile faded, and he gulped. He was either suddenly scared of the bet he made or trying to fool her into thinking he was scared. She didn't know which.

"My left hand?" he asked.

"Yes. Can you hit them with your left hand?"

"I guess we'll find out."

"I guess you'll find out." Although boastful in his voice, a tiny rush of dread seemed to brush against his nerves. His demeanor changed, and it was as though, even though he was accomplished with his right hand, his left hand proved a different story. He reloaded the pistol and readied to shoot once more. No matter his calming breaths, he missed each target one by one, and he growled as he turned toward her.

"Left-handed is always harder," she said.

"Yeah? Let's see you try it," he growled playfully.

Just as with her right hand, she hit every target with her left, shooting a perfect score with each hand. Through Craig's irritation, he couldn't help but laugh as she approached him, and he ducked his chin, shaking his head.

"All right. All right. You got me. You win. Where did you learn to shoot that good?"

"Just lots of practice." She glanced at Griffin, who laughed and patted Craig on the shoulders.

"I tried to warn you, Mr. Harrison," he said.

"Yeah, you did. I only wish I would have listened." Craig laughed, too. "That will be the last time I make that mistake."

He continued to chuckle as he walked back to the horses. Griffin remained at her side, walking several feet behind Craig.

"I tried to tell him," Griffin said, chuckling.

"I know."

"So, what did you two talk about?"

"Nothing that would interest you."

"Are you sure about that?" Griffin glanced at her, squinting one eye closed as though the sun was too bright.

"Yes, I'm sure."

They continued walking another couple of yards in silence before Griffin sighed. "Mr. Harrison seems like a good man."

"Yes, he is."

"He seems to enjoy your company."

"I suppose so." She raised one eyebrow as the realization of where Griffin was about to take this conversation churned in her stomach.

"You seem to enjoy his company, too."

Ava stopped and grabbed Griffin's arm, pulling him to face her. "What are you getting at?"

"Do you have to ask?"

"Yeah, I do. I don't understand the reason for this conversation."

"Don't play dumb, Ava. I see the way you both look at each other. You love him."

"No, I don't."

"All right. Perhaps you don't. But," Griffin pointed his finger in her face, "you're falling in love with him."

"You're crazy."

"Crazy enough to know I'm right. And crazy enough to know that he loves you... or he's falling in love with you. All I know is you both need to be honest with yourselves."

Before Ava could say another word, Griffin strode off, waving his hands as he muttered under his breath. She watched as the two men climbed onto their horses, looking at her to see if she was coming.

The truth of the matter sat on the tip of her tongue. She was falling for Craig. The only problem was, if he professed his love in return, would she want to stay or flee? Surely, some of her believed she would stay, but another part still screamed with an undying fear, telling her to leave and not even look over her shoulder.

"Are you coming, Ava?" Craig called out, waving at her.

Surrender.

Surrender the unknown to Him.

"Yeah." She nodded. "I am."

TWENTY-FOUR

AVA

"We could go in either direction." Griffin pointed at the hand-drawn map spread on a makeshift table. His fingertips traced the lines he'd drawn just that morning, and the gray lead smudged on his skin. "The new scaffolding is holding here and here, but..." He let his voice trail off.

"But what?"

"I don't think there is anything down there."

"Why do you say that?"

"We haven't seen any color in the shafts we've blasted."

"That doesn't mean anything, Griffin. You should know that."

"I know." He furrowed his brow. "What do you think?"

"She's got gold in her. I know she does. I can feel it."

"And where is this gold you can feel?"

Ava continued to study the map. She'd never met a mountain she couldn't beat, and although some tried, they all gave up.

Rattlesnake Mountain would, too.

"Well?" Griffin asked, cocking his head to the side.

"I'm thinking. Give me a minute."

Griffin folded his arms across his chest, watching her as she continued to look around the map. Although his eyes bore into the back of her head, she ignored him. He did this more times than she cared to think about.

Finally, after several more minutes, he dug into his pocket and yanked out his pocket watch. "Are you going to figure it out today or..."

"Do you have someplace to be, Griffin?"

"Kind of."

"Really? I thought you were joking."

He sighed and ran a hand through his hair. "Well, I was joking a little. But I was also a little serious. It will be quitting time here soon, and I promised Benjamin I wouldn't be late. Today was a rather important day at school for him."

"Why?"

"He had a spelling test today and was nervous about it. We studied for nearly two hours after supper last night." He shrugged. "It's probably silly, but I'm just a little worried about how he did. It would bum him out if he didn't get good marks from Miss Evans."

"That's not silly. It just shows you care about him."

"I do. Very much." Griffin's face lit up slightly. "He's such a great boy. He's bright and curious about the world—way more than I was at his age. Miss Evans gave me a couple of books the other students had all read, and he and I have been reading together in the evenings. He really enjoys those stories about knights and dragons."

Ava grinned, teasing him lightly. "Are you sure it's just the boy you've been enjoying? I hear his teacher is pretty nice, too, and you two talk a lot."

Griffin's ears turned a bit red, and he looked away. "She's nice, yeah. But it's not like that."

Ava chuckled. "Come on, Griffin. We've known each other long enough for me to tell when someone's caught your attention. I see the way you look when you talk about her. There's more to it than just 'she's nice.'"

He sighed, a small smile tugging at his lips. "Okay, fine. Maybe I do like her a bit. She's good with Benjamin. And she's kind and patient. It's just... I don't know what she thinks of me. And I don't know if it's the right time."

Ava laid a hand on his arm. "Griffin, life doesn't wait for things to be perfect. If you like her, you should tell her."

He shrugged. "I suppose, but it's complicated."

"Life always is."

"Yeah, but this is complicated. We just got into town, and who knows if we are staying. I don't want to start something I can't finish."

"That is understandable." She laid her hand on his shoulder. "Aside from life being complicated, it's also short. Don't miss out on something good because you're waiting for the perfect moment."

"Gold! Gold! We found it!"

Ava and Griffin spun as one of Craig's men ran through the camps, shouting at the top of his lungs. They looked at each other, and Ava's heart sank.

She rushed toward the miner, pushing through the crowd of other miners who had surrounded him. They all celebrated with hollers as they jumped up and down. More men joined the others, cheering so loud she covered her ears as she shoved a few out of her way, rushing toward the middle and the man who had been shouting about the gold.

"What's going on?" she asked him.

The worker turned toward her. His smile faded, and he furrowed his brow. "We won! We won, and you lost! Go pack up your stuff and get off Mr. Harrison's mountain."

"I'm not sure I should tell you. You're working for the enemy."

"Clarence, that's enough!" A voice echoed from the outskirts of the crowd, and as Craig weaved through his men, he patted several on the shoulders. "You don't speak to Miss Adams that way."

"But, Boss, we won!"

"I don't care. You won't speak to her that way. Do you understand me?"

"Yes, Boss." Clarence's shoulders hunched, and a dark cloud seemed to loom over the men. The celebration disbanded. The happiness was gone.

"You found gold?" Ava asked Craig, who remained near her while the men left.

Craig nodded. "We did. And it's one of the biggest strikes I've ever seen."

Her stomach clenched. While a tiny part of her was excited for him, she also knew Mr. Miller wouldn't take too kindly to the news that Craig had been the first to find gold. Surely, he would fire her, and what was she to do then? She couldn't return to Tonopah.

"Can I see it?" she asked.

～

Ava followed Craig through the tunnels. Dark and damp, the walls were lined with jagged rocks and wood scaffolding, and as they moved deeper, the air grew thicker with the musty scent of earth. Griffin trailed behind her, along with Mr. Cooper, and the four of them weaved through the mess of shafts.

They reached a corner, and as they turned and Craig lifted his lantern, the gold streaks between the rocks glistened in the glow.

"Well, there she is," he said. "This is one of the biggest veins I've ever encountered."

"It's enormous." Ava's whispered words were just breaths on

her lips. She'd seen strikes before that had taken her breath away, but this one was unlike anything she'd seen.

"Holy cow," Griffin whispered behind her.

Ava glanced at him and then at Craig. Her eyes widened, and she moved to the wall, hesitating as she reached out. "May I?" she asked Craig.

"Sure."

She traced the streaks of gold with her fingertips. The different hues of yellow gleamed brightly against the rough quartz. "This is incredible."

Craig nodded. "Yeah. The only problem is we must be careful with the extraction."

She furrowed her brow and then glanced at the ceiling of the shaft. She sucked in a breath, noticing a crack already forming and bits of dirt falling. "I see it. If you aren't careful…"

"The whole thing will collapse upon us." He finished her sentence.

"You're going to need to make sure everything is secure before you even start digging it out."

"Exactly. This gold isn't going anywhere anytime soon."

Griffin stepped up beside her, squinting as he touched the gold. "How far into the mountain are we?"

Craig shrugged. "I don't know. A couple of hundred feet."

"Do you have a map of where you've dug it out?"

"Not with me. It's back at camp. Why do you ask?"

"I'm just wondering how long this vein runs and where your shafts are compared to ours."

"Are you trying to cheat, Mr. Baker?" Mr. Cooper asked.

"What? No." Griffin shook his head.

"Do you think we crossed into your side of the mountain? Because we didn't. I can assure you. I drew the map myself."

"I don't think you did. I was only asking because—"

"Mr. Harrison isn't a cheater! And I'm not one either!" Mr. Cooper lunged forward, but before he could get more than a few inches, Craig rushed between the two men. He pressed his hands on Mr. Cooper's chest.

"Wyatt, that's enough," he said. "You have no right to accuse them of what you have."

"I just thought it was an odd question for him to ask."

"I didn't." Craig released the young man's shoulders. "It was a thought that crossed my mind, too."

"I don't understand."

"If this vein runs the whole length of the mountain, it's on their side, too."

"But they didn't find it. We did. So, we win the bet. This mountain is your mountain."

"Not yet, it isn't."

"But—"

"We need to fetch Mayor Duncan and send a telegram to Mr. Miller. I can't claim victory until we do." He patted Mr. Cooper on the shoulder. "Why don't you head to town and find the mayor?"

"All right. I'll do that." Mr. Cooper backed a few steps before he turned and meandered his way back through the mine.

Just as he vanished into the darkness, a sudden, loud explosion echoed through the shaft. The ground shook, and dust and debris filled the air.

"What was that?" Ava asked Griffin. "Was that from our side?"

"It shouldn't have been. I told those men not to blast anymore today."

Another explosion rocked through the shaft, shaking the walls. More dirt rained down upon them, and they lifted their hands over their heads.

"What are those guys doing?" Griffin shouted.

Before they could do anything, a third explosion boomed through the shaft, raining even more dirt and rock down upon them. The walls groaned and creaked.

"We need to get out of here," Craig said urgently. "Everyone, out! Now!"

Craig reached for Ava's hand, but several scaffolding boards buckled and fell before she could grasp it. Dust engulfed them as her body slammed into the ground. Pain shot through her shoulder, running down her arm.

"Ava! Ava, where are you?"

The rest of the scaffolding crashed around her, dropping one by one; each board fell inches from hitting her. Rocks wiggled loose from their homes, tumbling and rolling, and the debris kicked up even more dust, clouding her vision and burning her eyes. She curled her legs up into her chest and wrapped both her arms over her head, forming a tight ball with her body. Dirt filled her lungs, choking her as she sputtered and coughed.

"Ava!" Craig's voice sounded distant, almost as though he was miles away instead of mere yards. "Ava, where are you?"

The hole in the ground caved in on her, and a board landed on the side of her ribcage. She gasped, unable to speak. More dirt caked her mouth and throat. Another board hit her leg, pinching the skin, while a third and fourth board pinned her to the ground. Rocks continued to drop, falling and hitting her in the back, the arms, and the legs.

Her whole body writhed in pain.

As sudden as the shaking started, it vanished within seconds, yet it felt like it lasted for years.

"Ava! Ava!"

Her eyes watered, yet even the tears couldn't smother the fire burning in them from the rubble.

"Dig her out!" Griffin's voice drifted to her ears.

She opened her mouth, but words evaded her. Dirt stifled her voice, and her lungs begged for even the slightest bit of air. She tried to move, but the weight of wood and stone forced her stillness. Faint sounds of picks and shovels thumped against the stone. The sharp sound beat in her temples. Craig and Griffin both continued to bark orders. Fear hitched deep in their voices, the pitch one she'd never heard from either of them before.

"Ava! We're coming for you. Just hold tight." Craig's voice echoed through the walls.

Rocks crumbled, and the sounds became louder and louder.

"She's over there."

Within seconds, hands lay upon her shoulders, and Craig shouted in her ear. "Ava. Ava. Speak to me."

TWENTY-FIVE

CRAIG

The two men removed the boards and rocks that had fallen on her one by one. With each breath she attempted, she coughed, and Craig yanked a handkerchief from his pocket, wiped her face, and held it close to her nose.

"This will help keep her from inhaling any more debris," he said to Griffin before turning his attention back to her. "Ava?" Craig's fingers clutched her chin, and he gently moved her face toward him as he continued to whisper. "Speak to me. Come on. Speak to me."

Her eyes were closed, and although her lips parted, she didn't say a word. He reached up to her neck, pressing his fingers into the skin near her jaw below her ear. "I can feel her pulse. It's faint, but she's still alive."

"Let's get her out of here and back to town," Griffin said.

Craig rose to his feet and bent down. "I've got you, Ava. I've got you." His arms slid under her knees and around her shoulders. He cradled her, carrying her so close to his chest that she could hopefully hear his heartbeat. After a few steps, she reached up, her fingers grabbed his shirt and clenched as though she clung to his warmth, holding on with the last of her strength.

He ran through the mineshaft as Griffin trailed behind them. Both men choked on the dust floating in the air.

Sunlight hit their faces, and Ava coughed as the fresh air filled her lungs. Craig laid her down on the ground, brushing away the dirt from her face with the sleeve of his shirt.

"Get me some water," he barked to Mr. Cooper. The young man fumbled to the bucket, spilling half its contents before reaching Craig's side.

Craig yanked the handkerchief off and dunked it in the bucket. He wiped Ava's eyes, nose, and mouth, dunking it again and again, wringing out the water every few strokes.

"We need to get her to town and to Dr. Sterling. Now." He looked at Griffin, who nodded.

"I'll get the horses."

∼

CRAIG

Craig didn't know how many times Ava had fallen asleep during the ride back to the inn, but each time she awoke, his heart found hope. Her body was like a ragdoll against his, and he held her tight against him as he wove his horse through the trails back to town.

His mind raced with the unknown.

Had she broken anything? Did she have injuries they couldn't see? Internal ones that could kill her? Had she taken in too much dirt into her lungs?

Every one of his questions fired off in his mind over and over. Surely, most of them would be answered when they reached the doctor, but until then, he didn't know what would happen, which scared him more than anything.

Their time together had been limited to moments in the last few months. But in those moments, the notion he'd found a kindred spirit beat like a drum in his chest. He didn't want to wake up in a world where she wasn't in it.

"Lord, please," he whispered. "Please don't call her home. She's not ready. I'm not ready. I want more time with her."

They reached town, and after he halted the horse in front of the inn, he wrapped his arms around her and climbed down, tucking her tight against his chest. Mr. Baker bounded off his own horse and ran past Craig, shoving the inn's door open.

"Mrs. Holden! Mrs. Holden!"

The inn owner and the pastor came running into the foyer as Craig carried Ava through the door.

"What happened?" Mrs. Holden asked.

"Mine collapse. Get Dr. Sterling."

Without hesitation, Pastor Boone strode for the door. His boots echoed across the porch.

Mrs. Holden motioned toward Craig. "Let's get her up to her room. I'll fetch some hot water and bandages from the kitchen."

Craig cleared the stairs and headed down the hallway. Mr. Baker led the charge, opening the door to her room.

By the time Craig laid her on the bed, Mrs. Holden came into the room. "Dr. Sterling shouldn't be long. Is Miss Adams breathing?" she asked.

"Yes, and she has a pulse."

Mr. Baker moved over to the side of the bed, kneeling beside her. "Ava? Ava, wake up. Ava, open your eyes."

Upon hearing his voice, Ava's eyes fluttered.

Craig rushed to the other side of the bed and grabbed her hand. "Ava? Can you hear us?"

She nodded slightly, moving her head only a little. She licked her lips, opening her eyes a little more.

"Oh, thank God," Mr. Baker whispered. "Ava, are you hurt? Where do you hurt?"

She jerked her arms, pointing toward her whole body.

"She's not bleeding anywhere. That's a good sign," Mrs. Holden said. "Did anything fall on her?"

Craig nodded. "She was hit by some debris—boards from the scaffolding and rocks. I think she did a pretty good job of protecting herself. We found her curled up."

The two men and the inn owner remained by her bedside until the doctor knocked on the door.

"Good evening," he said, nodding toward everyone before moving to the bed. Mr. Baker backed away a few steps, giving the doctor some room. "Good evening, Miss Adams. I'm Dr. Sterling."

She blinked and smiled, giving him a slight nod.

"Are you having any trouble breathing or moving?"

"No," her voice cracked. "I don't think anything is broken."

"All right. Well, let's look and see if I can find any signs of internal injuries." He glanced at the two men. "You both may step out into the hallway. I will let you know when I'm finished."

Mr. Baker shook his head and folded his arms across his chest. "I'm not leaving."

"Mr. Baker, you need to let the doctor do what he needs to help Miss Adams." Mrs. Holden moved toward the young man, brushing his arm with her fingers.

"He can do whatever he wants. I'm just not leaving the room."

"Mr. Baker, he needs to undress her."

Griffin's laugh echoed through the room. "Mrs. Holden, do you think this is the first time I've seen this woman without clothes? It's not. Do you know how many times I've had to undress her because she got herself caught up in a mine collapse, or thrown from a horse, or came home a drunken mess? I know you'd like to think I haven't seen her in all her bareness, but unfortunately, that's just not reality."

"It's all right, Griffin." Ava's voice rasped and cracked

through her whispered words. She opened her eyes just long enough to catch the grimace spread across Mr. Baker's lips. "You need to fetch Benjamin from the school."

"I'm not leaving you."

"I'll be fine. Get Benjamin. He'll be worried about you."

"Miss Evans can bring him to the inn."

"Go," Ava said, glaring at him as she growled.

Although Mr. Baker looked like he would argue again, he didn't. Instead, he unfolded his arms and heaved a deep sigh. He walked over to the bed, looking down at her. "Fine. But I won't be gone for long. All right?"

"Don't worry, I'm not going anywhere."

After he moved away, Craig moved over to the bed. He smiled, trying to make light of the heavy moment. "So, you've been a drunken mess a time or two, huh?"

"He's lying," Ava muttered, licking her lips again. "I've never been a drunken mess. I don't even drink."

Craig glanced at Mr. Baker, who was standing by the door with his hand on the doorknob. He shrugged, chuckling. "Sorry. The joke was just too hard to pass up on."

Craig smiled slightly, making his way through the door into the hallway. After shutting the door behind them, Mr. Baker patted him on the shoulder. "I hope such things don't offend you. She's like a sister to me. Don't worry. I don't look at her the way you do."

"The way I do? What's that supposed to mean?"

"Like you love her."

"That's not—I'm not..." Craig sucked in a breath. The words of denial rested on the tip of his tongue, yet no matter how much he tried to utter them, he couldn't. For if he did, they would be a lie.

Griffin patted Craig's shoulder again. "No need to deny what we can all see."

Before Craig could say anything else, Mr. Baker waved and

strode away, shouting that he'd return as soon as possible before trotting down the staircase.

AVA

"Can you sit up, Miss Adams?" Dr. Sterling asked after the two men left the room.

She nodded, wincing with every movement. "I don't think I'm hurt too badly, Doctor."

"Why don't we let me be the judge of that? Open your mouth."

She did as he told her, and he checked her mouth, wiping a piece of cotton against the sides of her cheeks. "Your mouth and throat seem to be clear. You might need to rinse a few more times. Try not to talk too much; you'll strain your throat if you do."

She nodded.

"Can you move your arms and legs?" he asked.

She nodded again, lifting her arms and moving her legs. The soreness made her wince even more, but the pain wasn't enough to believe anything was broken.

"Well, that's a good sign." He glanced up at Mrs. Holden. "I should check her for internal injuries. Can you help me with her clothes?"

Mrs. Holden moved to Ava's side, helping remove her boots, pants, and shirt. The cotton material brushed against the raw scrapes along different parts of her body, and she hissed through the pain. Once she was left in just her undergarments, she laid back down, and Dr. Sterling covered her with a blanket, checking different parts of her body.

"Well, Miss Adams, you've already got some mighty fine bruises. Those will need weeks, if not months, to heal. They are the deepest shade of purple I think I've ever seen." His cold fingers pressed into her side, feeling up her ribcage. Pain ripped through her. Her scream rattled through the rafters.

"I'm sorry," the doctor said.

"It's all right. I know you are just doing what you have to do."

He pressed against her again, and she bit her lip to keep from giving them another reason to argue. "I don't think you broke anything, and I don't see any signs of internal injuries. I think you got lucky and will be pretty bruised up."

"That's good to know." She shifted her body, reaching for a blanket with the bit of strength she could muster. "Lucked out again."

"Again?"

"It's not the first time a mine has collapsed on me."

"Perhaps you should look into a different line of work."

She snorted. "I don't know how to do anything else, Dr. Sterling."

"Well, something to think about. Get cleaned up. I'm sure Mrs. Holden would be more than happy to help." He glanced at the inn owner, who nodded and helped Ava into a nightdress. "Then get some rest. You're going to be sore for a few days. Stay in that bed as much as possible until you start feeling better." He straightened up, grabbed his doctor's bag from the floor, and set it on the bed. "I'll come back tomorrow to check on you and see how you're doing. If there's any change in your pain or you get a fever, send someone to fetch me immediately."

"I will. Thank you."

With one last nod, Dr. Sterling left the room. Before he shut the door, Craig returned, and the two men shook hands before the doctor left. Craig's shoulders were hunched as he made his way over to the bed and slid both hands into his pockets.

"Did Dr. Sterling find any injuries?" he asked.

"No."

"That's good."

Mrs. Holden cleared her throat. "I've got water heating up in the kitchen. I'll fetch it, and we will clean you up, Miss Adams."

She left the room too, and silence fell between Ava and Craig as she shut the door.

"So," Craig rocked back and forth on his heels. "I know this is probably a stupid question, but how are you feeling?"

"I'm just sore... and a little embarrassed."

"Why embarrassed?"

"I don't know. I should have been smarter."

"It was a mine collapse, Ava. You couldn't have predicted what happened."

"Then I should have been faster."

"Any one of us could've gotten caught up in the debris."

Before she could give another reason, the door opened, and Mrs. Holden strode back inside, carrying a bucket of water in each hand. Water sloshed but didn't spill as she meandered around the bed to the wood stove and set them down. "I'll grab the chair, and if you can sit, we will start by washing your hair. Once that's done, we'll figure out the rest."

As Ava began to move the blanket off her, Craig darted toward her and helped her stand. She took a step, limping on her bruised legs, and she closed her eyes, trying to ignore the pain.

Craig tucked his arm under hers and scooped up her legs, carrying her to the chair and setting her down as lightly as he could.

"Sorry if that hurt," he whispered.

Although the stiff wood pressed hard against her aching bones, she shook her head. "It's all right. It didn't."

Mrs. Holden reached into the bucket and pulled out a bar of soap. Before she could even begin, Craig motioned toward the buckets.

"May I wash her hair at least?" He paused, glancing at Ava. "Is—or is that odd to ask?"

While a tiny part of her thought it odd, a bigger part didn't—and she almost wanted him to more than anything in the world.

"No. It's not."

Mrs. Holden smiled and clasped her hands. "Why don't I go downstairs and make you something to eat? Not too much, but something warm to fill your belly?" The inn owner patted Ava on the shoulder, then left the room, shutting the door with a click.

"I hope this isn't too odd," Craig said. "I just want to help."

"I know, and I meant it when I said it wasn't."

"All right. Well, let's get to it, then." Craig chuckled slightly, as though he wasn't sure exactly what he'd said he would do.

For a moment, Ava thought of asking him if he really wished to help, but she stopped herself as he grabbed a rag and dunked it in the water. He started with her cheeks, working his way around her face, neck, and the backs of her ears, wetting her skin first and then rinsing the suds away. With her face cleaned, he moved to the back of the chair, cradling her head as he collected her hair. He draped it over the back of the chair, letting the dirty mess hang before he fetched one of the buckets and dunked her long strands in the water before he set the bucket back down. While the water cascaded back into the bucket, he grabbed the soap, spinning it between his hands.

After getting what he thought was enough soap, he began working her curls into a sudsy lather, massaging her head and neck with a slow and steady rhythm that threatened to put her to sleep. It was the most romantic gesture given at her most weakened time, leaving her wanting nothing more than to wrap her arms around him and never let go. She'd always prided herself on her independence and strength, never allowing herself even the slightest moment of vulnerability. It wasn't that she thought being weak was bad. It just didn't fit into her world of working in the mines and working with men.

"I'm not hurting you, am I?" he asked.

"No."

After rinsing her hair, he searched the dresser, finding her brush among the other belongings she'd left beside it. He brushed the strands, working gently around the knots until they were smooth. By the time he finished, the door opened, and Griffin came inside carrying a tray laden with food. He paused, staring at the scene in front of him.

"He washed my hair," Ava said to her friend.

"I see that." Griffin continued to stare, then slightly shook his head. "I have your supper. Mrs. Holden had to see to a few people in the dining room, but she said to let her know if you need anything else."

"Oh. All right." She grabbed the chair's armrests and tried to stand. Her legs were still a little wobbly, but as Craig reached out to help her, she could steady herself by holding onto him. "Thank you," she whispered.

He nodded and helped her back into the bed, propping up her pillows and laying the blankets over her so Griffin could set the tray beside her.

"If you don't mind, I'm going to see to Benjamin. Make sure he's got supper and doesn't need anything, and then I'll be back."

"Yeah. Sure. I'm just going to eat and try to get some sleep."

"All right." Griffin nodded. "I'll check on you in a little bit." He glanced at Craig, motioning toward the door as if silently telling Craig he wanted to speak to him in the hallway.

Craig cleared his throat. "I'm going to head downstairs for a bite to eat myself. If you need anything, let me know."

"I will."

The two men left the room, shutting the door behind them. She would have followed them to hear the conversation if she knew she wouldn't fall flat on her face when she tried to get up.

∼

CRAIG

Craig followed Mr. Baker into the hallway and softly closed the door behind them. The muffled sounds of the bustling dining room drifted up from downstairs, starkly contrasting the tense silence between the two men.

Mr. Baker stared at Craig briefly before inhaling a deep breath and folding his arms across his chest. "So, care to tell me what you think you're doing?" His voice was low but firm, and his eyes narrowed.

Craig's heart thumped. "I don't understand. What do you mean?"

"Washing her hair, caring for her like that. What are you playing at?" Mr. Baker's frustration was evident, his posture rigid, and his voice carried an edge of anger.

Craig sighed, rubbing the back of his neck. "I just wanted to help. She was hurt, and I did what I could to make her comfortable."

"Falling in love with Ava isn't going to help her, Mr. Harrison. You know that, right?"

Craig's eyes hardened. "I don't understand. How would it not? I mean, I'm not saying that I am, but how can it not?"

"What happens now that the bet is off and you've won? What do you think the future holds for her in this town once Mr. Miller finds out he lost? Do you think he's going to take it lightly? Her life might be at risk, and she won't be able to stay here. What do you think that will do to her?"

"Her or you?"

"This isn't about me. It's about her."

"If you're worried I won't protect her, you're dead wrong. I won't let anything happen to her. I promise you that."

Mr. Baker stepped forward, leaning his face inches from Craig's. "You better mean that because if you don't, I'll be the first to make you regret it. Ava doesn't love easily; she can't with her past. But when she does, it's for life. If you're not ready for that kind of commitment, you need to walk away now before it's too late."

Craig glanced at the ceiling while his thoughts raced. He had been so focused on protecting Ava and caring for her that he hadn't fully considered the implications of his growing feelings. But now, faced with Mr. Baker's concerns, he realized the depth of what he was getting into.

"I don't want to walk away," Craig said, lifting his gaze. "I care about her too much."

Mr. Baker studied him. His eyes narrowed, then relaxed. "All right. I'll believe you. But you need to be sure. She isn't something you can back out of once you're in it."

"I know. She's safe with me. I'll do whatever it takes to be there for her."

"That's good because I have a feeling when Mr. Miller finds out you've won that mountain, she will need both of us. Mr. Miller doesn't seem like the type to take this lying down. He seems ruthless, and I don't think he cares who has to hurt to get what he wants."

"I'm not afraid of Mr. Miller. I never have been."

Mr. Baker sighed, running a hand through his hair. "For Ava's sake, I hope you're telling me the truth."

TWENTY-SIX

AVA

Ava rolled over, staring at the sheer curtains hanging around the window of her room. A curl of her hair fell into her face, and the scent of soap wafted into her nose. She inhaled, moving her hair as she thought of how Craig had washed it only hours ago. It had been something no one had ever done for her, and while she had loved every second of it, it had also terrified her more than she wanted to admit.

One never knows why they choose whom to love or why they choose one person over another, just as no one knows why their heart longs for one in particular.

People aren't born knowing who will catch their attention or make them forget their thoughts. They don't grow up with a person's face branded in their minds, so while they sift through the people they meet daily, they know when they see the familiar set of eyes or the perfect set of lips.

They could find them at any given moment, from their first breath to their last. It's never planned for, and it's never prepared for. If they could, they might find that their quest for love distracts them from the daily struggles that make them who they are to begin with. The constant search for their chosen would control their minds and actions, leaving them on a quest for nothing else.

No. It isn't supposed to be that way.

Love is supposed to shock them when they least expect it.

It's supposed to shatter all the preconceived images in their heads, leaving them in the position to let the pieces fall to their feet as they rush toward the person, even if they are just slightly scared to do so.

She'd forgotten what love was like. She'd cast it aside for insecurities that she masked with reasons she believed were valid—or at least she told herself she believed they were.

Yet, now, all those reasons suddenly didn't make sense.

Suddenly, they sounded nothing more than foolish notions she'd made up, even if she'd done so to protect herself.

A hand knocked against the door.

"Come in," Ava called out.

"Good morning." Griffin entered the room, carrying another tray of food for breakfast. He shut the door behind him before making his way to the bed. "How are you feeling this morning?"

"Stiff but otherwise unbroken," Ava said. She snorted a slight laugh as she sat up and leaned against the headboard.

"I'd be surprised if you weren't." Griffin set the tray on the bedside table, removed his hat, and sat on the edge of the bed. The weight of his body moved the whole mattress, and he tilted his chin as he studied her with an odd look.

"What's the matter?" he asked.

"What do you mean?"

He leaned toward her and pressed his finger into her forehead. "You have a deep wrinkle formed right here. The one you always get when your thoughts are bothering you."

Ava brushed his hand away. "That's not true."

"Ava, how many years have we known each other? I know you, even if you don't like that I do—which I know bothers you sometimes—so just make it easy on yourself and me, and tell me what is troubling you."

"It's nothing."

"Thinking about Mr. Harrison?"

"No."

"You know I don't believe you, right?"

Ava crossed her arms, glaring in Griffin's direction as a slight growl rolled through her chest. She didn't know what she hated more: his smugness or the thought of not telling him what bothered her.

She needed to change the subject.

"Have you ever thought of living another type of life?" she asked. Her fingers fidgeted with each other from the nervousness swimming in her stomach. Surely, the question proved innocent; however, the reasoning behind it was far from such a notion.

"What do you mean?"

"Have you ever thought of doing something different? Away from mining, like living a life with a house and a wife in some city or on a cattle ranch where your source of income doesn't come with the risk of death?"

Griffin scratched his chin, and a soft chuckle shook through his shoulders. "Well, I don't know if a cattle ranch is all that safe. I've heard some of those bulls can get quite mean."

Ava playfully slapped the side of his shoulder. "That's not what I meant."

"I know." He chuckled. "I suppose I've thought of marriage—especially now that I have Benjamin. I know he'd benefit from a mother figure in his life. But living in a city, moseying around in some expensive suit, carrying a newspaper, and working in some office building? I don't think I could live that life. I wouldn't know how. But busting each day as a muckman... I know that life. It's hard work, but it's all I've ever wanted to do."

"I understand." She inhaled a deep breath, searching for the right words. "I never grew up desiring to spend my life in the dirt." Ava laughed before the seriousness in her thoughts stole her smile. "But the mines and thoughts of finding gold do kind of just grab hold and don't let go. It gets in your veins."

"I'm sure successful businessmen say the same about their careers, as well as married couples about their spouses and cattle ranchers about their herds—that their choices in life grabbed hold of them and wouldn't let go."

"I suppose you're right."

"So what brought on all these questions?" Griffin asked.

"Just thinking. I suppose I'm simply curious."

"What happened yesterday wouldn't have anything to do with this curiosity, would it?"

Ava shrugged her shoulders.

"You're not thinking it's time to stop mining, are you?"

"No. I'm not. But mines run dry. We both know that."

Griffin nodded. Words seemed to evade him as he studied the breakfast plates on the tray. Morning sunlight filtered through the window, casting shadows on his pale face. "You're different," he said, exhaling a deep breath before continuing. "Something happened to you in that collapse."

Ava opened her mouth to argue but couldn't. His chosen words gnawed at her, and she couldn't help but feel they did because she knew he spoke the truth. Blinded by the years of living only for herself, she'd closed off the notion of anything else as the change was too uncomfortable to take on. However, she knew it was in the shift she'd grown the most. It was a constant in her life that she tried to ignore every day because she knew deep down admitting to it would confess her own weakness—while she believed she held all the cards in this game, she didn't. Had she become someone else? Had she lost what made her, well, her? She'd like to think no, but she couldn't be sure. Would one even see themselves change without someone else noticing it first? Or was it the ones around you who enlightened you to the new person you've become?

"How do you think I'm different?" Ava asked.

"You let a man wash your hair."

"It's not like I could have done it on my own."

"The Ava I knew wouldn't have let him do it. You never let me. Sure, I helped you change your clothes or get you fixed up when an accident happened, but you never let me help clean you up."

"It wouldn't have been proper for you to."

"Proper? We're muckmen, Ava. We left proper behind the second we stepped into the mines the first time." He chuckled. "The Ava I knew would have walked out of that collapsed mineshaft on her own two feet. The Ava I knew would have washed her own body, cursing through the pain like a howling wind, and I know this because you have done so in the past."

"I don't curse." Her eyes met his. Frustration ripped through her voice as she rubbed the back of her neck with her hand so hard her skin whitened from the pressure.

"You're right. You never have." He narrowed his eyes and cocked his head to the side, blowing out an inhaled breath. "So, what's going on? You meet some stranger, fall in love, and then suddenly want a house and children because gold mines can dry up?"

"Craig has nothing to do with this."

Griffin scooted closer to her, the blankets bunched at his hips as he reached for her hand, gently squeezing her fingers. "Why did you let him wash your hair if he doesn't?"

The pit of Ava's stomach churned. She withdrew her hand from his and slid from underneath her blankets, limping to the window. She folded her arms across her chest. Even with the heat from the sun through the glass, her body chilled. Soreness spread through her limbs, but she didn't care. She cared for nothing except facing the awkwardness of telling him the truth.

Her words mocked her, taunting her with their unspoken meanings.

Long ago, she'd sworn off having a man in her life who she could depend on. With thoughts of independence fulfilling her dreams, she vowed only to rely on herself. It was everything she'd wanted.

Or at least everything she thought she wanted.

She never allowed herself to even think about how much she missed a partner, someone she could love and trust to take care of her. However, the truth of the matter was she did. For once in a long time, she felt like someone else could hold her up should she choose to let herself fall. Of course, she didn't know if she could face this notion, yet she wanted to grasp it with all her strength and never let go.

"You know why," she muttered.

"You're right. I do."

"Then why do you ask the question?" She faced him as he rose to his feet. He strode toward her, grabbing her shoulders with his hands.

"Because I wanted you to say it. And not just to me. But to yourself."

Ava faced Griffin, not knowing whether she wanted to throw something at him or forgive him and forget the last several minutes of this conversation. His intentions to shove her into the truth were obvious.

"I hate you, you know that?"

Griffin smiled. "I hate you, too."

Ava opened her mouth, but a knock sounded on the door, stopping her. She glanced at the large chunk of wood as Griffin walked toward it, grabbing the doorknob and twisting it. The door popped open.

"Good morning, Mr. Harrison," Griffin said.

Ava's stomach flipped.

"Good morning, Mr. Baker. I just came by to see how Ava was doing."

"Well, why don't you ask her yourself?" Griffin opened the door wider, motioning for Craig to come inside. He smiled as soon as he saw Ava. "Good morning," he said to her.

"Good morning."

"How are you feeling today? I see you're out of bed."

"Yes, I needed to move around a little. I'm sore but otherwise fine."

"That's good to hear."

Silence fell over them as Ava glanced between the two men. Griffin smiled, also looking at her, then at Craig before he dropped his gaze to the floor, chuckled, and shook his head.

"I've got to get Benjamin to school," he said. "I'll head to the mine when I'm done and get back to work." He glanced at Craig one last time before stepping out and pointed toward Ava. "Good luck with that," he said to Craig, then shut the door behind him, leaving the two alone.

"What is that all about?" Craig asked. He raised one eyebrow, glancing from the door to Ava.

"Just ignore him." Ava waved her hand toward the door. Her heart thumped. If Griffin were still here, she would have smacked him in the back of the head for that.

Craig nodded, and although he looked like he didn't know if he should drop the subject or not, he did. "Well, you look better than you did yesterday. Have you eaten this morning?"

"Griffin brought my breakfast." She pointed toward the tray sitting next to the bed.

"You should eat it before it gets cold."

"I will, although I'm sure it's still good cold. Mrs. Holden is a fabulous cook."

"Yeah, I agree with you on that. I'm surprised everyone in town doesn't weigh four hundred pounds." A slight chuckle whispered across Craig's lips, and he stepped a few more steps toward her. "I take it you slept all right?"

"Yeah. Slept fine."

He moved even closer, inching toward her until he was beside her. She inhaled a sharp breath.

"I—I hope it's all right to say I worried about you."

"Why wouldn't it be all right?"

"It's just—when I found you under all that debris..." He trailed off, shaking his head. "I can't even think about it without feeling sick."

"Well, I'm all right. Thanks to you and Griffin." Her heart pounded so hard that the beat deafened her ears.

Craig shrugged. "We were just doing what anyone would do."

"I suppose that's true. But you did it. You saved my life."

He took a deep breath. His gaze dropped to the floor, his eyes moving from side to side several times before he looked back up at her. His expression changed to utter concern, nearly taking her breath away.

"I can't stop thinking about what could have happened," he whispered. "I don't know what I would have done had I lost you."

Ava's heart skipped a beat at his words. She looked into his eyes, seeing the depth in the hue. "You didn't lose me. I'm right here."

"And I'm so grateful for that. But that's not what I meant."

Although she wasn't sure she was ready for the answer, she asked the question anyway. "What did you mean, then?"

Craig slowly leaned in closer, his face inches from hers. Ava felt her breath catch as he moved even nearer, his eyes never leaving hers. They stared at one another; the moment's intensity cloaked her shoulders. Ava's heart raced, and she could see the same mixture of fear and desire in Craig's eyes. Without another word, Craig leaned into her, pressing his lips against hers. She closed her eyes, losing herself as all her worries and pain melted away.

He pulled away, pressing his forehead into hers. "I'm sorry if I shouldn't have done that."

"Don't apologize. You haven't done anything that you shouldn't."

"I've wanted to kiss you from the moment I saw you at that restaurant. Perhaps even when I saw you at the train station."

"I have thought about it probably a little later than that." She chuckled. "But I have thought about it, too." Her smile faded, and she moved away from him. "There is just one problem, though."

"Let me guess. It's knowing what we do now."

"That would be the one."

Craig opened his mouth, but a sudden, deafening explosion cut him off.

The entire inn shook, walls creaking and floors trembling under the force. Craig and Ava's eyes widened in shock and alarm as they looked at each other, then simultaneously darted to the window.

Everyone in the streets had dropped to the ground, and horses hooked to wagons were rearing at the hitching posts, trying to break free. A massive billow of smoke rose from the mountain, the ominous dark cloud curling into the sky. Her heart pounded in her chest, the implications of the explosion instantly apparent.

Ava clutched her throat. "Is that from..."

"The mine," Craig said, finishing her sentence. "That smoke is coming from the mine."

Before they could even think about what had just happened, a second explosion rocked through town.

"That's a lot of explosives to be felt in town," she whispered.

Craig's expression hardened as he spun toward the door. "I

have to get up there. There are men up there right now. They're in danger or worse..."

"Craig, wait!" Ava called out, pushing herself to the dresser despite the stiffness and pain in her body. "I'm coming with you. I just need to get dressed."

Craig paused at the door, looking at her with concern and urgency. "Ava, you're not in any condition to—"

"I'm not staying here while all the men up there could be in danger. Griffin might even already be up there or on his way," Ava interrupted, her voice firm. "Just give me a moment. Please."

He opened his mouth as though he would argue again but closed it without a word and nodded. He stepped out into the hallway while she dug through her dresser, fetching pants, a blouse, and long socks.

She didn't know what she would do if anything happened to Griffin.

TWENTY-SEVEN

AVA

As soon as she was dressed, Craig wrapped an arm around her waist to support her, and they moved quickly out of the room and down the stairs. Mrs. Holden, Pastor Boone, and anyone in the dining room had already jumped to attention and were standing on the front porch with their hands shielding the sun from their eyes. Their gazes were all trained on the mountains and plumes of smoke.

"It's the mine, isn't it?" Pastor Boone asked Craig.

"Yeah. I need every man available to come with me."

The pastor and a few other men who had been enjoying their morning breakfast trotted after them to the livery to tack up their horses. Other men joined them, and after saddling and bridling their horses, they all galloped for the mine.

The ride to the mine was a blur of fear and determination. Ava clung to the reins, ignoring the pain spreading through her body with her horse's every stride. Craig galloped beside her, weaving through the trees, his jaw set with the grim thoughts on both of their minds.

As they approached the mine, smoke billowed through the trees. The clouded haze smelled of soot and ash, and men were darting in every direction, shouting at one another. A few lay in the dirt while others knelt beside them. The entrance to the main shaft had collapsed, and smoke and dust filled the air. Miners were gathered, some frantically digging at the rubble while others called out for missing friends.

"Griffin!" Ava shouted as they dismounted, and she scanned the crowd for any sign of him. "Griffin, where are you?"

Craig was already moving towards the entrance, his eyes sweeping the scene. "Wyatt! Wyatt, are you here?" He approached several men. "Have you seen Wyatt?"

One of them nodded and pointed in another direction. Ava followed the man's finger just as Craig did, and they both saw Mr. Cooper over by the entrance, grabbing rocks with his bare hands and tossing them aside. He was screaming for the men around him to do the same. Craig and Ava rushed toward him.

"Wyatt! Wyatt!" Craig wrapped his arms around the young man, embracing him tightly. The young man returned the grip. Sweat dripped down his blackened face, and the soot smeared as he wiped his brow with his sleeve. "Are you all right?" Craig asked.

"Yeah. I'm fine," Mr. Cooper shouted. "My hearing isn't so good. I'm sorry that I'm yelling."

"Don't worry about it. What happened?"

"I don't know. The mountain just... it just exploded."

"Are there men trapped inside?"

"Yeah. But I don't know how many. We hadn't started working yet this morning, but a few wanted to get an early start."

"Well, let's get back to digging then." Craig and the other

men began working on the entrance, grabbing and throwing rocks to the side.

Ava still looked around for Griffin, calling his name several times as she moved through the camps. Smoke clouded throughout the trees, burning her eyes and lungs. She coughed several times as she hobbled along.

"Griffin! Griffin!"

"Over here!" a voice called out. Ava spun and gasped as she saw Griffin emerging from the smoke. He rushed toward her, and she wrapped her arms around him.

"Oh, thank God," she whispered.

"What are you doing here? You shouldn't be here," he said. His brow furrowed as he pulled away from her and grabbed her shoulders.

"The explosion rattled the inn, and I—are you all right?" She checked him over, hobbling around him and looking for any injuries.

"Of course, I'm all right. I just got here a few moments ago. I had to get Benjamin to school, remember? I heard the explosion after dropping him off."

"Oh, thank God." She wrapped her arms around him again.

"Mr. Baker!" Craig called out. "We could use your help!"

Griffin pulled away from Ava once more. She moved to follow him, but he caught her arm, concern etched on his face. "You should go back to the inn."

"I'm not leaving, and you know you can't make me."

His jaw clenched, and his gaze hardened. He opened his mouth to disagree, but Craig called for him again.

"Mr. Baker, we could use you now!"

"Fine. But go help the men who are injured." He pointed to the left at the group of men still kneeling next to several lying on the ground, and then he pointed at her. "I don't want to see you near the entrance to that mine. Do you understand me?"

She folded her arms across her chest. "I thought I was the one who gave the orders around here."

"When you aren't healing from getting caught in a collapse, you are. Today, you aren't."

He darted away before she could say another word, joining the men still trying to clear the entrance. Ava hobbled over to the men lying on the ground.

"How can I help?" she asked.

As Ava bandaged the injuries she could, the men worked to get the shaft cleared.

"Mr. Baker!" Craig called out. "We could use your help!"

Griffin pulled away from Ava once more. She moved to follow him, but he caught her arm, concern etched on his face. "You shouldn't be here. You're still recovering."

"I'm not leaving, and you know you can't make me."

His jaw clenched, and his gaze hardened. He opened his mouth to disagree, but Craig called for him again.

"Mr. Baker, we could use you now!"

"Fine. But go help the men who are injured." He pointed to the left at the group of men still kneeling next to several lying on the ground, and then he pointed at her. "I don't want to see you near the entrance to that mine. Do you understand me?"

She folded her arms across her chest. "I thought I was the one who gave the orders around here."

"When you aren't healing from getting caught in a collapse, then you are. Today, you aren't." Before she could say anything, he trotted toward Craig, rolling up his sleeves. He jumped between two men, grabbing rocks without even pausing to think about how he would help.

The air was thick with smoke and dust, making breathing difficult. Ava's heart ached with every cry for help, whether from those injured or those still trapped. Every face that worked throughout the camp was covered in soot and fear.

Ava continued from man to man, wrapping and bandaging

arms and legs. She helped pass around a bucket of water, lifting heads so they could drink from the ladle easier. She dunked rags in other buckets of water, wiping down soot-covered faces and helping those who couldn't see or didn't want to open their eyes in fear of how painful it would be if they did.

"We need to stabilize this section before it collapses further," Craig called out, directing several miners to reinforce the entrance. "Keep digging, but be careful. We don't want another cave-in."

Minutes ticked by. Each one felt like years on their own.

"Keep going," Craig urged, his voice steady. "We need to get everyone out."

They continued to dig, their efforts driven by the cries and pleas of those still trapped.

After wrapping the leg of the last injured man, she knelt in the dirt, watching as Craig, Griffin, Pastor Boone, and several others lifted a heavy log. Their muscles strained against the weight of the wood. Sweat dripped from all their faces, and a few of them grunted so loudly the sounds echoed through the trees. Time seemed to blur as they worked tirelessly, and the minutes stretched into an unending effort to save those trapped inside.

She closed her eyes, willing for strength.

How can I have strength when I can't even help?

A slight growl vibrated through her chest, and her annoyance bubbled.

She needed to do more than just stand around and wrap wounds.

She needed to fix the mess.

She needed to move the mountain herself and rescue the men.

She lunged forward, but a voice whispered, stopping her after only two steps. "*Surrender.*"

What? Is this voice kidding? Surrender? Now?

She closed her eyes, shaking her head as she took another step.

"*Surrender,*" the voice said again.

She inhaled a deep breath, clamping her eyes tighter. A tiny part of her tried to fight what the other part knew she had to do. She'd always depended on herself, believing that even if she might need help, she wouldn't get it, so why bother asking in the first place?

"Surrender," she whispered. Her knees hit the dirt, and she inhaled deeply, lowering her chin.

Lord,
Please forgive me for not doing this right. I will get better. I promise. I know I haven't been the best at believing in the power of kindness and love, but I—I know you can do anything, and right now... well, I need your help. The men in that mine need your help. The men outside trying to save the men in the mine need your help. We all need you. Please help us. Help us free the trapped men. Help them survive. I don't know what else to say. Please help us. I pray this in Jesus' name. Amen.

∽

Hours passed, and more townsfolk arrived to help. Everyone dug away the rocks that they could until they finally uncovered a hole through the entrance of the shaft. Relief washed over everyone as the men emerged, one by one, their faces ghostly pale beneath the grime.

Ava rushed over to them, helping wipe their faces and giving them a drink of water. The camp was an echo of coughing men patting each other on the back while they asked one another if they were all right or needed help. While everyone seemed to take a deep breath, dwelling in the moment that at least people were safe, more townsfolk began to arrive, including Dr. Sterling and Mayor Duncan.

Dr. Sterling rushed around the wounded, apologizing for not being there sooner. One by one, he worked on each one and continued through the men, focusing on the ones needing care back in town first.

"Get everyone you can into my wagon, and I'll take them back to town," he said, finishing what he could to render them aid in camp.

With the help of a few others, Craig, Griffin, and Wyatt pushed through the crowds with those in need clinging to them. They helped all that needed it into the back of the doctor's wagon, and once everyone was secure, the doctor climbed onto the buckboard, grabbing the reins and slapping them on the horses' backs. The rest of the townsfolk and miners who stayed behind watched the wagon until it vanished down the trail.

A collective sigh seemed to wash through everyone in camp. Most of the men who hadn't been injured sat in the dirt, wiping their faces with wet rags. Exhaustion plagued their shoulders. A few made their way to their horses, climbing on and riding toward town, surely with their families on their minds. One of them, a young man, hugged Mr. Cooper before he left.

"Tell Rachel I'm all right," Mr. Cooper asked the man, who nodded and gave him a thumbs-up.

Craig, Griffin, Mr. Cooper, and Ava all turned toward the mine shaft, studying the damage to the outside.

"Do you think we should even try to see what the inside shafts look like?" Griffin asked.

Craig nodded. "It will take a while, but I believe it can be rebuilt."

Someone cleared their throat behind them, and they turned to see Mayor Duncan standing only a few feet away. His eyes were wide as he saw all the rubble, and he gulped before he spoke. His voice cracked slightly. "I—I'm glad no one died."

"We are, too."

"I suppose this means the bet is off, and there is no winner. I shall have to take the highest offer and award the mountain to Mr. Miller."

"What are you talking about?" Craig stepped toward him. His shoulders were tight, and his brow was furrowed. "I won the bet. I found gold just before the explosion. In fact, I think that's why the mine was blown up. Mr. Miller found out about the vein I discovered."

Mayor Duncan's mouth fell open. "That's a rather bold claim to make, Mr. Harrison."

"Bold, but true. Everyone here knows I found that vein, and each man can and will vouch for it. I won that bet, Mayor Duncan. Rattlesnake Mountain is mine."

"Well, now, just hold on a minute, Mr. Harrison. I didn't see the vein. How do I know for sure you found it?"

"You can't be serious." Craig clenched his hands into fists, digging them into his hips as he spun in a couple of circles. "Are you accusing me of lying?"

"All I'm saying is that I didn't see the gold. Therefore, I can't judge who won."

"How long have you known me, Mayor Duncan? How long has every man in this town known me? Have I ever lied?"

"Well, no, but—"

"Then why do you think I would lie about this?"

The mayor lifted his hands, holding them in front of his chest as if he meant to calm the anger Ava could see pulsing through Craig's whole body. Not that she blamed him. She'd be furious, too. In fact, she already was. If any man was the liar in this situation, it would be Mr. Miller, not Craig.

"We just need to get Mr. Miller here and have a meeting before any decisions are made," the mayor said.

Craig's nostrils flared, and he pointed at the mayor's chest.

"If that's how you're going to play, then I suggest you send someone to town to send him a telegram."

TWENTY-EIGHT

CRAIG

For our struggle is not against flesh and blood, but against the rulers, against the authorities, against the powers of this dark world, and against the spiritual forces of evil in the heavenly realms. **Ephesians 6:12**

Craig stood in the mayor's office, his jaw set with determination. The room was filled with the heavy silence of expectations he feared wouldn't be met and the tension thick enough to cut with a knife. He glanced at Ava, who stood beside him with Griffin and Pastor Boone to her left.

Different Bible verses circled his mind—verses about good and evil, verses about remaining steadfast and calm, even his favorite verses, even though they didn't make sense in this situation, just to distract him from the meeting about to start. He wasn't sure what the outcome would be or what Mayor Duncan would decide. Gut instinct told him he wasn't going to like it.

Mr. Miller stood to his right, leaning on his walking stick with his head cocked to one side. Flanked by Sheriff Thorn, who watched without saying a word, Mr. Miller's expression was a mask of indignant outrage with a hint of smugness, which did little to ease Craig's already burdened confidence.

This couldn't be it.

This couldn't be the end.

He'd found that vein fair and square.

Mayor Duncan sat in his desk chair and scooted it up to the desk. The legs scraped across the hardwood floor, making a sound that pierced Craig's ear as it echoed throughout the room.

"I had hoped that the bet between the two of you would have made the purchase of Rattlesnake Mountain easier. Unfortunately, that is not the case," the mayor said. He rested his elbows on the desk and clasped his hands together.

"I don't understand how it's not easy," Craig said, his jaw clenched. "I found the gold. I won. And because Mr. Miller knew that I'd found the gold, he blew up the mountain to hide my discovery."

Mr. Miller glanced at Craig with mild irritation glinting in his eyes. "You've made quite the serious accusation, Mr. Harrison. Tell me, do you have any proof to back it up?"

"I don't have to provide proof. I know the explosion at the mine wasn't an accident. It was sabotage. And there is only one in this room who was behind it."

"And just what makes you so sure of that?" Mr. Miller asked.

"Several things," Craig replied as he finally looked at the tall, thin man, his voice steady. "First, the timing. Mr. Miller's been desperate to win the mining contest, and he knows he's losing. Second, the method. The explosion was too precise, too targeted. It wasn't a random collapse; it was a deliberate act. Third, his reputation. He has a history of stopping at nothing to get something he wants, and he wanted that mountain for reasons I don't know, but I'm pretty sure I could guess."

"Well, I see I'm just an open book to you, Mr. Harrison. Tell me, what did I have for breakfast this morning? Or for lunch this afternoon? Since you know me so well, of course."

"Don't be ridiculous."

"I'm being ridiculous? I'm not the one making accusations I can't prove. Accusing me of sabotage is a low blow, Mr. Harrison, even for you."

Craig met Miller's gaze head-on, refusing to back down. "I know it was you, Mr. Miller. You've been trying to undermine me and secure a victory from the start."

Mr. Miller scoffed; his eyes darkened. "And yet you have no proof. Perhaps it was you who blew up the mine."

"Me? Why would I blow up a mountain and mine I'm trying to win?"

"To secure your victory. For all I know, this could be just another of your desperate attempts to discredit me." He stepped forward and turned toward all of them, leaning against the mayor's desk. "Or perhaps it was her." His chin motioned toward Ava.

Her eyes widened.

"She's your employee."

"Exactly. My employee. The one who is standing next to you and not me. Perhaps she blew it up because she wanted to win. Or perhaps you both dreamed up this scheme to win the mountain for yourselves." Mr. Miller's eyes narrowed. "This is a baseless accusation concocted by Mr. Harrison and Miss Adams to win the mining contest. They're trying to frame me because they know they can't beat me fairly. I know they had secret meetings behind my back. I caught them myself having lunch at the inn."

Ava turned toward Mr. Miller. "I would never do anything you have accused me of. That meeting wasn't about anything other than the safety of our men. You were willing to put lives at risk to get what you wanted. I wasn't."

"Again, another accusation you can't prove."

"Common sense proves it, Mr. Miller," Craig said. "We all know what you're capable of. Everyone in Featherstone Valley does. Don't think we aren't all aware of what you did in Deer Creek."

Mr. Miller laughed, a harsh, mocking sound. "Oh please, spare me the sanctimony. All I've done in Deer Creek is make the town money."

"We don't want your money in this town!" Craig lunged toward Mr. Miller, but Mr. Baker grabbed his arms, stopping him. Sheriff Thorn moved too, and as he looked at Craig, he shook his head as if to silently tell him no.

"He's not worth it, Mr. Harrison," Mr. Baker said.

Craig spun and walked away, heaving several breaths as he closed his eyes. As much as he wanted to lose control, he knew he couldn't. He had to hold it together. He couldn't let someone like Sidney Miller get under his skin and make him do something he would later regret—even if it felt good at the moment.

Pastor Boone walked beside him, laying a hand on Craig's shoulders. "Take a moment and remember to stay calm. *James 1:19*, My dear brothers and sisters, take note of this: Everyone should be quick to listen, slow to speak, and slow to become angry."

"Yeah, well, even Jesus flipped tables," Craig whispered.

Pastor Boone chuckled. "You're right; he did. But I would suggest not doing that right now. For one, there are no tables, and for two, I doubt flipping the mayor's desk would be easy or a good thing to do."

Craig snorted, smiling as he dropped his gaze to the floor and shook his head. "Mr. Miller will ruin this town. You know that, right?"

"I do. But how this unfolds is not up to us."

"Are you saying that we should sit by and do nothing because God might choose to bring a man like that into this town?"

"No. But I am telling you the same thing that I told Miss Adams. Surrender and have faith."

Craig closed his eyes for another second and inhaled a sharp breath. He turned back to everyone in the room and returned to the mayor's desk.

"Both of you have made serious accusations against one another," Mayor Duncan finally said. "And we need to address them properly, which is why I asked Sheriff Thorn to be present today. Mr. Miller, are you denying any involvement in the explosion?"

"Absolutely," Miller said without hesitation. "I had nothing to do with it. This is all a smear campaign by Mr. Harrison and Miss Adams."

The mayor looked at Craig, his expression thoughtful. "Mr. Harrison, without concrete proof, it's hard to take action against Mr. Miller. Do you have any evidence?"

Craig's heart sank. "Not at this time. But I'm sure after we've cleaned up the campsite and the mine shafts, we will find what we need to prove it."

The mayor sighed. "I understand your concerns about the situation, Mr. Harrison, but I can't ask the sheriff to act on accusations alone. I need proof." The mayor paused, unclasping his hands and pointing a finger at his desk, pressing down on the wood so hard his skin turned white. "I also need proof you found gold."

"Once we clean up the mine, I can show you where the vein was and prove it was on my side."

Mr. Miller chuckled. "Why does that sound like a ploy to get more time to mine for gold and win the bet?"

"Because it's not a ploy. I've already found the gold and know where it is."

"And I'm supposed to believe that?" Mr. Miller grabbed the bridge of his nose. "Mayor Duncan, I'm failing to see why you can't see that this man is a liar and a cheat."

"He's not a liar." Ava stepped toward the mayor's desk, barely glancing in Mr. Miller's direction. "I saw the vein myself, which was clearly on Mr. Harrison's side. He found it."

Mr. Miller rounded his shoulders, tucking his chin down momentarily while tapping his walking stick on the hardwood floor. "More lies? I hoped you wouldn't stoop so low as to have a woman lie for you, too."

"I'm not lying." Ava clenched her jawline.

"We all know there is no stock in a woman's word, Miss Adams. I suggest you remember that before opening your mouth."

Mr. Baker moved beside her. "Ava isn't lying, but if it's the word of a man you need, you can have mine. I saw the vein, too. Mr. Harrison was the first to find it. I can even show it to you on the map he made of his side of the mountain."

Mr. Miller stared at Mr. Baker. His eyes narrowed. "And we are supposed to believe you even though you are with her—the one who we obviously can't trust because she has shown her disloyalty to the company that employs her."

"Disloyalty?" She raised one eyebrow. "Don't think I don't know how you got me out here. Don't think I didn't figure it out. You called in a favor to the men who employed me, and they fired me, handing me your telegram and my last pay. You wanted me to win you a mountain, that's all."

"Which is something you failed to do."

"And tell me, would you have kept me around if I had? Or would you have replaced me with someone who didn't give a lick about that mountain or the gold underneath it?"

"People don't want you in this town, Mr. Miller," Craig said, moving slightly between Mr. Miller and Ava to show the man that he would protect her no matter what. In fact, he almost wanted to beg Mr. Miller to do something just to give him an excuse to knock Mr. Miller into next Tuesday.

"Do you think I care about that?"

"You should care. You've lost. It's time to leave and go back to Deer Creek. No one wants you here."

"I suppose you speak for everyone, too."

"He's not wrong." Pastor Boone moved back toward the group, standing next to Craig. "The people of this town don't want you here. That much I know. I've heard the talk. I've heard the prayers." He glanced at the mayor. "You need to deal with this."

"Actually, I don't." The mayor stood from his desk and grabbed a stack of papers.

"What is that supposed to mean?" Craig asked.

"Mr. Harrison, I believe you did find the gold first, and with that, Rattlesnake Mountain is yours for the sum of your last offer. Pay the bank, and he'll get you the deed." He paused, taking a few breaths as he moved around the desk. His steps were slow, almost calculated, with a mix of hesitation and something else—regret, perhaps. "It is for the betterment of this town that I have decided to resign as mayor, and in my resignation, I have also decided that since it is in the town's best interest, I choose to name my successor. This man will take over the duties as mayor until the next election."

"But that's two years from now," Craig said, a lump forming in his throat, nearly choking him. Although he tried to ignore the gut feeling stirring in his stomach, he couldn't. He could almost see the situation unfolding, and the desperation to stop it flooded his mind.

This can't happen.

"You can't pick your replacement. The Town Council will never approve of it because they are the ones who choose who will act as mayor until the next election."

"That's not always the case. Under Town Charter Code 1902.15, it states, and I quote, 'in the event that the mayor is unable to fulfill their duties due to extraordinary circumstances, they may appoint a temporary replacement for the good of the town who will act as the mayor until the next election.'"

"Don't you dare do this, Mayor Duncan," Craig said, shaking his head. "Don't you dare do what I think you're about to do."

"I'm sorry, Mr. Harrison. But it's my decision, and I would like to announce that my replacement will be Mr. Sidney Miller."

"You can't do this." Craig looked at Sheriff Thorn. "Please tell me he can't do this."

Sheriff Thorn dropped his gaze to the floor. His shoulders hunched.

"I'm sorry to inform you that I can do this, and I have. I'll be announcing it to the town later this afternoon."

TWENTY-NINE

CRAIG

Do not be overcome by evil, but overcome evil with good. **Romans 12:21**

Craig closed his eyes. In all the years he'd spent on this earth—and even those spent up in the wild dangers of the Klondike—he'd never thought he'd be facing what he was. So much of him wished he could pinch himself and wake up from this nightmare.

Surely, that was what it was, right?

A nightmare.

The thought of Mr. Sidney Miller as mayor of his town brought waves of panic and anger, flooding every inch of his mind until he thought he might go mad.

Just what on earth was Mayor Duncan thinking?

He stared at the plump man standing on the porch of the mayor's office. His shoulders were hunched, and his face was pale. He looked like death on legs as he faced the crowd of townsfolk who had gathered in the street to hear his announcement.

Craig looked around the crowd. The air was thick with

uncertainty, while everyone's faces were filled with confusion and concern.

"Thank you all for coming," the mayor said, pausing and clearing his throat. His voice slightly cracked as he continued. "I know there have been many questions and concerns following the recent events at the mine. I want to address those now. While we have not yet uncovered who is responsible for the explosion, we remain vigilant over Rattlesnake Mountain. We've started an investigation and hope Sheriff Thorn will get the clues he needs to solve the case. The mayor's office will, of course, help in any way it can. The safety of the mines and the workers is paramount."

"If you cared about us, you wouldn't have made the bet you did with Mr. Miller, putting his team so close to ours; it was just an accident waiting to happen!"

Craig glanced over to see Reed Hall, a young miner from his team, shouting with a hand cupped to one side of his mouth, making his voice boom from across the street. While a small part of him wanted to disagree that the teams working so close weren't the reason for the unsafe conditions, he couldn't deny he had hated the idea of them sharing a main shaft any more than his men did. Of course, if they hadn't worked together, however, he never would have gotten close with Ava. It was, by definition, a paradox.

The mayor squinted as he searched the crowd for the voice, finally finding Reed before the young man finished his sentence.

"Both Mr. Harrison and Miss Adams agreed to the terms, young man," Mayor Duncan said to Mr. Hall. "I suggest you take your complaints to them."

"I trust Mr. Harrison more than I trust you. If he agreed, it was because you and Mr. Miller forced him into it!" With Mr. Hall's shouted retort, several of the other miners the young man and his wife were standing with also shouted in echoes of agreement.

Mayor Duncan looked at Craig. "Do you want to do something about that?"

"What do you want me to do?" Craig asked, shrugging. "They aren't wrong. You set the terms, and there was no talking you out of them."

The mayor glared at Craig, cleared his throat, and continued with his announcement. "It was an unfortunate accident, and we should just thank God that no one was killed. Those who were injured are recovering, and Mr. Harrison and his company have been awarded the mountain for finding gold first."

While Craig's team cheered and gave each other high-fives, Craig glanced at Ava standing next to him. She smiled, slightly nodded, and grabbed his hand, squeezing it tight as she leaned in and rested her chin on his shoulder.

"You deserve that mountain. You found the gold first."

"Yeah, but at what cost?" He turned away from her, ignoring the questioning look in her eyes as he turned to Pastor Boone standing on his other side.

"How did it come to this? The townspeople don't even know their lives are about to change."

"Please quiet down!" Mayor Duncan raised his arms to gain everyone's attention once more. "Please. I have another announcement to make. It is with regret and hope that I announce to you all that I am resigning from office as your mayor."

Although most silenced themselves when Mayor Duncan asked everyone to be quiet, there were a few whispered conversations still going on when he started speaking again. By the time he finished his announcement, the streets were so silent that Craig could have heard a pin drop in the dirt.

Craig glanced around, watching as the townsfolk around him all looked at one another with wide eyes and mouths gaped open. This wasn't even the worst part of the announcement, yet he could feel the shock and speechlessness wash through the town.

"Due to the timing of my resignation, I have decided that since it is in the town's best interest, I will choose my replacement without the help of the Town Council."

"You can't do that!" a voice shouted. Craig noticed Mr. Rutherford, the livery's owner, weave through the crowd toward the mayor. He shook his head and pointed at the mayor. "The Town Council decides who will replace you until the next election."

"Not according to Town Charter Code 1902.15. The code states that should I feel my choice is best for the town, I can legally make the choice."

Craig closed his eyes, sucking in a deep breath. Ava squeezed his hand harder.

"So, who is your replacement, Mayor?" Mr. Rutherford asked.

Mayor Duncan glanced over to Mr. Miller, motioning toward him. "It's this man right here. Mr. Sidney Miller. Your new mayor of Featherstone Valley."

While a few people clapped two or three times, they were slow claps, like the ones that people give when they don't want to celebrate in any way but don't know what else to do and feel obligated to applaud. Everyone glanced around at one another. Men furrowed their brows, and women clasped their hands over their mouths. The collective shock sent waves of bubbling panic throughout the crowd.

"We don't want Miller in our town!" Mr. Hall shouted.

Several around him agreed, throwing their fists in the air. A chorus of agreement rose from the crowd, with Mr. Rutherford leading the charge. "That's right! We don't need his kind here, bringing in booze and women. It'll ruin everything we've built!"

Agreement spread throughout the townsfolk once more.

The only one who seemed even remotely happy with the notion was Mr. Whitmore, the bank owner.

Of course, he would be satisfied with the choice. If Mr. Miller brought more businesses to Featherstone Valley, that would mean more money for his bank.

He stood in the distance, leaning against a bench outside the newspaper office. Mr. Jenkins, the editor of The Featherstone Valley Gazette, stood with him, and the two men watched the scene, saying nothing.

The rest of the townsfolk—Mr. and Mrs. Lockhart, Mr. and Mrs. Gables, Mr. and Mrs. Benson, and Mr. and Mrs. Randall, to name a few—continued looking around at one another.

Craig turned to Pastor Boone, his voice low. "Is it just me, or have you considered how this situation doesn't add up? The way it all went down... Mr. Miller isn't even a resident of Featherstone Valley, and he doesn't seem to care about the mountain anymore."

"I've noticed it."

"I don't understand why, or why Mayor Duncan didn't even go to the town council about his resignation, or why he hasn't explained how this is in the town's best interest." Craig's eyes scanned the street, landing on Wyatt, standing nearby with Mr. and Mrs. Hall. His face was flushed with anger.

"Mayor Duncan?" Mr. Lockhart finally stepped forward, leaving his wife's side. "How can you allow this? How can this be good for Featherstone Valley?"

Several others began shouting in agreement, and a collective of 'yeahs' and 'hows' echoed through the street.

The mayor raised his hands, trying to calm the crowd. "Please, let me explain. I understand your concerns, but Mr. Miller has promised significant investments in our town. He believes this will bring prosperity and growth. This is why I believe it will be for the betterment of the town."

"Prosperity at what cost?" shouted Mr. Gables. "We don't want saloons and brothels corrupting our community!"

Sidney Miller lifted his hands as though to calm the town. Everyone in the street silenced, staring at him. "Townspeople of Featherstone Valley, I assure you, my intentions as your new mayor are to improve this town and nothing more. With my ideas, I will bring in new businesses, create jobs, and make Featherstone Valley a thriving community just as I did in Deer Creek."

Mr. Rutherford scoffed loudly. "And at what cost, Mr. Miller? We know what kind of business you bring to the table. We don't need your 'improvements.'"

"That's not entirely true," Mr. Whitmore disagreed. "I believe Mr. Miller's investments could benefit the town's economy. We need to consider all sides of this."

"It's not just about the economy, Mr. Whitmore. Of course, the owner of the bank will only see money." Mr. Rutherford looked at the men around him, and after they nodded their agreement, he pointed toward the bank owner. "It's about the kind of town we want to be. We don't want to compromise our values for the sake of profit."

The crowd erupted into shouts and arguments, and the street filled with voices. Craig exchanged a look with Ava, who shook her head in dismay.

"Had I only known..." she whispered. "I wouldn't have taken the job."

"He would have found another. The bet was set in motion long before he hired you."

Craig turned to Pastor Boone. "We need to do something. We can't let Mr. Miller take over this town without a fight."

The pastor nodded. "I agree. But not like this. Chaos will only make things worse."

Craig stepped forward, raising his voice to the unrest.

"Everyone, please! Arguing amongst ourselves won't solve anything."

The crowd quieted slightly, turning their attention to Craig. He took a deep breath, trying to steady his nerves.

"We all care about this town," he continued. "We've built our lives here and want what's best for Featherstone Valley. This is a big announcement, and we all need a moment to digest it. We can't just react out of fear."

"Thank you, Mr. Harrison." A smile inched across Mr. Miller's face.

"Don't you dare speak to me. I disagree with you standing up there and will never support you. I demand transparency and accountability through an investigation into Mr. Miller's actions to ensure that any decisions made are in the best interest of Featherstone Valley."

"Demand all you wish, Mr. Harrison. But no matter what, I've made the choice, and the choice is final. I understand your concerns," the mayor said, his voice wavering slightly. "But this is my choice, and as your mayor, you must respect it."

Without another word, Mayor Duncan and Mr. Miller turned and retreated into the mayor's office, shutting the door behind them. The crowd still shouted question after question, and some even rushed toward the door, pounding on the wood and glass.

Sheriff Thorn made his way over to Craig and rested his hands on his hips.

"A lot of good you did today," Craig said to him.

"What am I supposed to do? He's following the law. Even if I don't think it's right, I can't do anything about it."

"Did you look into this Town Charter Code 1902.15?"

"I did, and it allows him to do what he's doing. Now, if you can find me some evidence linking Mr. Miller to that explosion... well, then I have something to work with." The sheriff shook his head. "As it stands right now, though, he hasn't done anything that the law says he can't. I checked it twice."

"What do you think we should do?" Craig asked Pastor Boone.

The pastor watched the townsfolk, shaking his head. "Have faith for one."

"Well, yeah, I figured that. But I wasn't asking our pastor what we should do. I was asking the Texas Ranger what we should do."

Pastor Boone glanced at him. A slight flicker of amusement whispered in the glint of his eyes. He smiled. "Start cleaning up that mine and find Sheriff Thorn and me some evidence."

"I'll get my men started on it tomorrow."

While Pastor Boone and Sheriff Thorn left the street and headed with Mrs. Holden back to the inn, Craig stayed behind with Ava and Mr. Baker. The three watched the townsfolk continue to try to get into the mayor's office. Although Craig wanted nothing more than to join them, he knew that wasn't how. They couldn't stop this from happening any more than they could stop a train rolling down the tracks.

They'd have to beat Mr. Miller at his own game.

Pure and simple.

He heaved a sigh. "Well, I guess the work begins tomorrow. Do you two think you're up to it?" he asked Mr. Baker and Ava.

Ava blinked at him, brushing her hand against her chest. "Us?"

"Yeah, you two are working with me now. Aren't you?"

She glanced at Mr. Baker, who nodded. "I know I don't want to leave," he said. "I'm quite happy in this town, and Benjamin is too." He backed away a few steps. "And speaking of which, I need to fetch him from school. Don't worry, Mr. Harrison, I'll be at the mine in the morning ready to get my hands dirty."

"Sounds good."

They watched as he walked away, and as Craig inhaled, Ava turned toward him. "So, I'm your employee now?" she asked.

He chuckled. "Well, I hoped you'd be more than that. But that's up to you."

"More as in... your head foreman?" She cocked her head to one side, fluttering her eyes.

He chuckled again. "More than that even."

"Oh. Well, now I'm intrigued. Just exactly what position in your company did you have in mind for me?"

He licked his lips, giving her a coy smile as he stuck out his hand. "Partner."

"Partner? Like fifty-fifty?"

"Yeah. I suppose." He moved closer to her, wrapping his arms around her waist. "Of course, say down the road... maybe we can renegotiate."

"Renegotiate? As in how?"

"Well, don't married couples share everything?"

"Marriage? That's quite bold of you to say, Mr. Harrison."

"So, is that a no to the idea?" He kissed her, and she pulled slightly away, lowering her voice.

"No, it's not a no," she whispered. "It's certainly not a no."

∽

ELIZABETH

Elizabeth stood by the window of her hotel room, gazing down at the bustling town square. She could hear the men and women of the town shouting through the glass, but their words were muffled.

It didn't take much to figure out they were shouting about Mr. Miller and their... how should she put it... displeasure with him.

Of course, she was used to that.

There were always people shouting about how much they disliked him.

It was nothing new.

More often than not, she didn't blame them.

She didn't like Sidney much herself.

Although he would never know that. She wasn't stupid.

She'd be homeless, begging for food, if it weren't for Sidney Miller, which was precisely where he found her two years ago. She wasn't about to return to that life, even if she hated this one. Homelessness and hunger were far worse than having to entertain a stupid man for thirty minutes a few times a day.

Of course, now that she'd become one of Sidney's favorites, the time she spent with other men had lessened more and more. Now, instead of several men a day, it was only him, and it was few and far between that they did anything other than just lie in bed, fully clothed, while she listened to him talk about his grand plans in life. Not that she listened much, and she doubted he cared that she didn't. Or at least that was how she felt.

She pressed her hand on the glass, brushing the sheer curtains back with the other. A figure caught the corner of her eye, and as she looked down, the young man who had helped her with her luggage when she arrived looked up.

What was his name again?

Wyatt... something. Cooper?

Yes, that was it. Mr. Wyatt Cooper.

An eager young man who looked at her in a way most men didn't, and he caught her off guard. It was almost as though he saw nothing but a proper young lady and not the...

Well, not the woman of questionable morals, as one might say.

Did he not know who I was?

She stared at the young man through the window, and time seemed to stand still. She inhaled a deep breath as a knot tightened in her chest, and she shoved away from the window, crossing the room and fidgeting with her hands.

A knock rattled through the door, and before she could reach for the knob, it opened, and Sidney walked inside.

"Pack your things, Elizabeth," he said.

"Now?"

"Yes. I need you to be ready to leave in about ten minutes."

"Oh. All right." She turned toward her dresser, opening the top drawer. "Are we returning to Deer Creek?"

Sidney's gaze softened slightly, and he shook his head. "No. Well, I am, but you're staying in here."

Her brow furrowed, and she froze. "If I'm staying here, why am I packing?"

"Not here as in the inn. Here as in Featherstone Valley."

"I'm staying..." She hesitated, her thoughts swirling. "But why?"

Sidney approached her and laid his hands on her shoulders. "You're looking at the new mayor of Featherstone Valley."

"They—they made you the mayor?" Although she didn't mean to, her voice shifted oddly, as though, in her shock, it was hard to believe him. A hint of anger flared in his eyes, and she smiled, reaching for his hand to settle the beast before he could turn. "What am I saying? Of course, they made you mayor. They would be foolish not to."

The evil monster still lingered in his eyes, but he studied her and smiled instead of lashing out. "Just think about everything we will do with this town and the money we can make."

We?

"What about Deer Creek? What about the saloon?"

He shrugged. "Liam can run them. They aren't a concern anymore. The only thing that matters is this town." He paused, glancing around the room. "Now, finish packing. You're moving to the mayor's house."

THE STORIES OF THE RESIDENTS OF FEATHERSTONE VALLEY AREN'T OVER...

THIS IS STILL ONLY THE BEGINNING...

WANT MORE OF FEATHERSTONE VALLEY?

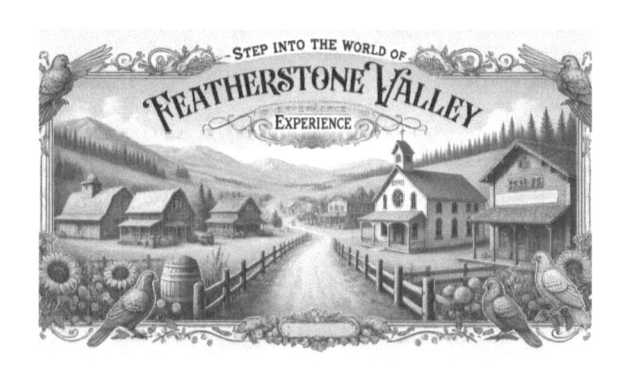

Step into *The Featherstone Valley Experience*—your chance to immerse yourself in the heart of this spirited Montana town! Each week, receive exclusive emails filled with heartfelt stories, delightful surprises, and exciting town happenings. Meet quirky neighbors, explore local businesses, and enjoy content from the *Featherstone Valley Gazette*, including gossip, coupons, and wanted ads. Interactive games, polls, and challenges make you feel like a true part of the community. It's free, fun, and the perfect way to enhance your Featherstone Valley reading journey. Don't miss out—sign up now and start your first adventure!

JOIN TODAY

WHISPERS IN FEATHERSTONE VALLEY

BOOK #3 ~ FEATHERSTONE VALLEY SERIES

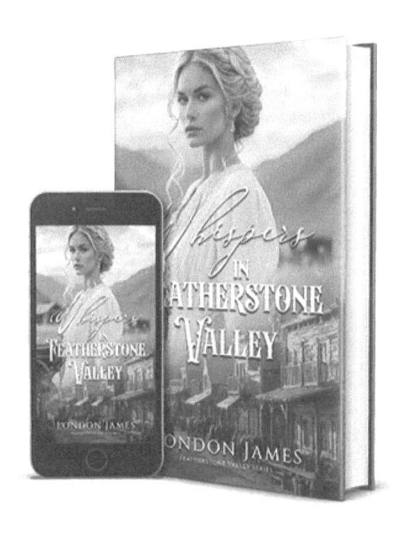

Will Elizabeth find the strength to reclaim her life and heart, or will the shadows of her past forever define her future? Journey with Elizabeth and Wyatt in a tale of love, resilience, and the transformative power of forgiveness and redemption.

WHISPERS IN FEATHERSTONE VALLEY

WAGON TRAIN WOMEN

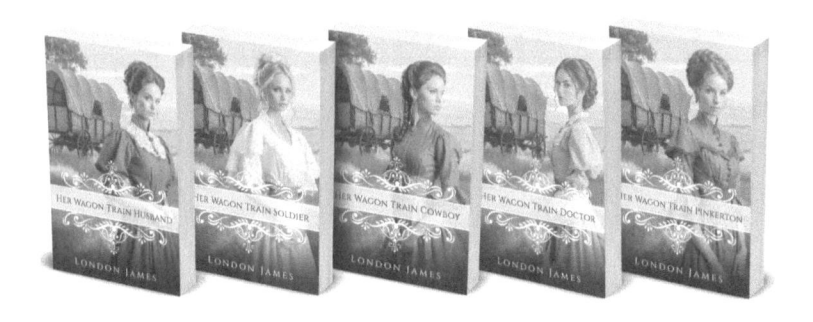

Five women headed out West to make new lives on the Frontier find hope and love in the arms of five men. Their adventures may be different, but their bond is the same as they embark on the journey together in the same wagon train.

CEHCK OUT THE SERIES ON AMAZON

OREGON TRAIL BRIDES

Four orphans and their headmistress set out for Oregon in search of men looking for mail-order brides. Will they find what they are looking for? Or will fate have other plans?

CHECK OUT THE SERIES ON AMAZON

BRIDES OF LONE HOLLOW

FIVE MEN LOOKING FOR LOVE...

FIVE WOMEN WITH DIFFERENT IDEAS...

ONE SMALL TOWN WHERE THEY ALL WILL EITHER LIVE HAPPILY EVER AFTER OR LEAVE WITH SHATTERED DREAMS.

CHECK OUT THE SERIES ON AMAZON

To my sister
Michelle Renee Horning

April 3, 1971 - January 8, 2022
You will be forever missed. I don't know how I'm going to do this thing called life without you.

LONDON JAMES IS A PEN NAME FOR ANGELA CHRISTINA ARCHER. SHE LIVES ON A RANCH WITH HER HUSBAND, TWO DAUGHTERS, AND MANY FARM ANIMALS. SHE WAS BORN AND RAISED IN NEVADA AND GREW UP RIDING AND SHOWING HORSES. WHILE SHE DOESN'T SHOW ANYMORE, SHE STILL LOVES TO TRAIL RIDE.

FROM A YOUNG AGE, SHE ALWAYS WANTED TO WRITE A NOVEL. HOWEVER, EVERY TIME THE DESIRE FLICKERED, SHE SHOVED THE THOUGHT FROM MY MIND UNTIL ONE MORNING IN 2009, SHE AWOKE WITH THE DETERMINATION TO FOLLOW HER DREAM.

WWW.LONDONJAMESBOOKS.COM

JOIN MY MAILING LIST FOR NEWS ON RELEASES, DISCOUNTED SALES, AND EXCLUSIVE MEMBER-ONLY BENEFITS!

COPYRIGHT © 2024

COVER DESIGN BY ANGELA ARCHER, LONG VALLEY DESIGNS

THIS BOOK IS A WORK OF FICTION. THE NAMES, CHARACTERS, PLACES, AND INCIDENTS ARE THE PRODUCTS OF THE AUTHOR'S IMAGINATION OR ARE USED FICTITIOUSLY.

ANY RESEMBLANCE TO ACTUAL EVENTS, BUSINESS ESTABLISHMENTS, LOCALES, OR PERSONS, LIVING OR DEAD, IS ENTIRELY COINCIDENTAL.

ALL RIGHTS RESERVED.

NO PART OF THIS PUBLICATION MAY BE REPRODUCED, STORED IN RETRIEVAL SYSTEM, OR TRANSMITTED IN ANY FORM OR BY ANY MEANS (ELECTRONIC, MECHANICAL, PHOTOCOPYING, RECORDING, OR OTHERWISE) WITHOUT PRIOR WRITTEN PERMISSION OF BOTH THE COPYRIGHT OWNER AND THE PUBLISHER. THE ONLY EXCEPTION IS BRIEF QUOTATIONS IN PRINTED REVIEWS.

THE SCANNING, UPLOADING, AND DISTRIBUTION OF THIS BOOK VIA THE INTERNET OR VIA ANY OTHER MEANS WITHOUT THE PERMISSION OF THE PUBLISHER IS ILLEGAL AND PUNISHABLE BY LAW.

PLEASE PURCHASE ONLY AUTHORIZED ELECTRONIC EDITIONS AND DO NOT PARTICIPATE IN OR ENCOURAGE ELECTRONIC PIRACY OF COPYRIGHTED MATERIALS.

YOUR SUPPORT OF THE AUTHOR'S RIGHTS IS APPRECIATED.

PUBLISHED IN THE UNITED STATES OF AMERICA BY:

LONG VALLEY PRESS
NEWCASTLE, OKLAHOMA
WWW.LONGVALLEYPRESS.COM

SCRIPTURES TAKEN FROM THE HOLY BIBLE, NEW INTERNATIONAL VERSION®, NIV®. COPYRIGHT © 1973, 1978, 1984, 2011 BY BIBLICA, INC.™ USED BY PERMISSION OF ZONDERVAN. ALL RIGHTS RESERVED WORLDWIDE. WWW.ZONDERVAN.COM THE "NIV" AND "NEW INTERNATIONAL VERSION" ARE TRADEMARKS REGISTERED IN THE UNITED STATES PATENT AND TRADEMARK OFFICE BY BIBLICA, INC.™

Made in United States
Troutdale, OR
08/08/2025